THE EYES
of
THE QUEEN

THE EYES *of* THE QUEEN

An Agents of the Crown Novel

OLIVER CLEMENTS

LEOPOLDO & CO

ATRIA

NEW YORK LONDON TORONTO SYDNEY NEW DELHI

An Imprint of Simon & Schuster, Inc.
1230 Avenue of the Americas
New York, NY 10020

This book is a work of fiction. Any references to historical events, real people, or real places are used fictitiously. Other names, characters, places, and events are products of the author's imagination, and any resemblance to actual events or places or persons, living or dead, is entirely coincidental.

This Leopoldo & Co/Atria Canadian export edition October 2020

LEOPOLDO & CO/ATRIA PAPERBACK and colophon
are trademarks of Simon & Schuster, Inc.

Interior design by Kyoko Watanabe

Manufactured in the United States of America

1 3 5 7 9 10 8 6 4 2

ISBN 978-1-9821-6475-1
ISBN 978-1-5011-5471-3 (ebook)

For my mother, Andrea Valeria, who lived multiple parallel realities simultaneously, in many universes that were entwined and united in her mind. She manipulated her reality, carved away the excess, chiseled its form: she was a great sculptor, but her subject was life itself. She always said that Astrology was the poetic sister of Astronomy, and John Dee would certainly have concurred.

I'm forever honored to be her disciple.

—LEOPOLDO GOUT

PART | ONE

CHAPTER ONE

Saint-Marceau, Paris, August 24, 1572

It starts with a bell in the night, just as he always knew it would.

"Oh, what is it now, for the love of all that is holy?" his wife says, sighing. "I've not slept a wink and already it is dawn."

"Shhhh," he whispers. "It's not yet daybreak. Go back to sleep. It'll soon stop."

But it doesn't. The bell rings on, dismal and insistent, and after a while Francis Walsingham leaves his wife, very hot and already grown overlarge with child, in the bed, and he makes his way to the window. He lowers the shutter and looks north, over his neighbors' modest rooftops, toward the city itself, whence comes the bell's toll.

"It's Saint Germain's," his daughter tells him. She is awake in her truckle bed, by the side of the big bed, down by his ankle.

"You have good ears," he whispers.

"What's happening?" she asks. "I have been having bad dreams."

He soothes her with some vague words and fumbles for his doublet.

"Francis?" his wife asks.

"I will be back by dawn," he tells her.

He goes out into the corridor where he finds Oliver Fellowes, his intelligencer, already awake in doublet and breeches, with a candle lit. He is a young man—the son of Walsingham's old friend John Fellowes—twenty to Walsingham's forty, handsome, with reddish hair and a neatly barbered beard.

"Well met, Oliver," Walsingham starts. "Are you just up from down, or in from out?"

Despite the anxiety the bell is causing, Fellowes laughs.

"Working, sir," he lies.

Walsingham laughs too.

It is the last time he will do so for many days.

"What do you think it is?" Fellowes asks.

"Nothing good."

They descend the narrow steps where the porter—a stocky Frenchman of the Reformed faith—waits with a bull's-eye lamp, ready to unbar the door. When they meet the warm August air of the courtyard, all three stare into the star-speckled darkness over Paris.

"Is no fire," the porter says. "A fire, you see from many leagues at night, and smell, too."

"What then?" Fellowes asks. "Some saint's day?"

"Is Bartholomew's in the morning," the porter tells them. "But no, is not that."

Then Fellowes speaks quietly.

"It cannot be Coligny, can it?" he asks. "Not so soon?"

That had been Walsingham's first fear too: that Gaspard de Coligny—the leader of France's Protestant Huguenots—had died of his wounds. Someone had tried to kill him two days ago, with an arquebus, from an upstairs window, but had only managed to cap Coligny's elbow and blow off his finger. Unless and until the wound became infected, he was not thought likely to die.

Unless now he has?

And if so, then there is no knowing what will happen. Will the Huguenots seek revenge against the Catholics? Or will the Catholics preempt the Huguenots and come for them? Paris is a tinderbox. France is a tinderbox. The whole of Christendom is a tinderbox.

"No," Walsingham tells Fellowes. "Listen: my daughter is right. That bell: it is Saint Germain's, the king's chapel. The Catholics would never mourn Coligny."

Fellowes agrees, but knowing what it isn't doesn't help them with what it is.

Just then another bell joins it, then another a moment later.

Oh by Christ, Walsingham thinks, *they are passing a signal.*

His guts roil. This is it. This is what they most feared would happen.

"Send someone to rouse Sir Philip, will you?" he tells the porter. "As well as Tewlis and the rest of his men. Have them keep the fires covered and the women within."

The porter grunts and sets off to wake Sir Philip Sidney, Walsingham's secretary, and Tewlis, the commander of his guards. Walsingham turns back to Fellowes.

"Oliver," he confides, "before this turns ugly, we need to perform a little task. Can you dig up a couple of swords—and anything else if you have it—and meet me at the stables as soon as you can?"

Fellowes raises a brow.

"Shall I summon a troop of guards?"

"No," Walsingham tells him. "This had best be just the two of us. No undue attention."

Fellowes looks sharp.

"Is it Mistress Cochet?" he asks.

Walsingham almost smiles. *Ah*, he thinks, *another of us enslaved by Isobel Cochet's charms.*

"No," he says. "She remains at the Louvre palace, I hope. She will be safe there, whatever happens."

Yes, Isobel Cochet will be safe wherever she goes and whatever happens, he thinks. Or hopes: it was he, after all, who sent her into the Louvre to be his ear to the door, his eye to the keyhole, so if anything has befallen her, then it will be him, Francis Walsingham, who will have to face her daughter—who must be what, six, by now?—to tell her that her mother is dead, just as he had once had to face Isobel herself to tell her that her husband had been killed in his service.

Not long later he meets Fellowes at the torch-lit stables behind the residency, watched over by a doubtful ostler. Walsingham straps on the unaccustomed sword belt and loosens the blade in its scabbard. Then he leads the horse out into the yard, with Fellowes behind.

Sir Philip Sidney is up, no cap, hair a little on end, standing in the yard.

"What's happening?" he asks.

"You are to take command of the residency," Walsingham tells him. "Oliver and I will be perhaps an hour, two at the most. You will know what to do if we are longer."

Burn everything and evacuate the residence. Yes. Yes. He knows. But concern creases his handsome face.

"Can I not go in your place?" he asks, knowing the answer.

Walsingham mounts up.

"Good of you, Sir Philip, but this is . . ."

He trails off.

They all three know.

"Ready?" he asks Fellowes.

Fellowes nods.

When they open the gates, it is still dark, but the sky to the east is blood red, limned with green, and every bell in Paris is ringing. Off they set, up the road toward the Petit Pont, with the gates closing behind.

Saint-Marceau is a modest, mostly Reformed area, all Walsingham can afford on his daily *diet*, and all along the wayside, worried householders have come out to stand before their doors, pale linen gleaming in the gloom, listening to the bells, asking for news.

It comes soon enough; before Walsingham and Fellowes have ridden a hundred paces: a single rider, coming too fast and scattering the watch on the Porte Saint-Marcel.

"They've killed Coligny!" he shouts. "The Catholics! They threw him out of a window! Now they're coming this way, killing everyone! Run! Run! For the love of God! They'll kill you all!"

He doesn't stop, but thunders past, and there is much screaming and shouting, and Walsingham's neighbors scatter back into their houses.

Walsingham heels his horse onward toward the bridge, Fellowes at his elbow.

"Where are we going, sir?" he asks. "What are we doing?"

"To Notre-Dame," Walsingham tells him, "to see a priest."

Ahead in the growing light, the road is filling with a tide of people flowing toward them. The horses jitter. Walsingham clings on as people swarm around them.

"Go back!" they shout.

"The Catholics are coming!"

But Walsingham and Fellowes force their way through the swelling crowd and through the first gate. A trap, it must be a trap. Everything within tells him to turn and fly. The road is narrowing between taller houses ahead. Still the bells ring, and still men and women—in the hundreds now—push by. Some are in their finest, some still in nightwear, each clutching whatever they can, infants mostly. They come with heads crooked over shoulders, faces streaked with terror and tears.

"They cut her hands off!" a woman cries. "They cut my mother's hands off!" She holds up her own, astonished to still have them.

"They are just—*butchers*!"

"Thieves!"

"Animals!"

Walsingham's anger is like a physical force, like a gorge. It fills his throat. How can they? These Catholics? How can they turn on their fellow Christians and slaughter them like pigs in autumn? He wishes he were back at home, in England, and far from these papist animals with their insatiable bloodlusts and their ancient, twisted superstitions. He has long feared something like this would happen.

Beside him, Fellowes rides in tense, pale-faced silence.

They smell it before they reach the bridge: blood. It fills every cranny, with a coppery, intimate tang. It makes the horses shy and stamp and toss their heads.

"Come on," Walsingham encourages his horse—and Fellowes. "We've got to get across the bridge before they close it."

But they are too late. The road ahead empties, and the great gates at the southern end of the Petit Pont are heaved to. The city is sealed off. May the Lord help those trapped within.

Fellowes waits, hoping perhaps Walsingham will turn back, but he will not give up yet.

"We'll try the river," he says.

And he leads them eastward along the rue de la Bûcherie where the smell of the old blood between the cobbles is strong enough to mask that of the new.

"In here," he says, and they dismount, leading the animals into a yard that isn't too bad. They hobble them to a post and leave the other way, down some steps toward the river's bank. It is light now, and so they can easily see the men on the Île de la Cité, right under the shadow of the steeple of Notre-Dame, pushing a dead woman's body into the river. She's naked and has only one arm. When she's gone, the men look up and wave the arm at them. They laugh and cheer, then move off, chanting some song, the words of which Walsingham cannot catch. They brandish the arm as if it were a monstrance, and they were beating the bounds in spring, in search of someone else to kill.

Walsingham could gag.

The riverbank is muddy and unkempt hereabouts. They find a boat dragged up out of the river and hidden under a sagging wooden canopy. Its guard has probably run with the rest of them.

There's an oar and a boat pole, and they haul the boat down into the fast-flowing brown waters.

"Master, are you sure?" Fellowes asks.

"We've got to," Walsingham tells him.

One heave and the boat is in. Walsingham takes the pole, Fellowes the oar, and the boat spins in the current. The water is deep and Walsingham cannot touch the river's bed with the pole. Fellowes works the oar like a Venetian, but still they drift downstream, westward, toward the bridge. There's a body in the water.

Not a dog. A human. Naked and fat, the skin of his back opened with a whip.

Above them to the right, twenty paces away, the sun shines on the jagged lines of the roofs of the great cathedral and the other houses on the Île de la Cité.

"Come on," Walsingham urges Fellowes.

By God's grace, no one sees them from the bridge as they spin through its arches and grind against the huge pillar. In the sudden darkness Walsingham grabs an iron chain cemented in a pillar and they are quickly out of the boat, scrabbling in the ooze. It stinks of shit. They drag the boat out of the current and up into the darkest shadows where they hope to return to find it. Walsingham wishes he had eaten something.

Along the bank, there are some steps up to the cathedral precinct, but before they climb them, Walsingham stops.

"Quick," he tells Fellowes. "Cut a strip off your shirt."

He's seen each of the men wearing armbands, simple white kerchiefs knotted around the muscles above their right elbows, presumably as a signal. They each had a white cross pinned to their caps, too, but there's nothing Walsingham can do about that. He and Fellowes cut strips off their shirttails and tie them on for each other. When they are finished, they look at each other.

"Do I look Catholic?" Walsingham asks.

Fellowes manages a laugh.

"Enough," he says. "But sir—"

He touches Walsingham's arm, and Walsingham knows what he is going to ask and cuts him off.

"I know this seems insane, Oliver, and I would not ask you to do it if . . . if England's whole future did not hang in the balance. But it does. If we cannot find our way to the cathedral today, then a great chance to do great good will be gone."

He grips an imaginary thing, as if it were chance to be seized.

"What is that?" Fellowes presses.

Walsingham knows he owes his intelligencer something more than this vague assurance, but secrecy is his second skin. It is very hard to tell him more, and he must force himself to do so.

"Some information," he begins, speaking quickly, knowing that if he stops he will never start again. "From the logbook of Admiral DaSilva."

Fellowes's eyes sharpen. He is about to repeat the Portuguese admiral's name aloud in incredulity but stops himself. He looks very boyish, then—just a youth in a borrowed beard.

"Is it . . . what we have been looking for?" he asks softly.

Walsingham nods, as if not trusting words spoken aloud.

After a moment, Fellowes turns shrewd again.

"Wherever . . . wherever did you come by it?"

He means two things: How did you come by it without my knowledge? And: Can it be trusted?

"We can talk about this at a later date," Walsingham says. "But for now we must retrieve it before we leave Paris for good."

Fellowes is convinced. Good.

"Come on then."

They start up the steps. Halfway up they meet blood running down, pooling in the worn stone treads before overflowing to the one below. They must step through it. At the top, they find a kind of hell: immediately there is a pile of naked corpses from which seeps the blood, pressed out of those below by the weight of those above. Beyond, between Walsingham and the steps of the cathedral, the precinct is turned into an abattoir where strong-armed men engage in a wild frenzy of slaughter and butchery. They hack at the living and the dead with cleavers, and halberds, and foresters' axes, parting them limb from limb with a dedicated, competitive ferocity, using both hands, as if this were a saint's day fair, and they do so to impress their sweethearts.

On the steps, above the worst of the blood, stand the massed ranks of clerics of Notre-Dame cathedral. They are in celebratory red, and they have brought out their monstrances, and while the thurifers swing their censers, the choir sings the "Te Deum," but you can't smell the incense for the blood, or hear the singing for the screams.

"Dear God," Fellowes says, clamping his hand over his mouth.

More victims are dragged in from the surrounding streets by their hair, by their nostrils, by their feet. Some are already dead, some still screaming, retching, wailing, and naked. Spaced around the precinct are more berms of corpses, each leaking its spreading crimson skirt, and Walsingham feels his boots letting moisture in and looks down: he is standing in a great pool of blood.

"Come on," he says.

They set off, making their way through the frenzy. Walsingham knows that he will never forget the grunts of the butchers and the sound of their cleavers in flesh. He will never forget the faces he sees: both killers and victims. He will never forget the charnel house smell of blood, shit, and sweat.

As they approach the cathedral steps he can hear the choir now, singing their thanks to God. The smell of the incense mingles with blood.

They pass up the steps and into the cathedral not quite unignored. A man—an actual butcher—from the kitchens of the Louvre, has taken a break from his work to refresh himself from a flagon of the thin red wine he likes to drink in the morning, and he sees the two men moving against the flow of all others. He thinks he recognizes the English ambassador from the time he paid court to the king and balked at eating horsemeat. He nudges his mate and picks up his cleaver, its blade blue black with blood, its handle gummy with gore, and they set off across the precinct, tracking bloody prints as they go.

Walsingham and Fellowes enter the cathedral through a smaller door inset in the larger west door. It booms shut behind them, and within the nave they are plunged into sepulchral silence. There is no one about until, suddenly, a priest, or some such, stands before them, with thin lips and a pale, shiny face like the new moon. Walsingham dips his fingers in the holy water and crosses himself in the Catholic style. Fellowes copies him. The priest seems reassured. Walsingham sees Fellowes has left a pink mark on his forehead. *The door handle*, he thinks. *There was blood on the door handle.*

He tells the priest he would like to pray in the chapel of Saint-Clotilde.

"It is shut, monsieur," the priest regrets.

A coin is proffered. The chapel is open, but only very briefly.

The priest guides them to the side chapel on their left. They leave footprints on the flagstones. In the chapel there is a memorial to a long dead canon, and a tall window of fine colored glass. The small altar is covered in a cloth but is otherwise bare.

"What are we doing?" Fellowes whispers again.

The priest lingers to collect his next coin.

"Distract him, will you?" Walsingham asks Fellowes. "Only for a moment, otherwise we will have to kill him."

They hear the door through which they came boom shut behind someone coming in, or going out.

Fellowes approaches the priest. Both speak Latin, Fellowes not too well.

"Confession?" he asks.

The priest's eyes light up, and Fellowes follows the priest out of the chapel to be out of Walsingham's earshot. Before he goes, Fellowes glimpses Walsingham bending to kneel before the altar. A dead-letter drop.

Fellowes kneels before the priest, and remembers the old words, and they come to him now, and when he has recited them the priest blesses him and starts the questioning. Fellowes has not confessed since Queen Mary died, but he can hardly tell the priest that. He makes something up, but the priest hardly cares; he wants to delve into the proper sins, those of which Fellowes is most deeply ashamed and Fellowes is reminded how intrusive the sacrament of confession is.

"Lust, my son?"

He is about to shake his head and deny it when he thinks—*my God. Isobel Cochet.*

The priest seems to read his thoughts.

"A woman?" he presses.

Fellowes can only nod. What did he expect? He hears footfalls in the church behind him. Stout boots on marble flags.

"Who is she?" the priest persists. Fellowes feels the priest's breath gusting on his face, garlic and meat and wine. "Is she married?"

"No." Fellowes laughs. "She's a widow."

"A *widow*?" The priest is disgusted. He does not want to hear of an old lady. But Isobel Cochet could not be less like that. Fellowes wants to proclaim that she is nothing like that. But as soon as he starts to think what she is like, all he can see is the flash of her smile, the curve of her lip, that questioning look in her eye. More than that, though: the shape of her throat, her shoulders, her hips, the way she laughs. The smell of her as she passes. *My God*, he thinks. He flushes scarlet at the memory of a loose strand of her dark hair in the spring sunshine on the river's bank. He has only seen her a few times, always with Master Walsingham, always in the Louvre, though, no, once at the residence, in Saint-Marceau, and then once again, that time on the river's bank. The moment he saw her, his life changed, and from then on, he was always aware that somewhere she was out there, sometimes close, sometimes farther away. A lodestone, if she but knew it, around which he rotated. There must be others besides him, he knows that. A fraternity. He feels no animus.

He wonders if adjusting his clothing will break the seal and sanctity of the sacrament? This is no time for that.

The priest wishes to know if when Fellowes thinks of her he spills his seed, as did Onan in the Bible? Another time Fellowes might laugh.

"Oliver?"

It is Walsingham. Fellowes turns.

"We must go," he says.

"Wait!" the priest snaps. He claps a surprisingly steely hand on Fellowes's wrist.

But Fellowes has just seen the two men looming behind Walsingham.

"Master!" he shouts.

Walsingham turns.

Fellowes wrenches his hand free of the priest, sending him sprawling. He draws his sword. In a church? Why not? Walsingham too.

The two men they face are smeared and flecked with blood. One—with the cleaver—wears clogs. The other wears a leathersmith's apron and carries one of those knives they use in slaughterhouses. Something purposeful with no name. Both have bloodstained rags tied around their right arms.

"I know you!" the clog and cleaver man shouts at Walsingham. Walsingham doesn't know him, exactly, but can guess enough.

"Sanctuary," Walsingham tries, reminding them all of their location. It is not clear if he means it, but the cleaver man is confused enough to need to look to the priest for guidance.

"They are English," the priest says from the floor. He has bloodied his nose in the fall. "Huguenot."

Fellowes has never cut a man deliberately, let alone killed one. But the clogged man comes at him so fast he has no choice. He leaps back. He flicks the blade from his right knee up across the man's face. The man is left-handed, and he'd hoped to bring the cleaver down on Fellowes's head. Instead Fellowes's blade bites deep into his wrist and the cleaver flies spinning in the air to clatter to the ground well away. The man screams. Fellowes steps aside to let him blunder on a step or two and then he plunges the point of his sword into his liver. The butcher squeals, arches his back, then falls to his knees, nearly pulling the sword from Fellowes's grasp. The man in the smith's apron turns and runs.

"Damn you!" Walsingham cries as he sets off after him.

Fellowes joins him, but the man is fast, and running for his life. He cuts this way and that across the nave, nippy as a terrier. He crashes back out of the door into the precinct before they can catch him.

Fellowes and Walsingham crash against it. They exchange a look.

"Did you get it? What we came for?" Fellowes ask.

Walsingham pats his doublet and nods.

"Let's go, then."

"Not this way."

"No."

They start back from the western end, running toward the altar. By now the priest is screaming and shouting. Most of the clerics are outside, watching the bloodshed, but there are still enough to come running to find the cause of the disturbance.

"We can't kill him, can we?" Fellowes wonders. He has developed a taste for it.

"You may have to," Walsingham says. "I am Her Majesty's ambassador to the court of King Charles. If I am caught like this—"

It doesn't bear thinking about.

"That'll be the least of our worries," Fellowes says, glancing over his shoulder. The west door is being opened, and men are forging through, and they can hear a great hubbub of voices without.

"Jesus."

They both start sprinting. There must be a way out through the sacristy or one of the side doors in the transepts.

They hear a shout behind them and a great charging scuffle of feet as the crowd of Frenchmen push through the door and run down the nave after them.

Christ, Walsingham thinks, *this has gone very badly*. They may not live to find out if it was worth the risk. They stop in the apse under the spire, two rose windows on either side, the sun blasting through that to the south, but a breeze coming in from below that in the north. The side door: it is open.

They run toward it.

"Can you swim?" Walsingham asks.

"Not a stroke," Fellowes admits.

"Nor me," Walsingham says. "Always promised I'd learn."

They are both breathless as they emerge into the shadows of the cathedral's north side. Here, too, is another pile of corpses, this one being picked over by a crowd of women and boys, while two men wait to load them into the bed of a cart. Beyond, fifty paces or so, is a line of houses, and beyond them, the river again.

"Look natural," Walsingham says.

Fellowes almost laughs. He tries, but it is hard, and their stiff-legged walk only attracts suspicion. It is the boys who look up.

Even though both Walsingham and Fellowes have their blades drawn, the boys know weakness when they see it.

Walsingham tugs on his armband, to emphasize its presence.

"Huguenot scum!" he says, nodding at the pile of dead people.

But he can't help but glance over his shoulder at the cathedral's side door. The first of the Frenchmen is there now. He looks like the dead man's older brother.

They start running again.

A street curves to the left, leading them westward. Merchants' houses, three or four stories high, lean in to greet one another. Ordinarily peaceful enough. Today there is a chain across, manned by five or six men with those white crosses on their hats.

The men are working their way down the street, emptying some houses, leaving others, and right now they are pulling two screaming women and three children from one of the houses—one of the women is clinging to the doorjamb while a man repeatedly punches her—so they do not see Walsingham or Fellowes who slip around the chain and disappear into an open doorway.

Inside they close the door. There is a locking bar, which they drop. In the gloom they look at each other once more. There is nothing to be said.

The back.

They turn and run down the narrow hall. It's a cloth merchant's house, and his stock-in-trade is piled in one room along with various coffers as well as lecterns and benches for his apprentices. A low door gives out into a high-walled, brick-floored yard at the end of which: a privy. Two-seater. A drop into the river. Too small for a man to fit through. They are trapped.

Fellowes finally says it: "Fuck."

He cannot help but look at Walsingham's doublet, where he

knows his master will have tucked the documents. They need to get rid of them. Imagine if the French got hold of them? England would be at her mercy.

But Walsingham shakes his head.

"Not yet," he says. "Not until we have to."

The roof.

They run back inside. The French pound on the door. Dust falls from the ceiling and light blinks in the cracks around the doorframe each time they land a blow. Up the steps they go: one, two flights, then it is just ladders for the servants. Up they clamber, Walsingham first. The ceilings are lower, and the windows smaller, and the comfort less, the higher they climb, until finally they are under the eaves, in total darkness. Fellowes pulls the ladder up behind them, using it to smash through the slates, letting the shards crash around their shoulders. Light floods in. Two children are revealed in one corner, hiding behind a mattress: whimpering, huge-eyed, and the room smells of mice and fresh urine.

Neither says a thing.

Walsingham is first out onto the roof. It is turning into a very fine morning, though a fire has started to the south, in Saint-Marceau, and smoke hazes the air. He thinks of his wife and his child, and of the others at the residency. Sir Philip Sidney is capable enough. Walsingham crawls toward the front edge of the roof. Down below the scene is carnage, and while many men are pulling others from their houses—some alive, some dead—many more are waiting below, waiting for those who chased them from the cathedral to break down the door.

"Bring the ladder!" Walsingham instructs.

Fellowes hauls it up through the hole they've made, and they use it to climb up a wall onto the roof of an even taller house.

From here they can see across to the north bank of the river, to the palaces and the castles, to the church of Saint-Gervais, where the bells still ring, and where down on the riverbank the slaughter continues. Men hunting men. More corpses pile up. Others are being pitched into the water.

There's a narrow gap above an alleyway that only the most athletic might jump, but they cross it with the ladder—a slender confection of planks and nails more suited to the weight of a house maid, or a boy perhaps—which creaks and sags horribly as each man crawls across the alleyway. Walsingham slips and grabs the riser. He drops his sword. It spins down and bounces on the stones, fifty feet below, where two men sharing a flagon of something start and look up. They shout and go running out into the street to raise the alarm.

On the other side of the alley is a roof on which laundry hangs from a tired old string, and there's a hatch but it is locked from the inside. The slates are hot under their hands and covered in bird shit. Pigeons erupt from unexpected places. On they go, relieved and even congratulating themselves on their progress, their ingenuity, when they hear the first boom of a gun, and a ball thrums through the warm air overhead. They stop and look at each other, and back, just as there's another thunderclap, and the wall next to Walsingham cracks, showering them with fragments of brick. Behind them three men are ranged along the skyline, and more coming, powder smoke lingering above their heads. The one from the church leads the way, Fellowes sees, only he's found himself a short-handled ax.

They drop behind a palisade and one after the other slides down another roof, their heels scrabbling against the slates, to butt up against a low wall.

Where the terrace ends.

"By Christ, what now?"

The ladder is useless and they can hear men scrabbling across the roofs after them.

Fellowes leans over the edge and feels sick with dizziness.

It is easily fifty feet to their deaths on the road below.

"We have to break in," Walsingham says, and they start ripping at the tiles, prying them up. Fellowes cuts his hand, a deep gash across the palm. He curses but carries on.

The sun beats down, and even up here they can smell the blood from the street below. Or maybe it's Fellowes's. They keep pulling at the tiles, but each is held in place by the one above it. Fellowes makes a small hole, smashing it with his heel. There is another gunshot from the advancing Frenchmen. They duck but don't see where the ball goes. Now suddenly there is a riot of men's voices, much closer. They've come up through one of the other houses: the one with the laundry.

But now there is just enough of a hole to slither through into the baking darkness of the attic below.

Fellowes tells Walsingham to go first.

"I will hold them off," he says. "They can only come in one by one."

It is a good idea, but Walsingham will not allow it.

"You go first."

Fellowes does, slithering through the hole they've made, feeling his way among the smoke-blackened rafters. He can hear rats squealing in alarm in the eaves and behind the wainscoting. He drops down onto the bare boards of the attic: straw and horsehair beds, a broken pot, a single shoe, and pigeons escaping through an unshuttered window. A moment later, Walsingham drops behind him and staggers a few paces.

"I'm getting too old for this," he says.

Down they go. Fellowes leading the way. Fellowes knocks the ladder to the floor. This is the house of a well-to-do man of law—featherbeds and painted hangings on the walls, even this far up the steps—and the family are present, but they are pressed to gaps in the shuttered windows, watching the scenes below. Each turns and screams when they see the filthy, blood-smeared men in armbands, one carrying a sword. But Walsingham raises his hand to placate them. He and Fellowes hardly pause as they run stamping down the stairs.

The ground floor is given over entirely to an office, with one wall of shelves completely filled with rolls of paper; the shutters are drawn, and two men in sober suits are pressed to the door, looking very tense. Neither have armbands, but both have weapons: one a fine but useless sword, the other a rough but ready kitchen knife. Walsingham holds up his hands in peace. The men turn and stare openmouthed.

For some reason, Fellowes thinks they might have gotten away with it, and that if they somehow exit the back, say, and onto the road, they may yet return to the little boat and make it across the river, or float downstream to Issy, to safety. But then he hears a crash somewhere in the fabric of the house above, several guttural screams, and the thunder of footsteps down the stairs.

He turns and runs toward the back of the house. Walsingham follows. They run through a smaller study, where a shrill lapdog barks fiercely, and then a deserted kitchen that smells of bacon. A door out into the yard, and against one brick-built wall: a wood stack. Fellowes clambers up it, sending loose logs skittering below. Walsingham swears as one catches his shin.

Fellowes hauls himself up to straddle the top of the wall. There is a flow of men, walking to and from the bridge to the north bank. Some stop to watch. He indicates his armband.

"Huguenot scum!" he says, aping Walsingham.

The men are unconvinced. They still stand and watch. They are armed and very dangerous, looking for someone else to kill.

"Oliver!"

It's Walsingham, below, still in the garden with his arm upstretched.

The running footsteps in the house are accompanied by bellowed shouts and desks screeching across the floors. They are coming through the house, this way. Fellowes leans down to haul Walsingham up. His cut hand throbs with pain, all the way up to his elbow. Walsingham scrambles up and over the wall. He lands in the street below just as the man they'd chased in the cathedral comes hurtling out of the house. He sees Fellowes on the wall and cuts that way. He is bellowing with rage and hate, his ax raised, and he's followed by many others.

Fellowes swings his leg over and drops down beside Walsingham. Together they face about ten curious French Catholics, each with a band around his arm, and a cross on his hat. Each with a weapon. They have, naturally perhaps, formed a semicircle around the two Englishmen, pressing them to the wall. But they are not even the real danger. The real danger comes from behind the wall.

"Master Walsingham?" Fellowes says. "I think we had best say our prayers."

"Oliver," Walsingham starts, "I am sorry I have gotten you into this. There was no need—"

Just then the Frenchman from the cathedral appears on top of the wall. He is bellowing with rage, lunging at them with his newfound ax. Fellowes ducks and turns. *If I can kill one more man*, he thinks, *let it be this one.*

But before he can move, there is a boom, and the Frenchman's head rocks back, and the ax spins from his grasp. When his head rocks forward again, there is what looks like a third eye in the very middle of his forehead. The man disappears behind the wall.

Walsingham and Fellowes turn back to the bridge. There is a closed caroche, fifty yards away, at the head of the bridge, and perhaps twenty men on horseback. A man stands upright by the coach's driver, and the puff of pale smoke identifies him as the marksman. The crowd in the street gasp in awe and back away, while those in the courtyard behind are shouting and arguing to see who should next put his head over the parapet. The horsemen come riding forward, and the rioters scatter out of their way.

"Thank God!" says a relieved Walsingham.

They are King Charles's personal bodyguard, in extravagant blue-and-yellow livery, well-armored with helmets, breastplates, pikes, halberds, and guns. Their captain is shouting and gesturing, commanding everyone to move away from Walsingham and Fellowes. Fellowes might weep with gratitude. He has never been so pleased to see anyone his entire life.

"But what in God's name are they doing here?" he asks as they descend to the courtyard. "And why do they wish to save us? How do they even know who we are?"

"M'sieur," the captain greets Walsingham with a lazy touch of the brim of his helmet.

"I am indebted to you, sir," Walsingham says. "And especially your markman."

Fellowes can feel his entire body trembling with relief.

"Don't thank me, m'sieur," the captain says. "Thank her."

He indicates the caroche.

"*Her?*"

Fellowes peers. A window is lowered and a red-sleeved arm waves. It is not a summoning gesture, as he might have expected, but one of pleasure, of glee even, and the arm is long and slender and belongs to a woman.

Fellowes and Walsingham turn to each other.

"Great God in heaven," Fellowes breathes.

It is Isobel Cochet.

CHAPTER TWO

Paris, same day, August 24, 1572

Mistress Cochet pulls back her hood to reveal she has lost her cap, and that her hair—dark with a tinge of red—has escaped its confines. Fellowes feels his mouth go dry, for her beauty is the sort to make any man—and woman, and child, and horse, and dog even—stop and stare: to open and turn toward her like a daisy to the sun. They wait to be warmed by her smile, to be lost in her brown-eyed gaze, to be lifted up by just a moment's attention, and here is Fellowes sitting on a bench in a caroche, with his knee touching hers. Though there is another man in the cabin with them, and though all are turned to the window, struck by the horror unfolding in the streets, a little part of Fellowes is concentrated fiercely on his kneecap.

"How did you know it was us?" Walsingham asks.

"I saw you on the wall," she says. "I thought, my God, I recognize that rump. It is Master Walsingham's."

Walsingham reddens.

"It was not very dignified," he admits.

She flicks her wrist. Her bracelets chime. She is in dark blue linen, with those red sleeves, but she has on her feet very fine riding boots, heeled, chisel toed, and polished like a fresh-spring conker.

"Some things are not worth preserving," she says.

"But where were you going?" he goes on. "And how did you come by this caroche? And a guard of the king's troops?"

"I persuaded the Queen Mother to send them to Saint-Marceau," she tells him. "In case the mob had reached the residency yet. And I thought I should come, too, just in case."

Walsingham sits back, finally believing what he is seeing, and laughs sibilantly.

"My God, Isobel, my God. I knew you would be able to look out for yourself, but for us, too? You have my gratitude."

She smiles distractedly. She is looking out of the window but winces when a moment later a hand bangs against the shutters and there is a growl of command and the stamp of horses' hooves. Soldiers struggle to keep the crowd back while the gates open to allow the caroche off the bridge and onto the south bank.

"What happened?" Walsingham asks.

"No one knows yet," Isobel tells them. "But either the Queen Mother or the Cardinal of Lorraine ordered Coligny murdered in the night. They went to his bed and threw him out the window, and then the king's Swiss Guard evicted every Huguenot from the palace and murdered them in the street. Women and children, too, with those halberds of theirs. Then Saint Germain's was set to ring, and every man in Paris took to the streets, and so it began."

"So it is planned?"

She shakes her head.

"I am not certain," she says. "To begin with, yes. The Swiss Guard, by God. You should have seen them. But I think all this"—

she indicates the streets—"was unexpected, but there is such fear: you can see. Look. They are almost relieved to be doing it to others before it is done to them."

My God, Walsingham thinks, *she is right: it is relief.*

"This is the start of something terrible," he says. "Something that will consume all Christendom. Catholic will kill Protestant, and Protestant will kill Catholic. And this time, there will be no crowd of groundlings to stand and watch: All must play their part. All must bloody their hands."

Fellowes is hardly listening. He stares at the skin of Isobel Cochet's throat where a pulse beats so prettily.

"But what were you doing in Paris, Master Walsingham?" she asks. "So far from home?"

Walsingham makes a small movement of his hand that she understands: *you do not need to know and it is better you do not*. But Fellowes sees a tiny splinter of steel appear in her eye. She is not used to being checked, of course. She glances at him and tries to hide it with a smile that melts his bones. He finds himself gabbling something about his gratitude to her for having saved his life, and that he would unquestionably and unquestioningly do the same for her if ever the opportunity arose.

She smiles with gentle amusement and he feels somehow shut out of something, like a child in conversation with adults.

Walsingham pats his arm.

"Well," he says, "there is a chance you may soon redeem your obligation, Oliver."

Fellowes turns to him, finally relieved not to be consumed by the sight of Isobel Cochet's skin.

"Sir?"

"When we reach the residency, I'd like you to take Tewlis, and half his men, and be ready to lead the party to the barge at Issy."

Fellowes is perplexed.

"You are not coming?"

"No," Walsingham says. "I will stay here in Paris, to keep the residency as long as possible. In case of more incomers."

Now Fellowes is crestfallen.

"Sir Philip might serve," he suggests. "Or Tewlis himself? My place is here, sir, by your side."

Though the thought of spending so many days by Isobel Cochet's side is no mean consolation. However, Isobel speaks.

"I will likewise stay in Paris, Master Walsingham," she says.

Fellowes feels a swoop of disappointment.

Walsingham frowns.

"Are you sure? Are you not worried about young Rose? Or will Rose not worry about you?"

A shadow crosses Isobel's face.

"My daughter is with my father," she says, her voice low and sorrowful. "She is quite safe, but— I will send word, with you, if I may, Master Fellowes?"

She knows his name. Fellowes blushes. "Of course. It would be my pleasure."

Walsingham looks at him beadily, but they are nearly in Saint-Marceau now, on open ground, and before he can add anything they see over the shutters of the carriage a group of men dragging a screaming naked woman into a field by her hair. Isobel lowers the shutter and shouts at the French captain who halts the coach. A moment later, there is a boom of a gunshot from above, and one of the men in the field jerks his head to one side, and then falls away.

"What a markman!" Fellowes says.

"He is Scottish," Isobel tells them, as if she has found a new milliner.

"The first time in my life I have reason to be grateful for the Auld Alliance," Walsingham mutters.

Three horsemen ride out after the rapists. They kill two with their swords, or wound them so badly they might as well be dead, and the others scatter across the fields. Another shot rings from above, wounding one by the hamstring. The horsemen don't bother to finish him off but ride back. The woman sits up, now saved, and tries to cover her breasts.

"*Allons-y!*" the captain calls, and the coach lurches to life.

Ahead is the residence, surrounded by a small crowd that retreats at the sight of the king's guard. The caroche comes to a halt before the gates, and Walsingham calls out to Sir Philip Sidney, who raises his handsome face over the parapet, laughs at what he sees, then drops down. A moment later the gate is opened. Walsingham helps Isobel out, and they turn to thank the captain and the marksman.

The captain nods at the driver's bench and clicks his fingers. "*Écossais*," he says.

The man watches them with a reserved, dispassionate gaze from his seat. He is tall and rangy, with a broad, freckled face, probably ginger under his helmet. He carries an arquebus of greater than ordinary length.

"Wherever did you learn to shoot like that?" Walsingham asks.

He says something that is utterly unintelligible. A place name? An insult? A threat? Who knows.

"Well," Walsingham says, "please take this, as a token of my gratitude."

He finds in his purse only a single coin, an angel, and passes it up. He curses silently, for an angel is three weeks' wages for an ordinary man and will have to be accounted for. The man reaches down to take it without a word, and it vanishes into a fold in his doublet.

"Well," Walsingham says, somewhat discomfited. "Good-bye."

The man nods but says nothing more, and Walsingham can feel his cold-eyed stare as he turns and steps back into the yard, grateful to be safe once more.

The yard of the English residence is fifty paces by fifty paces, and it is now filled with carts, horses, dogs, and people, all milling around anxiously waiting for the gates to open, so they may start their journey to the barge at Issy. Smoke from a nearby windmill set alight and from the bonfire—to destroy any incriminating documents—hazes the sky.

Walsingham seeks out Fellowes, who is overseeing the creation of some documents they wish to leave only half burned—a letter from Sir John Hawkins, for example, which overestimates the speed at which the naval commander can build his still-unknown ship design by five times—and he takes him to one side.

"Oliver," he says, "I have had no time to look at this, but you know the pains we went to get it, so you know how seriously I take it."

Fellowes nods.

"I think it best it goes with you straight back to London, as fast as you can, to be placed directly into Lord Burghley's hands. No one else's, you understand? Not Leicester, not Derby, and certainly not Smith. Burghley's and Burghley's alone, when he is alone."

Walsingham withdraws the package, sealed in waxed linen, and he palms it in through the points on Fellowes's doublet.

"I still do not know where it came from," Fellowes says.

Walsingham smiles. "We will discuss it all over something hot and sweet when we are both back in London," he reassures him. "Until then, next to your heart, yes?"

Fellowes nods. They shake hands, one last time.

"See you in London, sir."

"God bless you, Oliver."

Neither notices Isobel Cochet until she is almost between them.

"Master Fellowes," she begins, "I am sorry to intrude, but I wonder if it is not too late to take you up on your kind offer to assist me, and whether I might join you in your party back to England."

Fellowes is delighted, Walsingham surprised.

"I have been thinking what you said about Rose," she tells him. "I have not seen her for a month or more. A six-year-old shouldn't be without her mother."

And so it is agreed.

Fellowes is indescribably pleased. He offers to find her a horse. Walsingham leaves them to it and goes to find his wife and child sitting with the other women and children, in the bed of the cart by the gate. He kisses each, one last time.

"I will see you safe, back home in London," he promises.

He shakes Tewlis's hand and salutes the departing soldiers. The gates open. The French soldiers are still there, holding back a sparse crowd with ease. The first carter lashes the first ox and the cart's wheels grind across the stones. The second carter lashes his, and out they go. Walsingham holds his wife's gaze and mimes a blown kiss.

Oliver Fellowes rides alongside Isobel Cochet. They make a terrifyingly handsome couple and despite his gloomy turn of thought, Francis Walsingham cannot believe God would let anything happen to such a pair.

And yet. And yet.

"Godspeed, Oliver," Walsingham says, and God bless.

When the convoy is gone, and the gate is shut, Walsingham retires to his chamber. He kneels and prays for the safety of his wife and his child, and that with God's grace, his scheme will play out to England's advantage.

Sir Philip Sidney comes later and asks how he is.

"As well as can be hoped," Walsingham tells him.

The convoy—two carts, eight horses—passes a loose group of men in sober black cloth with those white crosses daubed on their hats and white kerchiefs tied around their arms. They are gathered amid the posts where the women would usually wring their laundry, but today they've murdered someone and there's a dead body on the ground between them. They look up and watch the English pass, and then they leave their victim and fall in behind.

The road runs westward, past windmills and onion and cabbage fields, across low ground that is marshy come winter, where the smell of dyers' yards and tanners' pits enriches the air. Ordinarily a traveler might fear wild dogs or pigs, or feral children with stones to hand, or the roads pitted so deep a man might easily vanish up to his chest, but today there are mobs of men and even women on the wayside, crosses daubed on their hats, to spit at the English as they pass, and to shout foul curses, and threaten acts of violence. They laugh at the terror of the English women and children, but they are mindful of Tewlis and his four soldiers with their smoking fuses. No one wishes to be the first to die.

But that will change, Oliver Fellowes knows, and fear claws his heart.

"Nurse your flames," Tewlis tells his men. "And shoot the big ones first."

On they ride. The crowd becomes louder, closer, denser. The

horses' eyes roll, and their ears press flat. There is a chant of a sort Fellowes does not wish to know the words. He feels Mistress Cochet watching him, from where she rides talking to Mistress Walsingham like mother and daughter, and he is determined to impress them both.

Something foul is thrown.

"Do not react!" he calls. "Do not."

The people in the crowd jeer and press close. A pale-skinned baby's arm, hacked off at the elbow, is made to make obscene gestures. More join the crowd, and the road is almost blocked ahead. They are having trouble keeping their line. A pisspot is thrown but ducked. A soldier fires his gun and the crowd flinches like a single animal. A moment later it pushes back, closer than before. A woman draws a finger across her throat. A horse rears. A man bellows something, his mouth holding a single tooth.

Steady, steady, for the love of God.

Fellowes enters a state of extreme calmness, where the sounds of the menacing mob are muffled as if by oakum in his ears, the image of men as seen through cheap church glass. Isobel Cochet watches him with steady intent.

Oliver smiles.

She does too.

The provocation continues until at last they reach Issy, late in the afternoon, when the first stone catches Fellowes just above his right eye, a ringing bang, and then blood is half blinding him. A soldier shoots a boy in the crowd. The crowd recedes like the ebb of the tide, then surges back. Every man raises his sword. The soldiers grip their guns. Ahead is the choppy broth of the Seine where the bargemaster waits aboard his craft.

Another stone and then one more. A gunshot. Then a flurry of them. The crowd scatters but only for a moment. Then more stones. Cobbles the size of fists. Screams. A howling child. Another gunshot. This one French. A soldier staggers, bellowing, clutching an arm that hangs limp in his burning sleeve. Fellowes feels a glancing blow. His horse rears as if wasp-stung. He slides from the saddle, and lets the horse go, bucking downriver.

Tewlis has spread his three remaining men in a fan, but they have not loaded yet.

"Get aboard!" Fellowes shouts. "Get aboard!"

The bank at Issy is built up, and the river is low, and the gangplank is level. Fellowes runs to help the women and children from their carts. The ground is tussocky, stone. Mistress Cochet is still mounted, turning her horse this way and that. Men pluck at her cloak. She has a whip and uses it with precision.

She'll soon be pulled down, though. Fellowes helps Mistress Walsingham across the gangplank. She is frozen, terrified, so finally Fellowes wraps her in his arms and carries her. He deposits her on board, into the arms of the master, and turns and runs, his heels slipping on the greasy planks, back to Isobel Cochet.

He runs up the incline. A glancing blow on his shoulder. Shrugged-off hands. A fist connects. Good. Isobel is still mounted, her horse terrified, ten paces away, but a man has the hem of her skirt, and another her boot.

She lashes both with her whip.

From behind, Fellowes pulls one man and spins him away. He holds up an arm, imagining she will slide off her saddle and under it as if it were a wing.

She does, and they are, for an instant, face-to-face and he might kiss her on any other occasion, but—

Something is wrong.

A great heat swarms in his chest. As if he is being crushed. He can't breathe. Can't move. He opens his mouth to bellow, to push

Mistress Cochet away, for she is very close now and one arm is around him, and the other holds a—

A knife.

He clamps a hand over his breast. Blood. He looks at her face. Pure sorrow. Pity. Regret.

"Do not struggle," she says. "Embrace it as you would embrace me."

A blue blade. A stiletto. Hidden where? He reels. Falls. Darkness closing, life narrowing.

Life. Gone.

CHAPTER THREE

Mortlake, England, August 25, 1572

Dr. John Dee cannot sleep, but when he does, he dreams of angels, and he wakes with the word *biathanatos* on his lips.

"How's that?" his mother asks, cupping a hand to her ear.

"Violent death," he tells her, speaking loudly.

"That's not what you want," she says. "Is it? Not when you've got your interview to come?"

"No," her son agrees.

He breaks his bread and dips it in his ale, then chews slowly, thinking about this most recent dream of his. He has become sure, of late, that they are encrypted communications from elsewhere. Angels? Men smile when he suggests this, but Christians are required to credit far more outlandish beliefs, and he is certain that had he the grammar of the communications, or their key, he might prove to be right.

The river, through the open door, is bad this morning, but the tide is on the turn, and soon its foul cargo will slip back downstream to London, where it belongs. He watches his mother fussing with the bread oven, obsessively sweeping out the ashes, and he wonders further about his dreams. He has many theories about their meanings, but like so many of his other theories, as yet they evade the pins of proof.

His mother is still sweeping.

He gets up, crosses to her shoulder, and turns her gently from her task.

She stares at him, half in terror, half in confusion.

"All's well, Mother," he says. "All's well. Come now, let us sit awhile."

She allows herself to be led to the bench by the door. They are both used to the smell. Lord, they smell that way themselves. Dee sits her down. She mews gently and yields up her brush of hawthorn twigs. He puts it aside. *She has forgotten who I am*, he thinks.

Just then, from the front door comes a booming knock.

His mother bends her head.

"Is it the Queen?" she whispers, her eyes round as new-minted pennies.

"Not today, I think," Dee says, but he does not move to answer the door, to find out who it is, for he knows well enough.

"Because she's been before, you know?" his mother continues. "To see my son. My son, John."

He listens to her, just as he listens to the voices now raised at the front of the house. Both are painful in different ways. He supposes he has the count of twenty before the men from the front appear at the back.

"I must leave now, Mother. Don't answer the door."

"Are you in trouble?"

"I will be, if you answer the door."

"I'll not answer it then!" she says with a smile.

He kisses her lightly on her cap and then turns and takes up his traveling bag—weighty with lumpen objects—and his green doublet, and he slides through the back door, and a moment later is running down through the orchard to the river beyond.

When he is gone, the knocking grows louder.

"All right, all right," his mother says. "I am coming."

The man at the door is big, with a fat round face on a neck so thick it would take three hands to strangle, but with close-set eyes and a head polished to a brilliance. He carries a stout oak staff and, tucked into a thick leather belt that hardly restrains his bulging gut, is a well-used cudgel. The man behind him is slighter, narrower, but lithe and as mean-looking as a blade.

"This the residence of John Dee?" the first man asks.

Dee's mother shakes her head.

"Never heard of him," she says.

"You witless old sow," the man tells her. "He is your son."

She frowns.

"No," she says. "You are the witless one, for I have no son."

"You do. He is John Dee. And this is his house."

And now she remembers.

"You are right!" she says. "I do. And this *is* his house."

"And is he in?"

"Oh no. He is not here. He is on his way to the university at Cambridge, there to see the dean of Saint John the Evangelist, whom he says is to offer him a teaching post!"

The man smiles toothlessly. He thanks her and wishes her God's blessings, and the two men go on their way, and when she closes the door on them, Widow Dee allows herself the simple, satisfied smile reserved for a proud mother.

Her son meanwhile hails a boat on Mortlake shore, and soon enough is following the tide of bobbing ordure down the river Thames to London. He sits with his bag on his knees, keeping it out of the boat's lees. It contains a change of linen and three books, an astrolabe, the globe made by his friend Mercator, and another device of his own fashioning, with which he is very careful.

Fine weather and good luck bring him to Cambridge before sundown two days later, and he passes the lepers' house just as the bell of Little Saint Mary's rings curfew. That night Dee stays at the house of his friend James Pewlit, who has a house on Jesus Lane, and who has expended much social capital to get Dee the next day's interview, but who, despite this, stays up with Dee into the short hours, talking of the rules of proportion and perspective in relation to accurate maps. Much wine is drunk and many sheets of paper are despoiled and set aside before they fall into bed with Mistress Pewlit and their newborn, to snore through what remains of the night, waking the next morning frowsy-headed and malodorous.

Noon, though, finds Dee well breakfasted and standing at a lectern before the stone-faced master, the dean, and some of the Fellows of the College of St. John the Evangelist. He knows his linen is fit only for the fire, and he wishes he had taken the time to visit a barber, but still, he thinks, they need not sit and stare at him like that.

Only the dean, the only working brain among a lot of dry old sticks, is following Dee's thoughts on the subject of the moon's influence on tidal ebb and flow with nods and murmurs, usually in the right places. The majority are unswayed, particularly by Dee's device—made himself, somewhat crudely, but what do you expect?—which he holds aloft again to show how it predicts the risings and fallings of tides on any given shore, in any part of the world.

"You mean to tell us that that *thing*, that bollock of brass and leather, can predict the height of the tide in far distant Cathay?" the master asks.

"The height *and* the time," Dee reminds him. "And yes, I'd stake my life on it."

"I hope there is no need for that," the dean says.

Nervous laughter. Queen Mary has only been dead fifteen years or so, and the reality of death at the stake still lingers like smoke in the air.

"Imagine the advantage it might confer on any nation who possessed such foresight!" Dee rolls on. "Even apart from its scientific use, it has mercantile, exploratory, and of course, military applications that . . . well . . . These are dark times for this country, as is well known. Imagine if the Spanish possessed such a benefit."

The dean murmurs agreement, but the other Dry Sticks are on the master's side, and they remain unmoved even when Dee concludes his pitch, and the dean stands to thank him.

"Dr. Dee," he starts, "we all know there is hardly a man alive more gifted than yourself in the field of applied mathematics, nor one so well connected to men of great learning across the sea."

He nods at Mercator's globe.

"And we all know that having you enhance our fellows' table would be a garland, as well as provide much needed rigor . . ."

Dee has felt the "but" coming from the moment the dean opened his mouth.

"But?" he asks.

There is an uncomfortable moment. The dean defers to the master, who hauls himself to his feet. He is bulky, gray bristle chopped, with a mouth downturned at each end.

"But look at yourself, Dr. Dee," he says. "You appear hardly fit to muck out the pigs, let alone teach some of our country's finest young minds."

"Mere hazards of the road"—Dee waves away his objection—"such as might befall any man coming from Mortlake."

He places a hand on his breast, in part to suggest sincerity, in the other part to cover a wine stain.

"Besides, I do not wish to teach, so much as to learn, and to pursue knowledge through the intertraffic of minds."

The master's sneer remains fixed.

"But there remains your reputation to consider," he goes on, and Dee feels ice cold and boiling hot at once. It was going so well, or not too badly, and now this.

"My reputation?"

"Such as it is."

"Meaning?"

"Dr. Dee, were you, or were you not, imprisoned in the Tower in London on charges of sorcery and treason?"

"The charges were brought maliciously and were dropped by order of the Queen herself, may God keep her."

"Yes, but she then banished you from court!"

"Over a simple misunderstanding."

"You punched the Queen's Privy councillor Earl of Leicester in the face. You call that a simple misunderstanding?"

"He dishonored Her Majesty."

"Nevertheless."

Dee wishes to punch the master, just as he once did punch the Earl of Leicester, but the dean intervenes.

"Dr. Dee," he says. "Sir! No one admires your intelligence as much as we, nor your passion for learning and teaching, but—"

"But?"

"But it is our judgment that your name is now blackened beyond reclaim!" the master interrupts in return. "And we cannot risk the reputation of this university by having the two yoked once more as one."

Dee has heard it all before, expressed more clearly: he is a companion of hellhounds, and a conjurer of wicked and damned spirits, yes, yes. He does not thank them for their time, or wait for an apology, or bid them farewell. He simply turns, collects his orb and his globe, and walks out of the chamber, and the house, into the quadrangle beyond.

Four days' travel and an hour's humiliation and for what?

God damn it! He needed that job. And he feels bad about his friend Pewlit, who had persuaded the dean to at least interview him in the first place.

And so what now?

Sell some books?

He already has nine hundred and twelve books, and they fill his house in Mortlake so he had to build them another room, but he needs each, and many more, to finish his work.

Dee empties his purse into his palm: five shillings and thruppence.

Home in meager comfort, or an afternoon at the Swan with Two Necks?

The Swan with Two Necks it is.

Dee sits at a table behind a pie of various meats and he has ordered only his second jug of ale when two men enter the inn towing a square dog on a short lead. Every man there recognizes them, if not specifically, then generally. Some as potential friends, but most as men whose eye you do not wish to catch.

Dr. Dee sighs.

He knows how it will go.

Sure enough, it takes only a moment before they identify him and make their way over. This is more proof of his theory that every object in the universe—perhaps a human most of all—emanates a force that influences all other objects—perhaps other humans most of all—without physically touching them. He has developed this theory from watching his lodestone, which can both attract and repel other objects without touching them. He, it turns out, has attracted these two men, all the way from Mortlake.

"John Dee," the bullish one begins. "You are under arrest for debts owed to his Grace the Bishop of Bath and Wells amounting to the sum of five marks, eight shillings, and sixpence."

That seems far too much.

"May I at least finish my pie?" he asks. "It has swan in it, I am sure, which I have had before, only once, many years ago."

It is a memory, nothing more.

The bull—who is called Bill, it turns out—agrees. He summons another jug of ale for himself and the narrow-set man, who tells Dee his name is Robert Trunk.

"I shall call you Bob," Dee tells him. "It is more pleasing that way, don't you see? Bill and Bob. Bob and Bill. What about that?"

He laughs.

The ale comes, and they sit and watch Dee set about the rest of his pie in silence.

This could be awkward, Dee thinks, but a bottle of what the landlord swears is French brandy later, and they are firm friends.

"Do you know what?" he tells them. "Do you know what? They claim—the master, those bastards, all of them—they claim to be . . . to be men of learning. They probably speak Greek while they are swiving their bumboys. I don't know. I don't care. What a man does, you know, is up to him. And his God. That is me. I am like that. But don't talk to me about learning. About mathematics. About . . . about. *Things*. When you have your arse greased like a . . . like a beaver . . . and it is stuck in the air for . . . for a turd in a loaf such as . . . such as I don't know what. The Earl of Leicester. And don't you ever, ever talk to me about reputation!"

Three hours after this, getting on toward sunset, the bull sleeps with the polished head on the board while the other is leering about the place, hopelessly confused, while the dog is licking his own testicles.

"Do you have transport?" Dee asks, suddenly sober.

"Huh?"

"A cart? A carriage even? Surely you are not proposing we walk back to London? They will want me in the Guildhall looking my best, won't they?"

They don't have a cart, or horses, but once the men are roused enough to buy one more bottle of brandy to take with them—"against the cold"—and have settled the reckoning, they find a sumpterman with space enough to take all three as far as Bishop's Stortford for a price Bill fumbles in his purse to pay. Dee sits up front while Bob and Bill sleep in the jouncing bed of the cart behind, wrapped in each other's arms. The sumpterman is silent, but Dee has a nice light baritone and while the cart rolls on into the evening, he sings the songs he learned in Leuven, in Flanders, until the sumpterman asks him to stop. The dog they've forgotten in Cambridge.

Two nights later and they are nearly at Ludgate gaol.

"One last drink?" Dee suggests.

And Bob and Bill agree. Their attitude to Dee has softened over the last two days: growls have turned to eye rolls, to laughter, then to thundering pats on the back, depending on the time of day, and the quantity of ale drunk. He has become their pet, he thinks, replacing their dog, and if he could but lick his own testicles then the masquerade would be complete.

Dee knows the keep at the Bull: a man named Chidiock Tunstal, with a forked red beard and a belly as if he were about to birth a bullock.

"Bring us ale, Chidiock," Dee tells him, "and anything you have that is wrapped in greasy pastry."

And when he does, Dee tells his companions that it is apt they should be spending their last evening together at the Bull.

"For you, Bill, seem to me a fellow born under an earth sign, such as Taurus, as, I am bound to say, do you likewise, Bob, though I should say you are more of a Capricorn. Good health."

They drink. Neither man is interested in astrology for neither knows in which year he was born, let alone which month, let alone which day, but knowing himself to be a goat or a bull gives each a stake in the conversation, and it takes Dee only a moment to set them on the road to strife. It is basic stuff, and he need only nudge it along now and then—"Mars ascending, I should say: forever a cause of mischief and destruction" and "I see the scorpion's heart in your chart"—and soon the two have seen the worst in each other. John calls to the fore something that happened with a purse that went missing in the village of Rotherhithe.

"Is there a star sign for thieves, Doctor?" Bill asks.

A drink is thrown, then its mug. Stools are kicked back. The whole bench too. Dee snatches up the jug of ale—still half full—just as the table's legs splay under their grappling weight. He stands to watch for a moment. It is astonishing to see two large men fighting with no restraint. They kick, bite, gouge at each other, rolling off the table and in among the filthy rushes. Their blows connect with concentrated fury, and the sounds of each set the air rippling.

Dee steps away, and some time later, he finds himself on Billingsgate steps with five shillings, thruppence, and an empty jug of ale. It is a warm night, with a heavy yellow moon that hardly raises a reflection on the lugubrious river's surface. A boatman agrees to take him under the bridge and upriver for one of the shillings. He is a nice old fellow, who has been on the river since he was a boy, and he does not mind Dee singing. An hour later, just a little before midnight, Dee is back in Mortlake, wiping the mud from his boots on the long grass of the orchard below his own house.

"Is that you, John?" his mother calls from the still open door.

CHAPTER FOUR

Sheffield Castle, August 29, 1572

Her third husband, James Hepburn, fourth Earl of Bothwell, had shown her how it was done.

Lightly so there is no bruising of your pretty wee neck, see?

Once she had overcome the terrors of having his hands around her throat, and of the darkness hazing the edges of her vision, she had to admit the effect was extraordinary.

It is not the only thing I have to show you, he'd told her.

And he was right: it was not. But he was dead now, she thinks, or imprisoned somewhere, and so might as well be, and so is she. Sometimes, at night, alone in her bed in Tutbury, or Sheffield, or Chatsworth, or any of the other castles she is shuffled between, she thinks about that.

But she is spoiled to any other way now, for nothing else delivers her in transport in such a violent fashion, and so she has taught this girl when and where to apply her fingers—*just here, and here, when I signal*—and she goes at it fairly regularly, though under orders of her confessor, she tries to keep it down to once a day.

But by Christ she is so bored.

All she has to look forward to is that, and needlework with Lady Elizabeth Talbot.

And so now, why not?

"Margaret?"

Margaret Formby knows what she wants, and she sets aside her own circle of stitching and crosses the small room while Mary lies back on the large bed. She is a handsome, severe girl, Margaret, who was initially awkward and scared of what she was asked to do, but she has learned well and now her touch is firm at the right time, and delicate when it is not the right time. Mary tips her head back and sees rain on the gray glass of the window behind her. She wishes she might have it opened and that she might have a view of the countryside. She cannot do the first, and nor has she the second, and so she allows Margaret to lift her skirts, and part her braies, and she devotes herself, for the moment, to such pleasures as she can get.

After the passing of time during which a man might say the first cycle of the rosary, Mary takes over from Margaret, as they have practiced. Oftentimes, in the past, the earl used to insert into her anus a stubby, knobbled length of silver that he called his "other *membrum verile*," which, when she was on the point of her delivery, he would slowly withdraw. The first time he did this, she fainted. He spoiled her, she thinks, just as he spoiled so many women.

"Now! Now!"

Margaret presses. Mary cannot breathe. The light fades. She can see worms in the peripheral of her vision. Hot. Waves of pleasure swell through her body, and she thinks this is what transubstantiation will be like. This is rapture. This is what it will be like when she is finally lifted up by the angelic host and borne in bliss to heaven. But then the pleasure becomes intense—violent, and in its extremity it becomes pain. Her mind is collapsing; her body is killing itself.

She jerks upright on the bed, throwing Margaret away. She draws in great gasps of air. Her face is scarlet; her entire body feels afire. She feels cored out, caved in.

Margaret never knows if this is what she wants.

"Get away," Mary tells her, for now she cannot stand to look at her.

Mary rights her braies and pulls down her skirts and after she has regained her breath, her composure, and her sense of solidity, she stands. Her heart beats in her temples.

Margaret is back at her stitching.

Time gathers weight. Heavier and heavier. Mary feels it everywhere, pushing her down, crushing her. She is crushed. By time. By despair. By misery. She turns back to the bed and falls on it, lying facedown, and she lets the tears come.

Later that afternoon, she receives her gaoler, Sir George Talbot, Earl of Shrewsbury, with no fewer than four of his guards, each with a sword, primed to act as if she would attack their master.

"God give you good day, Your Majesty," he says, bowing low, maintaining the pretense that he is other than her keeper. He wears broadcloth breeches, a finely stitched doublet, and a wide, furred cape, which opens to reveal a surprisingly modest, though pearled, codpiece that fails to catch her slightest attention.

"And unto you, Sir George."

"I trust you are well? You look somewhat downcast."

Downcast? *Downcast?* She thinks to give him downcast.

"I am quite well," she tells him instead. "Tired is all."

He glances over at Margaret, whose hand is paused midstitch. Of course she is a spy. Does she tell him all?

By the Mass, who cares.

"What is it you want, Sir George?" she asks.

Now he comes to it, and it is a good thing.

"The Queen sends permission that you should be permitted to walk our grounds."

She is pleased but will not show it.

"Your grounds? Why, Sir George, I shall scarcely set off before I shall need to turn about."

"The Queen has given permission for you to take your hawk to the park."

Now she cocks her head. This is news indeed.

"My hawk? In the park?"

Shrewsbury smiles.

"Today," he says. "This very afternoon."

It is no better a pastime than pleasuring herself, she thinks to say, but holds her tongue.

She is in grosgrain and linen, for it is an oppressively warm day, and she rides on an elegant roan, with red leather saddle and reins. She carries her hawk in its polished leather hood, and Sir George is at her side, though a little behind, as befits his rank. He concentrates on the greenery of the oaks and the elms that fill the far end of his park, perhaps five hundred paces away, whence he supposes the birds will come. The tip of his tongue is very pink between his bearded lips, but he probably has no idea what he looks like. He and Bess of Hardwick? She doubts it.

But she is not interested in birds. She is tensed for something else, and she believes the hawk, a merlin, senses her tension unlike the other men, especially not the pathetic little huntsman who is so eager to please. He hops from foot to foot, trying not to point out the various birds that are even now scattering for their lives. Her hawk's leather-helmeted head turns this way and that, this way and that. *It might almost twist off*, she thinks, and for a moment she is seized by the idea of grabbing it in her fist and doing just that. Its head would fill her palm as a satisfying ball. Imagine Sir George's face!

They ride up onto a ridge like a causeway above the river. The sky is filled with alarm calls and fleeing birds.

"Sir?"

It is the huntsman, following along with all the guards, twenty paces behind. Sir George quiets him with a glare. They all know the hawk should have long ago been set at the birds. Why does she delay?

"Your bird is disposed?" Sir George asks.

She does not answer. Why should she? Why should she tell him she is not in search of any old prey?

At last they come to a promontory overlooking a fat bend in the river, beyond which are thick woods. There is, by now, not a bird in the sky and it seems to all as if she wishes it so. She reins in her horse to stand still and allows it to crop the grass. She is deliberate and slow, almost as if she is putting herself on show. She waits for a long moment and then removes the hawk's cap.

Instantly the hawk becomes another being.

Its eyes permit no secrets.

It turns its head like the mechanical devices Mary used to see in Paris. This way, that. Now that she can see its eyes, she does not wish to pull its head off. She wishes to let it fly, to give it freedom, just as she wishes it for herself.

Up it goes, to become a distant dot in the sky and there is always the fear that it will never return. And just when she can hardly see it, from the fringes of the wood beyond the river's bank, comes a fluttering pale bird. A pigeon? A dove! It seems not to have seen the hawk. But the hawk sees it. It returns in screaming vengeful fury, descending with unnatural speed, and then—*pluff!*—the dove is hit as by a bullet.

Sir George makes a noise of admiration.

The two birds tumble to the ground. The dogs are into the water. The merlin perches above the dove and rips at its breast. The merlin departs from its prey only reluctantly, but one of the dogs retrieves the dove and brings it back in its jaws. The hawk meanwhile returns to Mary's glove. She replaces its hood and strokes its bloodied chest. The dog drops the dove at the huntsman's feet.

The huntsman looks puzzled.

"A dove," he says, as in *Where did it come from?*

"Bring it to me," Mary says.

The huntsman picks the bird up by its wingtip and brings it to her with a bow. She grips it in her gloved right hand. Under its feathers it is no more substantial than a mouse. The hawk arches toward it. She takes it away. The dove's eyeballs are burst, and there is a wound in the feathers from which spring scraps of pink flesh. She taunts the hawk with it. The hawk might bate at any moment, but it does not. She can sense the discomfort of Sir George and the other men, of Margaret, too, and does not care.

She can see it: a tiny ring of mottled silk, wrapped around the dove's ugly foot.

She turns away, and cuts the silk band with the edge of her ring, and then folds it between her fingers. The she turns back and tosses aside the dove.

"Sir George, I am tired," she says. "Have your man take my bird."

The outing is over.

Back in her room, she dismisses Margaret.

"Be gone from my sight. I will call if I need you."

Alone, Mary unwinds the silk ring. Within, she finds a folded piece of paper. She lays it next to the ewer, before the mirror. It is blank. Under her bed is her night pot, empty and washed. She crouches over it and urinates. With a puddle of piss in its bottom, she brings it to the table and holds Margaret's stitching into it for a moment. She cares not that Margaret will find her work stained and pungent. She lifts the stitching out, shakes the excess on the floor, and then places it on the table. She flattens the paper against the piss-soaked thread; the heat of the fresh urine works without her having to breathe on it, and the cipher emerges.

Her eyes are bad. It takes her a moment to read in the mirror the tiny numbers etched onto the scrap of paper, which she copies to another paper.

She rolls the first scrap into a ball the size of a dried pea and puts it in her mouth. Her urine—tinged very slightly purple—is royal urine. She chews once and swallows. The tiny scrap of silk follows the paper.

When this is done, she returns the pot to its place under the bed, and returns the mirror and Margaret's stitching too. Then she reaches for her Bible. With a pin she pricks out the words. It takes a long time, flipping to and fro, backward and forward. Kings, Judges, Leviticus. Verses 12, 18, 36, 4. With each number the word changes in relation to the word indicated. Before the bell rings the hour, though, she has the message.

She sits back in the window seat, Bible at her side, and she stares through the old glass at the wavering image of the castle's courtyard. She does not smile, but she breathes quickly, as if panicked. She knows it is hope that kills a prisoner. The hope of freedom, and the hope of triumph. She looks at the little pinpricked piece of paper.

This gives her hope.

Her friends give her hope.

She wishes one or two of them were with her now, so that she might share the news: They have it. They have the very thing for which her cousin of England most hoped, and the very thing her cousin of Spain will make most use of. And all because of that silly bitch Isobel Cochet and the love the woman bears for her whining daughter.

This, Mary thinks, *will change everything.*

But she will have to bide her time. She will have to be patient.

She chews and swallows the paper.

"Margaret," she calls, returning to lie on her bed.

Later that night, in the darkness, she hears Margaret breathing in her sleep. Mary thinks of James Hepburn, and the way he kept that silver *membrum virile* on his belt, and she wonders again where he got it from, and who made it, and how much it cost him. She thinks about how many women he had used it on, because you don't just keep a thing such as that about your person, and not make use of it, do you? She wonders: Where is it now? And then: Where did it come from?

CHAPTER FIVE

Whitehall, September 1, 1572

Heavy summer rain beats upon the shoulders of his cloak as Francis Walsingham hurries up the steps of the palace. He has not slept in five days, and whenever his eyes shut for longer than a blink, he relives the hellish days in Paris after Saint Bartholomew's. He can hear their songs, see their smiling faces as the Catholics laughed and danced and waved their bloody axes in the air. As if it had been *carnivale*.

Now, though, he is come fresh from home in Mortlake, chin shaved, mustaches tipped in oil, hair kept in place by a neat black velvet cap. His doublet is very dark, his collar broad and white as snow, and the only concession he has made to his journey across the Narrow Sea and up through Kent are his mud-spattered riding boots. He does not want to look too tidy.

Thunder rumbles in the south. He takes the steps three at a time and does not break stride as the two halberdiers before the door ground their weapons in salute and stand aside to let him pass. He marches straight into the long, paneled anteroom where he finds Robert Beale, another of his intelligencers, bent over a fire, busy feeding papers into its depths. He is dressed as soberly as Walsingham, though his collar is smaller. Beale starts when he sees Walsingham.

"So it is true?"

Walsingham nods once, keeps walking. He unties his cloak and throws it to a standing servant. Beale slides the rest of the papers into the fire. Together they walk the length of the room toward another pair of halberdiers guarding another set of doors at the far end.

"The lucky were cut down," Walsingham tells Beale. "The unlucky garroted."

Beale runs a finger under his collar.

"Dear God. Does the Queen know?"

"Only the half of it," Walsingham tells him.

"God save them," Beale murmurs.

"God save us," Walsingham corrects.

Beale is confused. He breaks step.

"Us?"

He has never known Walsingham to exaggerate.

"There has been a breach of— I have lost a document. To them."

"Something sensitive?"

They have reached the halberdiers at the second doors now, and Walsingham must begin his act, if his plan is to succeed.

"Enough," he says. "The DaSilva document."

The halberdiers ground their weapons and step back as the doors open.

"Leave me, Robert," he tells Beale. "This is my mess, and mine alone."

Beale says nothing. But he nods and steps back and away. Walsingham stands quite alone.

Through the doorway is a very fine room: tall windows, tapestried walls, a fire ablaze in a brick-built hearth. Walsingham notices none of this. He is fixed by the stare of the woman who sits in a tall chair at the head of a long table filled with the bulky shapes of her Privy Council. The eyes of this woman are the fiercest blue and see straight through him. He is grateful to have to bow his head and stare at the floor.

"Master Walsingham," the woman says. "We have heard dire tidings from Paris. Tell us we are misinformed."

He raises his head again. The woman is in silver, with a high collar, and her fiery red hair is tamed with a garland of gold, studded with rubies, emeralds, and diamonds.

She is his Queen.

Walsingham looks her in the eye.

Once again, he is caught unawares by the powerful effect she has on him, just as she has on every man in the land, from the Archbishop of Canterbury to the humblest turnspit. It is not that she is especially or particularly beautiful, but she possesses something no mere painted courtesan could ever hope for: an extraordinary combination of fragility and strength, of high seriousness with dark humor, of fierce intelligence and passionate sensuousness, of silk and steel. *That,* Walsingham thinks, *is what so unmans a man.*

Her question still hangs.

He gathers himself. "I regret I cannot, Your Majesty."

And now there is movement among the men gathered at the table, three of them, heads turning on collars like turnips on plates. Chief among them is Lord Burghley, the Old Fox to whom Walsingham owes much. He is gray bearded, dressed in rich red today, with a cloak of plum, his chain of office around his shoulders. He looks more fretful than Walsingham has ever seen him. Then there is Sir Robert Dudley, the Earl of Leicester, impressively dapper in mustard velvet, one eye always on the Queen to gauge her reaction, and change tack accordingly; and then there is Sir Thomas Smith, the sneering Secretary of State, who has lost much weight recently, so that you may see his skull beneath his skin. Perhaps only Walsingham knows why this should be: Smith has been trying to plant Englishmen in Ulster, in the north of the island, to civilize it, but the Irish have taken exception and killed many of the settlers, burned down their buildings, and scorched the earth. And though he persists in hope, Smith has already sunk and lost almost all his money in the enterprise and is forever on the lookout for more, most especially from the Queen, who will not give it to him.

Of the Privy Council, only Edward Stanley, Earl of Derby, is missing. Interesting.

There is a long silence. A peal of thunder overhead. Much closer already. Wind rattles the windowpanes. Smoke is blown back down the chimney.

"So then," she says. "We are alone."

It is dramatic, of course, but no one contradicts her. This is something they have all feared would one day happen: that France would fall to the Catholics, and now she has, and all Christendom is united under Philip of Spain. Only Reformed England holds out: lone, isolated, and meager-powered England.

Perhaps God has forsaken them.

"But it is not hopeless, eh? Walsingham?"

This is from Sir Thomas Smith. He is smiling at Walsingham, encouraging him, and yet—

Does he already know?

Walsingham remains silent.

"Well, since Master Walsingham chooses modesty," Smith continues, "then I shall have to blow his trumpet for him. He has—what word would you use, Master Walsingham? Procured?—procured for us, the most startling piece of intelligence imaginable, haven't you? Something to show that God has not entirely forsaken His English nation. Something to tip the balance of power in our favor."

The Queen is skeptical.

"What is this . . . intelligence?"

Walsingham closes his eyes. He waits.

Smith has the bit between his teeth. "It is material taken from the logbook of the Portuguese admiral Baltazar DaSilva."

Now Walsingham opens his eyes to find Smith smiling at him, but his eyes are alive with malice. Smith believes he is feeding Walsingham gallows rope. The Queen is looking pleased, albeit uncertain, as if she has been promised a great surprise for her birthday.

"And what does it disclose, this material?"

"I regret to say, ma'am, that I cannot say: for as I believe Sir Thomas knows full well, the material has been taken from us."

There is a slight recoil, not least from Smith.

"Taken from us?" he repeats. "Taken from us by whom?"

It is an act. It fools some, but not Walsingham.

"It does not matter," Walsingham tells them.

"By God it matters, Walsingham!" Smith bellows. "It matters a great deal. It has been taken by one of your 'espials,' hasn't it? Admit it, man! You have failed. This is what your nonsensical intelligencing has come to! Abject bloody failure!"

Smith is purple with rage. The Queen quiets him so that others may be heard.

"Explain, please, Master Walsingham," she demands. "Leave nothing out."

Walsingham takes a deep breath. He knows he is treading the

very fine line between success and having his head removed by an ax.

"The document," he begins, "which was two pages removed from Admiral DaSilva's logbook, came to me in Paris from a source in the court in Lisbon, just this last week."

"How did it come to you?" the Queen asks.

Francis Walsingham has eyes that some men have called hooded, and he uses them now to great effect, turning his gaze to the Queen. He need say nothing of the labyrinthine pathways that link Whitehall to the court of King Sebastião in Lisbon, and the Queen understands. She nods.

"Never mind," she says. "Go on."

"The recent tumult meant I had no leisure to study it, or make a copy, and so, believing our embassy to be in danger, I entrusted the document to Oliver Fellowes—may God rest his soul—to bring it back to London to place in the hands of Lord Burghley here."

Burghley looks mildly surprised.

"Unfortunately," Walsingham continues, "Oliver Fellowes was murdered before he left France, and the document was stolen."

There is a mumble of respect for the soul of the dead man before business resumes.

"You did not look at it at all?" Leicester asks.

"I did, my lord, but had no time to decrypt it before the tumult overtook us."

"It was *encrypted*?" This is from Burghley. He has removed his hat and is pulling his beard.

Walsingham nods. They all sit back and they all exhale. They know what that means: the Portuguese admiral Baltazar DaSilva is known first and foremost as a navigator, and an encrypted logbook can only mean one thing. He has been sailing in uncharted waters and has found something he does not wish to share with the world.

"And what do we believe he found?" the Queen asks for them all.

Walsingham must say it: "The Straits of Anian. Or so I believe."

"The Straits of *Anian*? The *Straits of Anian*? Dear God! You had information as to the *Straits of Anian*?"

A babble of voices. Ten, twenty questions. How could this happen? How could he allow it? The Queen's voice cuts through it.

"The Northwest Passage? He has *found* the Northwest Passage?"

For the last fifty years, every navigator in Christendom has sought the Northwest Passage to Cathay. It is the route to untold wealth, and the only way to break the power of Spain; the only way to ensure England's safety, her freedom.

"So I am led to believe," Walsingham tells them.

"Well," Smith says, a sneer on his face. "We'll only know for sure when we see Spanish convoys coming through, won't we?"

Now the Queen's eyes are very piercing.

"The Spanish?" she demands. "The *Spanish* have DaSilva's pages?"

"I do not know who has them now," Walsingham admits.

"Then who took them, Walsingham? Tell us that."

This is Smith, of course.

"A woman named Isobel Cochet," Walsingham answers.

"Cochet? She sounds like a Frenchy," Leicester says.

"She was married to one," Walsingham agrees.

"So it is the French who now know the location of the Northwest Passage? Not the Spanish?"

"I am sorry, Your Majesty, I do not know on whose behalf Mistress Cochet now works."

"And why is that?" Smith wonders aloud. "Is that because she is—or was!—one of your most valued espials, Walsingham? Is that it?"

Walsingham says nothing. He loathes Smith.

"But she turned her coat, didn't she?" Smith continues. "And now she acts for—*pffft!* Who knows? Not for Master Walsingham at any rate. Not for England. Not you, Your Majesty."

The Queen raises her hand.

"So let me see, Master Walsingham, let me see if I have this straight," she starts, her voice steely as a blade. "With our treasury empty of any coin for war; and with a Spanish fleet under Admiral Quesada sailing from Cádiz in order to land here, burn our country, suppress our religion, and replace me here on this throne with our cousin Mary of Scotland; and now with all hope of assistance gone from France, you have let slip through your fingers the one thing—the very thing!—the *only* thing!—that could conceivably have saved us from invasion? From the Inquisition? The one thing that would have allowed us to buy the ships and pay the men to furnish our defense? The one thing that would allow us to build up castles strong enough to repel a fleet of Spanish galleons? That would allow us to keep England free? And you have gifted it to Spain?

"Is that so?"

He holds the Queen's gaze, but thinks of Smith. He must allow him a glimpse of his panic. Just a glimpse.

"Your Majesty—" he starts, relying on being cut off. Smith duly obliges, performing for the Queen as a juggler, or a clown. If only he were so innocent.

"And you have given it away with one of your silly games of cloak-and-dagger!" he shouts. "Pissing about across the Narrow Sea, with your ciphers, and your codes, and . . . and whatever else it is you people do."

The Earl of Leicester looks calculating, but Lord Burghley does at least come to Walsingham's partial defense.

"Master Walsingham's 'activities' did at least yield the document in the first instance," he points out.

"The first instance matters not one whit!" Smith jeers. "What matters is how the thing plays out. And in this instance it has played out very badly. Very badly indeed. You're a bloody fool, Walsingham! An incompetent bloody fool!"

"Enough!" the Queen snaps.

Silence. She stares at Walsingham. He can taste his heart in his mouth. He knows his fate hangs in the balance. He might have misjudged this. The Queen might now call for those halberdiers outside. They'll happily take him under the arms and drag him to the Tower with the sort of pleasure of which they might later tell their wives over bread and ale.

She looks at him for a long time, sitting in judgment, waiting for him to justify her faith in him, and in that moment, he changes his mind: she is beautiful, in moments such as these, beautiful enough to stop a heart.

And finally she says: "If what you say is done, Master Walsingham, then for the sake of all England, it must be undone. You must make this right, or, God help you, I will find someone who can."

He breathes again. His lease of life is extended. But for how much longer? He backs out of the room, trembling, but bows extravagantly as he goes, and finds Nicholas Gethyn, Thomas Smith's private secretary, hastily retreating from his post listening at the door.

"Francis," he says, "may God grant you good day."

Walsingham smiles. Gethyn is an oddity at court: tall and shy, there against his inclination, and of the sort to believe every man can see his darkest secrets. As it happens, Walsingham can: Gethyn has against his better judgment allowed himself to be bullied into investing much of his wife's money in Sir Thomas Smith's Ireland colony, to the probable ruination of his family.

"Gethyn," he says. "How are you? How is your wife? All those children of yours?"

"Passing well, Francis. Good of you to ask. Ten of them now and have just welcomed another. Can never remember their names but I miss each one, very much. And my wife, too, of course, who sends love."

Romilly Gethyn was a great beauty, Walsingham recalls, though not seen since she took to childbed. He thinks he must do something for them—remove them from their obligations to Sir Thomas Smith, perhaps—but not right this instant.

"Nicholas," he says, "I am rather up against it at the moment. May we resume our conversation at a later date?"

They have slipped to Christian names.

"But of course, Francis. Of course."

Gethyn has something to tell him, of course, but what? Something about Smith no doubt, though Walsingham believes he knows enough about Smith for the moment. He will ask Beale to investigate, anyway.

Beale is waiting in the antechamber, pale and sick with fret.

"Walk with me," Walsingham tells him. "Back to Seething Lane."

The rain has let up, and Beale does so, along the Strand, for Walsingham is sick of taking ship. Beale fills in his master on all that has happened, insofar as he is able to, though it is obvious he believes his master already knows more than he, despite being so taken up in Paris. He tells him that the Queen has been very restless.

"It was the shooting of Coligny that started it all over again," he says. "It reminded her too much of James Stewart's murder."

James Stewart, first Earl of Moray, had been Regent of Scotland until he was shot with a gun from an upstairs window while riding through Linlithgow. The murderer had spread feathers on the floor to mask his movements and put up a dark cloth to hide the smoke from the fuse and the explosion after the gun had been fired. Walsingham had likewise thought of him when he had heard Coligny had been shot, though the man who shot Stewart was— He stops suddenly.

"Stewart's killer was never found, was he?"

Beale shakes his head.

"A man named James Hamilton," he says. "He escaped overseas. France, I suppose."

My God, thinks Walsingham. *My God.*

It is just one other thing to remember: Hamilton.

Beale sighs with displeasure. "It's a bad business," he goes on. "Anybody may now just take a shot at anybody from thirty paces. Thank God guns are so inaccurate."

Yes, Walsingham thinks, *well, we'll see about that, soon enough*.

"And how did the Queen greet the news that Quesada has set sail?" Walsingham asks.

"Not well," Beale admits, "but it is only five ships, and none of them big, so we do not fear imminent invasion."

Walsingham wonders if they have yet read his report that the comptroller in Bilbao is short of hay to feed the horses sailing with Quesada's fleet? Insignificant in itself, but horses mean troops, and a shortage means a greater than expected demand. And that there are fifteen ships, all of them big.

"How many will they need if they can free Mary of Scotland?" Walsingham asks Beale. "With her at their head, the north will rise as one behind her, and Scotland will send troops, too, of course."

It is a bleak picture. Beale flushes slightly, assuming Walsingham knows more than he does, which he does. He is a good man, Beale. The son of a mediumly well-to-do wool merchant from Cambridge feeling his way in a changing world. Dedicated, discreet, and loyal, with a sharp mind and sharp eyes, he will go far, Walsingham thinks. *Further than poor Fellowes, at any rate.*

Dear God. Poor Fellowes. He has had scarcely a moment to mourn the man or address his own guilt in that matter.

"While you were in Paris, Lord Burghley renewed his plea to have Queen Mary's head over Norfolk's rebellion," Beale tells him.

Norfolk's rebellion had been earlier in the year, when Queen Mary had promised to marry the Duke of Norfolk if he would free her and let her lead his army to replace Elizabeth on the throne and restore England to Rome. It was only thanks to Lord Burghley that the plot was foiled, after which Norfolk faced the headsman, but Queen Mary did not, and now she lingers like the sword of Damocles over all their heads.

"And still she will not allow it?" Walsingham supposes.

"No. Not without solid proof. And even then . . ." He trails off.

They have had this conversation so many times before: every threat to England exists only because Queen Mary lives still. She is the toehold that Spain has in England, and she is the pintle around which every secret Catholic plot in Reformed England turns. Without Mary alive, men such as James Hamilton would not now be prowling around the fringes with his arquebus; without Mary alive, the Spanish would have no pretext or cause to attack; and without her, there would not be this constant possibility of armed rebellion in the north. Until she is dead, these threats only loom larger and more deadly with every passing day.

"As long as that devilish woman is alive, Queen Elizabeth will never be safe on her throne," Walsingham tells Beale, again. "We must somehow, in any way we can, bring her to the scaffold."

There are times when he thinks that is his sole purpose in life, the reason he was put on this earth. But Queen Elizabeth will not countenance the killing of another God-anointed queen.

"She is moved to Sheffield, though," Beale tells him, "and George Talbot is told to double her guard."

"Yes," Walsingham murmurs: it was he who organized that. He wanted her in tighter containment for the next step in his grand plan.

Beale is quiet for a moment, then starts as if he has had something on his mind.

"Master Walsingham . . . ?"

"Mmmm?" He knows what is coming.

"Is it true? About Isobel Cochet?"

Walsingham can only nod.

Walsingham had heard the news later that terrible day, while he was still in Paris, and he had come back to England because of it, to be met at Sandwich by Tewlis, the erstwhile captain of his guards, who had seen some of what happened, and then later, when he got home to his wife, who had seen the rest.

"Stabbed him, and then ran," she'd said. "Among everything else going on, I hardly noticed, only that it was poor Oliver. Poor Oliver. And Isobel, too. My God, Francis, I never thought . . . well, you don't, do you?"

You don't, Walsingham had thought.

"And you definitely saw her take the document? From his doublet?"

"Oh yes. Well. It wasn't there when— Master Tewlis sent two of his men to bring him aboard. Just in case there was anything that might be done with him. He was carrying no document that I saw. Just a great hole in his heart. And oh my, Francis, so much blood."

He had soothed her then and asked after her health and had kissed his daughter, but he was summoned to Whitehall.

Now he walks with Beale, watching the shipping on the river.

"And how progresses Master Hawkins?" he asks. Admiral Hawkins has been promising a new, nimble, race-built design of ship that he says will be able to maneuver around the top-heavy galleons favored by the Spanish and pepper them with shot from a distance.

Beale is noncommittal.

"He tells us he cannot build ships out of air," he says, "and that his new designs cost money."

"So we are still—?" He does not want to say defenseless, but that is what he means.

"If they knew how weak we were," Beale says, "they would come now. With more than five ships."

Which they are doing, and which makes the loss of DaSilva's document all the more serious still.

When they reach Seething Lane, Walsingham checks to ensure the door to his inner chamber has not been opened since last he closed it, and when satisfied, he springs the three locks. Despite being Walsingham's right-hand man, Beale has never been in this windowless sanctum, and he stares amazed not so much by the ranks of well-ordered files and boxes of papers on shelves that line the room, as by the various ornately tooled contraptions, fabricated in gold and bronze and ebony. One with a small bank of plates bears all the letters of the Hebrew alphabet, and another consists of interlinking brass cylinders marked with tiny nubbles and indents. He gazes, furrow browed, trying to divine some understanding of these cryptographical devices, but it is no good: to the uninformed, they are enigmatic beyond comprehension.

Walsingham ignores him and lights a candle in a bull's-eye glass lamp. After a moment it sends out a focused beam of light on the wall where there are astonishingly detailed charts of the Western Approaches to the Narrow Sea, as well as various others, of islands and reefs Beale has never seen before, all pinned and marked, but Walsingham focuses the lantern's beam on a more familiar map of northern France, centered on Paris.

"Thoughts?" Walsingham asks.

This is the sort of test Walsingham often sets his men. Beale relishes the chance to prove himself.

"Isobel Cochet?" Beale checks.

"Yes."

"Motivation, first."

This is a puzzle. There is no obvious reason Cochet would betray all she had previously claimed to believe. She is not religious, or if she is, only mildly Reformed. Her maiden name is Pinkney, and she was born and grew up near Canterbury in Kent, with her loyalties undoubted. She has worked for Walsingham tirelessly and wholly successfully for five years or more, her judgment impeccable. Thanks to her dead husband, she is never short of money.

"Was she pressured?" Beale asks.

Walsingham nods. Her daughter, of course, would be a possible bargaining chip.

"Find out where she is, will you, Robert?"

Beale writes a memo.

"Who'd take her?" Walsingham tests.

Beale exhales loudly. He gestures at the map, sweeping his hand across it: all this, he is saying, means everyone. "Not Spain, though," he supposes after a pause. "Nor France. Had either known we had the DaSilva pages, they would have sent troops to take them."

Walsingham agrees. "Levers," he says.

Beale waits.

"Some powerless prince," Walsingham muses, "attempting to lever a king to act on his behalf."

"Christendom is full of powerless princes."

Walsingham agrees.

"So then who knew about DaSilva's pages?" Beale asks.

He does not expect an answer. He knows Walsingham will not tell him the details of how he came by them, anyway, because Walsingham is Walsingham, and he tells no one anything they do not need to know. Nor will he risk another of his networks being revealed from top to bottom through indiscretion. He has learned this the hard way, with the death of two of his best-placed espials, including Isobel's husband, Guy de Cochet.

Walsingham places his fingertip on the map: Lisbon. A courtier, Beale thinks, at the São Jorge palace, perhaps. Beale follows Walsingham's finger as it runs north over the map to Santiago de Compostela. A priest then, Beale supposes, or an idolater at the shrine of Saint James the Great. From there Walsingham's finger moves north again, across the sea, to La Rochelle on the French coast. A sailor, with the Italian admiral Strozzi, perhaps, involved in the sea blockade of the city. Then Walsingham runs his finger upward across the Bay of Biscay, through the Western Approaches to the Narrow Sea and then past Calais and into the North Sea, where it settles briefly on the Dutch city of Den Brill. *So a Sea Beggar*, Beale thinks; one of the Dutch pirates who have broken the blockade of La Rochelle, and who are holding out against the Spanish up there. From Den Brill the finger slides south to the French city of Rheims. Rheims! An English priest then. A Catholic. *A recusant, God save us.* From Rheims: a short stab westward across the map to Paris. That could literally be anyone.

"So," Beale prompts, "where is the weak link?"

In the gloom, Walsingham's eyes seem to sweat with the effort of thought. His fingertip hovers as he retraces the document's journey. It stops over Rheims.

"If there is compromise, it is here," he says.

"And Isobel Cochet?"

Walsingham taps the map.

"Paris, of course. The Louvre."

"And is there a connection to the handover in Rheims?"

"De Guise," Walsingham says.

"The duke?"

Beale refers to the Duke of Guise, the leader of the Catholic League in France, the man who perhaps ordered the first attempt on Gaspard de Coligny's life, and the man who hates Protestants above all else.

"The bishop," Walsingham corrects.

The bishop—of Rheims—is the duke's brother. He is the Cardinal of Lorraine, the man whom Walsingham thinks of as the Minister for Mischief, whom Isobel Cochet herself suggested might be to blame for ordering the second, final, and successful attempt on Coligny's life, and the massacre that followed. Both are uncles to Mary of Scotland, and each would stop at nothing to have her returned to a throne, any throne, but particularly that of England, to which—whisper it only—she has a good claim.

"A powerless prince all right," Beale agrees.

"And one who would not wish England to know the whereabouts of the Straits of Anian, that is for certain."

Beale and Walsingham look at each other in surmise.

"But who knowing it himself," Walsingham continues, "will use it to force King Philip's hand in any matter. Any matter at all."

Both are thinking of Mary of Scotland, and of the Spanish

fleet sailing under Quesada. Walsingham feels the wolves circling ever closer. Why cannot the Queen just have her cousin put to death? A stain on her hands, yes, but while she lives . . . He sighs in frustration.

"So," Beale asks. "Do we have anyone inside the bishop's palace?"

Walsingham shakes his head.

"No longer," he says. "Betrayed. They cut him open, wound his guts around a spinning wheel, and burned them from the far end."

Beale shuts his eyes and pinches the bridge of his nose.

"Could we get someone in to find Cochet?" he asks.

"We could, I suppose, but in to where? Where will she be? The cardinal will know we need to find her and will not keep her in Rheims. He will keep her close, surely, but he has properties all over France."

He taps from west to east, north to south.

"It is impossible. Like the needle from the proverb."

"And yet it is what Her Majesty commands we must do."

"But even if we should ever locate her, who could we send to get her out?"

After a moment's thought, Walsingham adjusts the lantern so that its beam switches to fall on the table before his writing stool, and on which sits a simple clothbound book, the sort in which any wool merchant might keep his figures of profit and loss. He opens it and reveals column after column of names.

"We need someone with something a little out of the ordinary," Walsingham says. He flicks over the pages until he comes to a back page on which is written a short list of names and numbers. He reaches for a freshly sharpened nib and runs it down the page. Beale can see the names and their attendant numbers, some crossed out, and he knows what that means. But some are clear and legible: 003 – Christopher Marlowe; 004 – Walter Raleigh;

006 – Francis Drake. Walsingham comes to the column's end, unhappy.

He shakes his head. "What do we know about the bishop?" he asks.

"He is a de Guise, first; a man of the cloth, second; and a Frenchman, third. In and out of favor with the French king and likewise the pope, fanatically dedicated only to his family's advance, most especially his niece Mary. He is believed to be trying to introduce the Inquisition to France, yet has an interest in the occult, and is an advocate of what he calls the intertraffic of the human mind."

Walsingham is silent for a moment.

"The intertraffic of the human mind, eh? Well, well, I believe I know just the man after all."

CHAPTER SIX

Mortlake, England, September 2, 1572

"John! Wake up, John! There's two men at the door."

It is his mother, and he knows there are two men at the door. Two men and a dog. Bill and Bob. Bob and Bill.

"Don't answer it, Mother."

Are we in trouble? she will ask.

Only if you answer the door, he will answer.

He is tying his breeches, lacing his doublet, his gaze roving the shelves in search of what to take, what to leave. His books—all nine hundred and twelve of them? Or his astrolabes, his globes, and all the various mechanisms of his own device? Hurry. Hurry.

"They say they want a word with you."

"I bet they do."

His hand falls on Mercator's globe. He is not likely to see his old friend again for a while, he supposes, and if he leaves it here, it is just the sort of thing a fool will melt to make a trinket for an even larger fool. He wraps it in a shirt, pushes it within his bag, and then makes for the rear window. The roof of his library abuts the house just below his window, and he balances himself on its apex, spreads his arms, and wobbles his way to the gable end. Below is an apple tree, fat with green fruit. A five-foot drop. *Bang.* Always more painful than he imagines. Apples thud to the ground. He is about to join them when the dog—last seen licking its own testicles in Cambridge—appears.

Dear Christ, it is an ugly beast. Of the sort that brooks no argument and will not let go. He knows that he will have to sacrifice his left forearm to its jaws and beat it to death with his right fist. But his moment's hesitation has cost him time he does not have, and now Bill appears in the orchard. He has a black eye and a puffed lip.

"John Dee," he says. "You are under arrest for debts owed to His Grace the Bishop of Bath and Wells amounting to the sum of five marks, eight shillings, and sixpence. Plus expenses."

Plus expenses? Dee clambers along a branch. He is only a few feet above Bill's head, but it is enough. If he can make it into the next tree and the one after that, and the one after that, then he might be near enough the river's edge to make a run for it. Can these sorts of dog swim? It does not look as if it might.

There follows a standoff.

Now Bob comes too. And he now also has a dog, of the same sort. White, but so short haired as to be almost pink, with red eyes and a lolling scarf of a tongue.

"Come on down, Dee," Bob calls.

"What are you going to do? Throw the dog at me?"

There is some head scratching.

"Could do," Bob says.

It is curious to look down and see his own shape among shadows thrown by the latticework of the apple branches.

His mother watches from the back door.

"Come down, John," she calls. "You'll only hurt yourself."

Bill and Bob below agree.

"They'll hurt me more if I do," he tells his mother.

"I'm sure they won't, will you?"

"'Course not."

But they will, so he shifts his weight and prepares to slide over to the next tree. At times like this he wishes he could fly like the angels. At times like this he wishes his mother did not have his trees pruned so carefully. The bough bends under him, slowly lowering him toward Bob's grasp, he being the taller of the two men. Both dogs growl. Dee makes a calculation. He leaps. His bag, with Mercator's globe in it, catches on a branch. He is pulled short, bouncing back. The branch gives and he slides and crashes to the ground, scattering dog and man below. But they are on him straightaway. One dog has his boot. The other his wrist. The strength they bring! They pull against each other, and he is pulled between them as if he were a bone to be tussled over. The two men stand watching with pleasure.

"Come on, then," Bill says, and he takes Dee's other heel, the one without the dog, and turns him, dragging him toward the orchard doorway. Funny to think Queen Elizabeth once stood exactly there. Different days perhaps.

Bob calls off his dog, and Dee's sleeve is released. It aches to the very bone, but there is no blood.

"Where are you taking him?" comes a voice. It is not Dee's mother.

"Marshalsea," Bill answers.

"I am afraid I have greater need of him than the Marshalsea," the voice continues, and both Bill and Bob look up and about.

Down by the river: two boats, oars up, nudging to land, each carrying men of the sort it is unwise to resist. At the bow of the first: a well-dressed man in good black cloth.

"Put him down, will you." It is not a question.

Even Bill and Bob know not to argue, though they try.

Dee looks up at the sun. He says nothing. He knows that voice.

"He is ours," Bill starts.

"He is a subject of Her Majesty the Queen," the voice reminds him. "And I claim his person in her name. Now put him down or I will shoot your dogs, and then you."

One by one all three let go of Dee's limbs, and a moment later, he is sitting up, rubbing his ribs, ruing his fall.

"You all right, John?"

"Yes, Mother."

"You'll have to pay us for him," Bill says. "Five marks, eight shillings, and sixpence."

"Plus expenses," Bob adds.

Francis Walsingham pulls a face and shakes his head.

"You'll have to invoice the Treasury."

"I think I'd rather go with these two gentlemen to the Marshalsea, if it is all the same with you, Master Walsingham," Dee says.

A spasm of irritation crosses Walsingham's face.

"You'll do as you are told, Dee," he says.

The two men and their dogs, and his mother, watch John Dee climb into the boat with Master Walsingham and settle himself on a thwart next to another man, who will turn out to be Robert Beale, Master Walsingham's right-hand man.

The oarsmen push off, and they row against the tide eastward, toward London. Little is said. Dee's arm aches, and there is a hole in his boot. It is a close morning, and a mist haunts the river, left over from yesterday's rain. After perhaps an hour, the boat brings them into the steps below the Tower, and despite himself, Dee shudders.

"Nothing to fear, Dr. Dee." Beale smiles. He seems reasonable enough.

"Not yet," Walsingham adds, with a rictus grin of his own.

His teeth must trouble him, Dee thinks.

They walk up past the Tower and up Seething Lane, escorted by five halberdiers.

"What is all this about, Walsingham?" Dee asks.

They are standing in Walsingham's curious garden, filled with knee-high hedges cut in geometrical patterns signifying nothing that Dee can determine. He knows he should be modestly impressed, but he has been all over Europe, so he is not.

Walsingham starts by admitting that they have not always seen eye to eye in the past, and that Dee's current predicament owes something to him, but, he suggests, they need to put all that behind them.

"Why?"

After much diversion, Walsingham eventually explains how he came to have, only to lose, the DaSilva paper.

Dee, being a keen cartographer, presses Walsingham on the whereabouts of the Straits of Anian and removes an object from his bag.

"Do you always carry a globe with you wherever you go?"

"Just show me," Dee demands.

But Walsingham cannot.

"The page was in code," he tells him.

"And you lost it? Everybody says how clever and careful you are, Walsingham, but I have always known you as a bloody fool. Do you know how valuable that information is? The Northwest Passage! By Christ, that could have been the saving of our country!

We could have broken the papist stranglehold on Christendom! The things we might have learned! And you lost it! Why, tell me, does the Queen permit you even to breathe? Your head should be on the bridge even now, providing thin sustenance for the crows! Dear God! How could you?"

"I did not plan it that way, Dee," Walsingham snaps. "I did not plan to have it stolen."

"Well, what are you going to do about it now?"

There is a moment's silence before Walsingham answers, as eloquent as any set of words.

Dee smiles at him.

"So," he says, "now you need my help."

Walsingham is momentarily disconcerted by the easy offer. But he is grateful.

"Yes," he agrees.

Dee almost laughs. How long has this been coming, he wonders, and he cannot help but recall the last conversation he had with Walsingham, after Walsingham had played a part in sabotaging his standing as the Queen's adviser on astronomy and astrology because he had a name as a sorcerer, a man who practiced magic. Dee had told him that it was not magic that he practiced, but technology.

"There is a divine force," he had told Walsingham, "created and controlled by God, that turns the planets, causes the sun to rise and set, the tide to wax and wane. The ancients understood this power, and they understood how to access it. But we have lost that knowledge, and all we are left with is superstition and ignorance, prey to easy exploitation. With time, and money, I could find the lost third book of Johannes Trithemius's *Steganographia* and with it regain that knowledge, and so come to an understanding of the use of that divine power."

This had cut no ice with Walsingham, who had told him the

Queen had no need of any companion of hellhounds, or a conjurer of wicked and damned spirits, and he was backed up by that fool, Sir Thomas Smith, with whom Dee had argued about his pathetic and dangerous colony in Ireland, which was just then sucking up all his money, and all that he could borrow from the Queen. It would have been far better for the Queen to spend her money elsewhere: specifically, in the New World. That was where the future lay, Dee had said, not Ireland.

Sir Thomas Smith never forgave him that.

And as for the unfortunate fracas with the Earl of Leicester, well, that was always going to happen. The man wore a mail shirt, for the love of God, because so many people wanted to kill him. Anyway, Dee was sent to pack his bags. He had returned to Mortlake unemployed and humiliated, never, he thought, to see the Queen again.

He had also thought that he would never forgive any of the men their spite, their machinations, and yet now here is Walsingham, begging for help, and Dee despite himself, gives him his ear and his time.

You will pay a hefty price for that, Dee thinks.

"I will need chambers," Dee begins, "and all my books brought from Mortlake. And my various instruments: my astrolabes; my cross-staffs, all three of them. And I will need to consult widely, with men such as—"

But now Walsingham puts a hand on Dee's arm as if he were trying to stop a friend embarrassing himself.

"No, Dee, listen," he says. "It is not that sort of help I need."

So it is Dee's turn to be taken aback.

"You do not need me to find the Northwest Passage?"

"No, I need you to find the pages. I need you to go and reclaim them for me."

Dee stares, unbelieving.

"You want me to *go* and reclaim them? To steal them back?"

"Yes," Walsingham agrees. "I am in need of your access to the parts of the world where I have none."

Dee is glad it is only Beale who stands as witness to his foolish hopes of tardy recognition. Meanwhile Walsingham ignores the expression on Dee's face and continues on. He tells him of how DaSilva's packet of pages was taken from an intelligencer named Fellowes, whom he says he loved like a son, and of Mistress Cochet, who murdered the man.

"And she was my best, and my brightest," Walsingham confesses. "Of great beauty, and with an astonishing brain, for a woman, and many other skills besides."

He leaves it vague what these might be. Dee is hardly listening. His core is molten with shamed anger. Yet Walsingham babbles, as if he believes Dee's agreement to help still applies. He tells him about the English College at Rheims, and how Isobel Cochet might have been forced to act as she has by the Bishop of Rheims, Cardinal de Guise. Guise and his interest in the intertraffic of the mind.

Dee is silent. He wishes with all his heart that he was alone. He would welcome a cell in the Marshalsea.

"I believe that is most likely where the document has gone," Walsingham concludes. "I believe you will find it with the cardinal. Since you spent time with Bishop Bonner, you are known to have Catholic sympathies. You may pass among them and know to ask the right questions."

He finally registers Dee's dismay.

"What is wrong?"

"No," Dee tells him. "No. I will not do it. Not your dirty work, Master Walsingham. You do that yourself."

"But Dr. Dee—"

There follows a torrent of promises: money for more books, money to found the national library Dee has always wanted, money to fund his speculative digs in the Welsh Marches for the buried treasure of the late King Arthur, a position at Trinity. Then come the appeals: to his better nature, to his patriotism, to his Reformist beliefs.

None of them work.

"No, Master Walsingham. I will not pretend I do not wish you had not lost DaSilva's charts to the Spanish, and that the benefits of such an advantage are not to come England's way, but you deserve to hang for this, and I will not be the one who moves to save you. You will have to find some other fool."

Walsingham hangs his head. He knows Dee has his points, and that there is no reason he should risk his life on his behalf.

"But for the Queen? *Your* Queen?"

Dee is briefly disconcerted. What does Walsingham know? What does Walsingham think he knows? He regains balance.

"This has nothing to do with her," he says. "Go on. You can take me back home now. Or, no. I see. The Marshalsea. I should have known. Still, I thank you for sparing me a no doubt uncomfortable journey with my bailiff friends and their dogs."

"I am afraid it will not be the Marshalsea, Dr. Dee. Not for you."

Dee looks skeptical, but Walsingham is flushed with purpose.

The guards are almost sympathetic as they hurry Dee down Seething Lane, past the well-kept houses of the aldermen, and out into the clearing around the Tower's moat. He starts to resist as they cross the bridge to the Byward Tower, but it is a totem, and before a man can say the Our Father, he is bundled up the steps of the Beauchamp Tower and into his old cell with a view, should he wish it, of the bluff side of the White Tower and of the scaffold in its keep. The door booms shut. The key turns. Dee is plunged in darkness.

"Oh fuck," he says.

Dee clenches his eyes and his hands. He sits with his back to the wall and waits. He has been here before, many years ago now. He is attuned to the rhythms of the place: the bells that ring, the doors that close, the clack of keepers' heels as they pass, the dismal caw of the ravens in the keep. He knows when the food will come; when the buckets will be emptied; he knows when the Queen's officers will start to circulate, and when he will have to muffle his ears against the screams.

At least he is not manacled.

If only they had let him keep his globe, he might usefully study that. Instead, though, he is without resource other than his mind. He might use this time for thought, but without pen or paper, and without reference, he finds his mind wandering. He thinks about Walsingham. Dee had only told him half the truth: everybody knows him to be clever and thoughtful, that much was true. What was not true is that Dee has ever thought him a fool. Which is what makes the loss of the DaSilva's paper so astonishing. It is disastrously out of character. If only they had them! If English mariners such as Frobisher, or Hawkins, or even Drake, could find their way through the Straits of Anian, then they might find Cathay, and conquer those lands just as the Spaniards had conquered New Spain. From this, untold wealth would pour back to fill England's coffers, enough to pay for more warships than Hawkins could even dream of, manned by a navy professional enough to see off every Spanish galley at sea, with enough left over to pay for the books to fill the library he—Dee—had been attempting to persuade the Queen to establish.

This would ensure England was forever ahead of her competitors in the fields of astrology, astronomy, navigation, mechanics, mining, and of course alchemy. She would take her place in the New World, to impose her own values and ethics, in place of those demented papists, and in time, even the Reformed religion would wither, as people relearned the wisdom of the ancients and learned to reach God through knowledge of the self.

But he refuses to think about Walsingham's ineptitude any further. He knows how a man can drive himself mad this way, without even the need to put him in the room with the brake or the rack, as they do in the Wakefield Tower. He thinks instead of his friends in Germany, and in Holland, and he thinks again about that third volume of Johannes Trithemius's *Steganographia*, which if he could only find it would permit him to communicate with men such as Gerardus Mercator, whose great map shows the rough whereabouts of the Straits of Anian, or Gemma Frisius, who had re-created the known world in a series of segments fashioned in copper and bronze. What would such men make of DaSilva's claim to have found the Northwest Passage?

At length, and at last, he falls into what his keeper, peering through the loophole in his door, believes to be sleep. But Dee is in a state of what he calls lucid wakefulness, in which he is able to see all past and sometimes even future events as present happenings. He dreams now of the events that led to his first incarceration here, under Queen Mary, more than fifteen years ago, when he had just finished his studies in the Low Countries and returned to England.

He had managed to secure the patronage of the young King Edward, which permitted him time to study the cause of tides, and the movement of the heavenly bodies, and he was enjoying some renown—along with his friend Jerome Cardan—casting horoscopes for those who knew their birthdates.

Among those whose chart Dee cast was the young princess Elizabeth.

She had, at that time, been in a strange limbo as the bastard half sister of the King, kept away from court in Woodstock. Yet, through various skeins of obligation, Dee had been summoned, and, intrigued by what he had heard of her, he went, in his scholar's gown and a fresh collar. He was first struck by her slim, flickering, and ethereal beauty, for her hair was fiery red like her father's, and her skin was so pale you might almost see through it. It was the acuity of her mind, however, and the clarity of her gaze that most impressed. *My God*, he had thought, *here is a mind!*

She had grown up in a strained fashion, and her predicament remained dangerous, but while others might have sought gentler comforts to soothe their isolation, Elizabeth chose to numb her pains with the acquisition of knowledge. She never ceased asking questions of him, from the moment of his first bow, until he was backing out of the door of her rooms. She was hungry for anything he could tell her about anything, and so it began: a system of writing that did away with individual letters, knowledge of the fortifications of the lock gates at Antwerp, familiarity with the medicinal herbs the Romans had planted on the wall in the northern parts, a device for moving heavy weights using levers and pulleys, flightless birds in certain islands off Africa.

She was above all fascinated by his astrolabe, and in every aspect of astronomy, as well as astrology and clairvoyance, and so, naturally enough, he offered to cast her horoscope. She was Virgo, he told her, the Ministering Angel, practical and hardworking, fastidious in her health, and mistrusting of fiery displays of emotion, though, in fact, this last characteristic did not apply.

But also: likely to be a spinster.

Does that upset you? he had asked.

She took a mouthful of the roasted swan they were served for supper.

We shall see, she'd said.

She was eighteen at the time, six years his junior, and any physical impulses he felt toward her were overcome by the thought of what her sister might do to his person were he to act upon them, and so he contained himself and worked to temper the girl into something he thought would one day be of very great use.

But what, though?

Meanwhile Jerome Cardan was invited to cast the King's horoscope, for the King was a sickly child, and the chart would help his physicians choose the correct course of treatment. Cardan divined the boy was threatened with a grave illness—which any man with eyes might see—but if he could survive it, he would live to a grand old age.

But the boy could not, and the next week he died.

Cardan fled the country, though it has always puzzled Dee how he managed it in time.

Despite the best efforts of some, Queen Mary took the throne, and set about reversing the religious reforms her predecessors had made.

For a few months, all was well.

Queen Mary even appointed Dee the court astrological adviser, and in this capacity he cast her horoscope: Sun in Pisces, Moon in Virgo, Mars in Capricorn. She was a fist, cold and efficient, occasionally impetuous when it came to enacting plans. These details he sugared. She was a dreary lover, and he did not see children. These details he kept to himself.

But then he made his mistake.

Princess Elizabeth asked to see her sister's chart, and he showed it to her.

What did it mean? Nothing, he thought. Or rather, he did not think. Elizabeth was just interested in it, as she was in everything.

But that is not how it appeared to all. Rumor spread, and it was soon believed Dee's intent was infinitely sinister; that he had bewitched children; that he had cast spells on a goodwife; that he was plotting to kill the Queen and replace her with Princess Elizabeth.

Spies placed in the princess's house informed the Queen that he and the princess had discussed the Queen's horoscope and within the week Dee found himself snatched from the garden at Hampton Court, bundled aboard a boat, and rowed downstream to the Tower. His lodgings were sealed and searched, and it was then that those wild accusations were first leveled: that he was a summoner of hellhounds, and a conjurer of damned spirits, unfit to be part of her household.

And so his reputation was broken, though not, unlike many, his body, for while others were racked and then burned, he—Dee—was held for weeks on end, and then summoned before the Star Chamber, where he was questioned almost endlessly about his intentions and practices, and he was held in various prisons in and around London, mostly in the Bishop's Palace, but for one strange week here, in this very room, in the Beauchamp Tower.

His bowels had turned liquid as they had brought him upriver that first time, in the falling dark, and to the sound of a tolling bell.

"I am no traitor!"

"Right."

He had prayed all through that first night and in the morning the guards had found him still kneeling.

"Thought you were godless?"

"No one is godless in the Beauchamp Tower," Dee told him. "Besides, it is more complicated than that."

They had taken him to the Star Chamber again that day, to be cross-questioned by judges and clerics, and with every question he had feared for his life, for even from the river, he had seen the sky to the north of the city smudged with the pyre smoke of burning martyrs. The air had seemed to crackle with their pain.

It was on the second day, returning after a morning in Westminster, that Dee saw her again. Elizabeth. She was walking on the wall between the Bell Tower and his Beauchamp Tower. She was dressed very darkly, and she looked ill, but there was no mistaking her. He effected a bow as best he could with his hands manacled, and his guards—four of them—were sympathetic to the princess's plight. She had been imprisoned not because she had asked to see her sister's future, but she was a party to Wyatt's rebellion against Queen Mary's marriage to Philip of Spain.

She had turned and watched Dee being marched to his tower, and she had raised a fist in solidarity. Once in his cell, with the door shut in on him, he had hurried to the window that, if he pressed his face through its aperture, also gave him a view of the wall on which she still stood.

"My lady!" he had called "My lady!"

And she had smiled at him, and wept with joy that he was still alive, and he wished he might extend a hand, just to touch the tips of her fingers again, but it was not to be.

They had, though, in spite of everything, passed the days often just as before; in long discussion, and even some laughter, and what might have been hellish became bearable because she would often call to him from her post on the wall, and though she was a prisoner, she was also the Queen's sister, and the guards would look the other way.

"Dr. Dee! Dr. Dee!"

The voice is insistent. But it comes not from the past, not from his wakeful dreaming, but from the present.

"Dr. Dee!"

It is a woman's voice, one that he has not heard for some time but cannot forget. His Queen. She is framed by the open doorway, in very dark blue linen, a tall collar, her hair under a jeweled net.

Dee stands. He dusts himself down. He bows.

"Your Majesty," he says.

"We didn't disturb you?" she asks, allowing him to take her hand and press his lips to the ridge of gloved knuckles. She is wearing four rings: diamond, two rubies, and one plain gold. She smells of myrrh.

"I was just this moment coming to the whereabouts of the philosopher's stone," he tells her.

"While snoring?"

"A ruse to ensure I go undisturbed."

"And how well does that work for you?"

"Not awfully," he agrees. "Though I did not expect houseguests. I should have baked a cake."

"We should have liked that." She smiles, but her smile is strained. "It will be better fare than I can expect at Hill Hall."

"Hill Hall? You are to see Thomas Smith?"

"Yes," she says with a sigh. "I need show myself to the men of Essex, they say, and so, to Hill Hall it is. I'd almost rather stay here, if I were able."

There is a pause. Dee can feel his eyebrow creeping up: Yes?

Elizabeth sighs. She is carrying a fan of meadowsweet against jail rot. Dee is suddenly conscious of the bucket stinking in the room's corner. The Queen crosses the room to the window, looking out over the bailey, over the scaffold toward the church.

"So," she says.

"So," he says.

"I regret to find you once more so constrained, John. It was not my intention."

"No? Master Walsingham exceeding his orders again?"

She sighs.

"He does what he must," she says.

"Must he threaten me with death?"

She smiles vaguely.

"Did he do that?"

Dee growls. Not really, he supposes.

"But I am," Elizabeth says. "I am daily threatened with death."

He sees that she has aged. Her skin, once lustrous, has thinned, cracked, dried. She wears powder under her eyes.

"You do look tired, Bess," he tells her.

She turns to him, a scribble of anger across her face.

"You are not to call me that again."

She glares at him, her eyes very blue even in the dark, and he remembers how those same eyes used to look at him, before she was queen, and they were fellow prisoners together.

"Preoccupied, then," he corrects himself. "Your Majesty."

She stares at him, and for a moment, he thinks he may have lost her. They have been strangers too long for such jokes, and to forge herself a queen, she has had to remake herself entire. Sadness and fear almost overwhelm him.

But at last she smiles and lets out a long sigh.

"It has been too long, John."

"It has, Your Majesty."

She nods. Her eyes dart around the room. She licks her lips.

"I am sorry to come to you only in this hour of my need," she starts, dropping the royal "we" and shape-shifting to become more like the Bess of old whom he might distract with descriptions of the kingdom of Prester John where milk and honey flowed freely; where poison could do no harm and nor did noisy frogs croak.

"But calamity has struck, and this country, our nation, and my very life hang in the balance. I know Master Walsingham has explained the threat that now hangs over us, and that he has made his appeal, and that you have found it . . . wanting."

He feels this painfully. He tries to frame the words that will explain his contempt for Walsingham that will not make him sound petty, but he cannot do so, though she divines the answer, of course.

"I know you have your reasons—good reasons—to dislike and mistrust Master Walsingham, but there is something about this business with Mistress Cochet that he is not telling you, which explains why he did not anticipate her as a threat to what otherwise might have been an intelligencer's coup."

Dee waits.

"Mistress Cochet. Isobel Cochet. The woman who took the document: she has a daughter. Rose. Rose is about six, and her father is dead. Dead in Walsingham's—and so my—service. By every account, Rose is all to her mother."

Elizabeth—who had just three winters when her father ordered her mother's head to be struck from her shoulders just yards from where she now stands—looks so infinitesimally sad as she says this that Dee almost crosses the room to put his arm around her. How badly would that go? Very, he thinks. Instead he waits for her to finish.

"But Rose has been taken," the Queen continues.

"Dead?"

"No. Taken. By someone. After the pages were taken, Master Walsingham sent men to the girl's house and found she had been taken from her bed in the night. Her grandfather—who is a warden of one of the Cinque Ports—hoped she might have gone wandering and sent men after her, in the hope she had perhaps fallen in a sawpit or pond, but closer inspection revealed a note."

"A note? Where was this? Where was the child?"

"Near Sandwich. Where the girl stayed when her mother was working for Master Walsingham."

From Sandwich across the Narrow Sea to France is nothing.

"What did the note say?"

"That the girl was safe, but they were to tell no one she had gone, save confirm it was so, should the mother send message to ask."

"When was this?"

"Two weeks ago."

"And the mother did send message to ask?"

"Yes."

Dee scratches his chin. *Clever*, he thinks. Or lucky. Or perhaps Walsingham should have done more to protect the girl if he was putting her mother in such jeopardy? Where would that end though? The mistake was that someone had discovered that Isobel Cochet was working for Walsingham. If one could find out who that might be, then one would know who had the girl, and with that, who had forced her mother into stealing the DaSilva documents.

"We do not know," Elizabeth tells him. "Walsingham believes it may be the work of the Cardinal of Lorraine, the Bishop of Rheims, who is our cousin of Scotland's uncle, and who has much to gain were she on England's throne in my stead."

"Yes, Walsingham mentioned de Guise."

"You know him?"

"A sly fox. He and Walsingham are of a pair, ever keen to have others do their dirty work for them."

"In this case the dirty work he envisages is to bend the might of Spain to turf me from my seat."

Levers, Dee thinks. *Levers to move a heavy object.*

"And where is he now? Rheims?"

Elizabeth shakes her head.

"Walsingham has someone in the English College. The cardinal has not been seen for a month or more. No one knows where he is."

So that is the problem, Dee thinks. *The old fox has gone to ground, dragging his prey with him. They'll only know where he is when he is the Archbishop of Canterbury.*

"You once told me," Elizabeth tells him now, "that there existed a force that mediated between all things in the cosmos. A power that has always existed, and the ancients understood, but we now give to God."

Dee nods. That is more or less it.

"You told me that a German meister believed that it might one day be possible to rediscover this power, a man might somehow insert himself into that power, and let it become him, and he it, and in so doing, influence that power to his own ends."

He knows what she will go on to ask.

"I will disappoint you, Bess, I mean, Your Majesty, but since our disputations at Woodstock I have spent a decade or more reading books that talk of books that talk of other books that are said to hold the key to such things. But though I have sought these books through all Christendom, from Cracow to Cádiz, from Paris to Poznan, I have met no joy. It is true I am yet to despair of ever finding them, for I am of an optimistic disposition, as you know, but I cannot see how I will ever do so while I am so constrained under the orders of Master Walsingham."

She is disappointed, obviously.

Seeing this, Dee goes on.

"Do you think if I could change the world I would not already have done so? Is not my being here in the Tower proof that I am unable to influence its mechanics? Who, Bess, would choose to shit in an old bucket?"

She laughs now, a sad laugh. She sees her hope was foolish.

"There are worse things," she tells him.

And he believes she knows them. Oh yes. She knows them all right. But now is not the time for that.

"Not if the bucket has not been emptied since the last guest," he jokes.

She looks away.

The church bell rings. She has lingered too long. She shucks her cloak about her shoulders.

"I was not such a fool to imagine you might change the world's course," she tells him. "But I always think of you as my eyes, John, able to see clearly in the night where others only saw darkness."

He looks down when she says this. He remembers. She used to call him her eyes, she said, because he had seen so much more of the world than she had—then—and she believed he knew how it all worked. Not just the planets and the stars and so on, but the world's men and women, too, and the ways of power and privilege, its uses and abuses. He had scratched a symbol on his wall for her, a silly thing: a pair of eyes shaded from the sun by a hand with the thumb sticking down. It had looked more like two zeroes and a seven. It was probably still there.

"I hoped you would help recover what is lost," she goes on, remembering their closeness. "If not for Master Walsingham's sake, then for your country, and if not for your country, then for mine. For me."

She stares at him for a long, comfortless moment. And Dee is lost for words. Then she leaves.

When she is gone, he finds his words, but by then it is too late to undo all that he has done, to do all that he has left undone.

That night Dee dreams of tides washing over broad sands, of a mountain, of a ringing bell, and of the Archangel Michael.

In the morning he calls out: "Fetch me Walsingham!"

CHAPTER SEVEN

Beauvoir, Normandy, September 9, 1572

John Dee does not dislike horses, but this one is slender, and pin buttocked, and he is pleased to be down from its saddle. He shields his eyes from the evening sun and looks south across the sea toward a distant pimple of rock, set far from the seashore—isolated; lonely; impregnable, castellated, and atop: an abbey spire pointing to God.

Mont Saint-Michel.

Property of the Cardinal of Lorraine.

He stands awhile waiting, watching the tide come in. It moves, he has been told, faster than any horse in Christendom, and when it comes, the landscape transforms into seascape at a frightening speed. He shivers and leads the horse along the newly engorged river's north bank, wishing he had come by boat after all.

"I don't like linear journeys," he'd told Walsingham, when they had stood by the wharfside in Sandwich, watching the boat being loaded with wools for the markets in Antwerp.

Walsingham had rolled his eyes.

"But are you sure about this, Dee? Revealed to you in a dream? We are . . . we are staking the nation's future on something you saw in your sleep?"

"Walsingham," Dee had said. "You will have to trust me."

The exact noise Walsingham had made could not be rendered in letters of any known alphabet.

"It is not me who trusts in you and your dreams, Dee," he'd said. "It is the Queen. All your dreams and intuitions. *Tcha*."

"They have never yet let me down," Dee had told him, not absolutely certain this was the case. But he had been absurdly pleased to hear of the faith Bess still put in him.

"We'll see," Walsingham had said. "So. Go with God, and we will send a ship to meet you off Nez Bayard in—"

"Yes, yes, Walsingham. On the old Feast of the Exaltation of the Holy Cross, I know. I shall expect the finest luxury: maidens, swans, samite, and so forth."

Walsingham had growled, and when at length the boat had docked in Calais, Dee was quickly into a saddle, brandishing the passport Walsingham had forged for him, and on the road to Avranches as soon as could be managed. If Dee's dream was wrong, then it would be best to find that out sooner rather than later. After five days' riding only the fleetest horses, he was at the Lion D'Or, saddle sore and sick of salty mutton.

"You are a pilgrim, m'sieur?" the innkeeper had asked, pouring him a big jolt of calvados and pushing it over the counter.

"I am," he had confirmed and had required another cup.

And now here he is, his boots tied and slung around his neck, waiting at dawn in the marketplace with the party of perhaps twenty French pilgrims, each one likewise barefoot. Their guide is a sullen Norman with a mustache the color of wet straw, in thigh-length boots of sealskin and an oiled hat, who tells them first how the abbey came to be built after the Archangel Michael appeared to the Bishop of Avranches, likewise in a dream.

"The bishop ignored the archangel not once, nor twice, but three times, until the archangel burned a hole in his forehead—like this, see?—after which Bishop Aubert thought he had best do as ordered."

And so the abbey was founded on an uncompromising rock in the middle of a sea of muddy sand and water, where the tides were fast, vast, and unpredictable.

"It is the most treacherous place in the world after London," the guide continues. "Most days the water rises three times the height of a man, and sometimes as much as five times. It comes in faster than a horse can gallop, and there are times in the day when the land you think you are standing on turns to water, and down you go. *Pop. Pop.*"

Despite the nervous laughs it is not funny, he says. Many pilgrims have died: drowned or sucked down by the liquid sand. This is why they must pay him to guide them through the mudflats to the rock itself, where the abbey spire dominates the land as far as the eye can see.

"You try to cross one moment too early: you drown. You try it one moment too late: you drown."

They set off through the dawn, the donkeys very strong smelling. A sea mist pleats and gathers in the wind. Dee shivers. He is not well. He nudges his donkey forward.

"Is the abbé here?" he asks, nodding forward into the mist.

"Of course," the guide tells him.

"Anybody else?"

The guide gives him a snide look.

"My sister," he says. "She is very busy."

He stretches the word *very*: ve-e-rry. A cook? A whore? He hopes she is better looking than her brother. Of course she must be. But what does it mean? They ride through the low marshland. Tall grasses sough in the salt-laden breeze. He can hear gulls but no sound of the sea. Then at last they emerge out of the mist and onto the flats. There, ahead, at the end of the long low causeway, is the mount itself. In certain lights it is magical, but this morning, daunting. A clutch of gray slate spires reach up to God, skirted around by a forbidding castle wall.

It is the only castle in Normandy not to fall to King Harry's English armies, and there is little wonder why. But the guide is more interested in the great swath of sand that surrounds the castle.

One of the French pilgrims—the least pious of the party, there to impress a woman, Dee surmises—asks if it is true that King Louis built a prison on the island.

The guide agrees.

"I heard there is one dungeon that floods at high tide," the pilgrim says.

It makes the Tower sound palatial.

"Certainly," the guide says. "And an iron cage, too, the size of which they can change to suit any man. Now, behind me in a single file. And keep up."

They ride out through the swath of sandy mud. Two bowshots, perhaps three, and to the south the surface seems to shimmer like potters' slip. *It even looks lethal*, Dee thinks. Behind him everyone is silent. They are stunned by the place, perhaps, or are thinking of their cold feet, and the dangers of the quickening sand that surrounds them.

They ride on until they reach the castle's outer gate, manned by five soldiers in steel helmets and traveling cloaks. A brazier of sea coal throws up a quantity of smoke, and for a moment Dee cannot see their colors. If they are not de Guise, then he has misinterpreted his dream. He steels himself to have been wrong in this, and to have to turn back, back across the sands, to beat the tide, and to ride for Calais, after two weeks' wasted effort, but mostly: wasted time. Time he does not have. He feels his heart screwing with anxiety.

At last one of the soldiers moves. His cloak swings open. No colors on show, because he is wearing a breastplate. Dee feels hopeful. Who wears a breastplate to protect a mere abbé? But then another man emerges with no cloak: his jacket is parti-colored, mustard and plum, the colors of de Guise.

Dee lets out a long plume of breath.

He is right: the cardinal is here.

But is Isobel Cochet?

The soldiers are bored enough to be interested in a party of barefoot pilgrims and stand watching them dismount outside the gates. Dee knows how to pass as a much older man and he huddles close to a pair of women from Angoulême as they pass through the first gate into a yard. More men in helmets. Ten so far. All in the colors of de Guise.

The guide tells them that they must keep their prayers short, and be back at these gates within three hours if they wish to ride back in safety.

"Stay any longer and you will be staying all night."

The guide waits with the first set of soldiers, sourly chewing the ends of his mustache, but the pilgrims must pass another gate, where stand another five or six. The pilgrims get down on their knees and begin the long crawl up the hill. The road winds around the mount, through a few tight-packed houses. It is cobbled, but cleanish, and there are more soldiers and a few of the abbey's servants up and about their business who stand aside to let the pilgrims pass with tuts and sighs of irritation. Dee feels a fool, but thank Christ they are not flagellants. Walsingham would have liked that.

The road leads them, winding through various buildings, and up numerous flights of steps. The higher he climbs, the further he works himself into the snare, and of course: the abbé's quarters—where they will be holding Isobel Cochet, for she is, as Walsingham said, a personable young woman—will be right at the very top. She will be locked in some antechamber with barred window and a long drop to the sea. Probably a peephole too.

While they are shuffling around a tight turn, Dee hears a coarse scraping and looks up to watch a sled packed with provisions being hauled up the side of the castle on an almost vertical ramp of stone. His curiosity is piqued. The sled ascends the ramp just as did the beetle he once designed for a play when he was at Cambridge, though here the lifting device is left obvious: a rope as fat as a man's arm. He imagines it must work on some sort of pulley system, though how is it powered?

The pilgrims' fervor increases as they approach the level of the abbey. Dee has crawled perhaps a thousand paces and the tops of his feet are now skinned, but he believes he has seen the lay of the island now. He can see the shortcuts through the dorters and refectories, the offices and the kitchens.

At some point he knows he is going to have to slip aside and set about finding Isobel Cochet and that will not be best achieved as a barefoot pilgrim on his knees. He allows the other pilgrims to overtake him, accepting their encouragement, refusing their offers of help, until he is at the back of the line. He steals away.

Ahead, under an archway, a flight of steps goes up to the left, a noisome little alley continues flat to the right. Dee pauses at the foot of the steps. He slips his bleeding feet into his shoes. His knees feel like eggs. He straightens himself, changes his hat so that he is wearing a biretta, and turns his cloak.

He is Père Dee.

He follows the alley into a courtyard, crosses that, and then walks through another doorway. Down some steps, and out through another arch onto the road he has just crawled up. Beads of blood in the dust.

He walks up as if he is making his way to the almonry, on business perhaps, and people nod and greet him politely as he goes. He passes his party of pilgrims and blesses them absently, before finding what he is looking for: a bookseller—shabby, and pale, with a very dark beard that covers his cheekbones—in the process of setting up his stall under an arch. He deals in religious tracts for the pilgrims and has some old scallop shells for sale to those who wish to pretend they are on their way to Santiago. Dee engages him in dunderheaded nonsense about the quality of his books—which are bad in every sense.

"It is a pleasure to have such conversation," he tells the man, "after coming from Paris."

"Have you come with the cardinal?" the bookseller asks.

Dee is evasive but tells him he has just arrived on the island. "At my master's orders."

"Is it true what they say, that the cardinal is waiting for a Spanish fleet?" the bookseller wonders. "Leastways, that's what one of the Spanish gentlemen told me."

"Ah, that would be Señor—"

"Not a señor: a padre. Like yourself. Padre Adán."

"Padre Adán? I had not realized he was a book lover."

"Oh yes, Father," the bookseller assures Dee. "He was after books about hidden writings, what he calls steganography, from the Greek, you know. He found my offerings far too humble for his esoteric tastes."

The man has a high-pitched nervous laugh. Dee smiles. He is closing in, he thinks.

"And where will I find Padre Adán?"

"He stays in the abbé's quarters, with the cardinal."

The bookseller gestures. Dee turns. Above is a handsome stone building, its heavy door guarded by two more halberdiers in mustard and plum, and one of those curly-haired hunting dogs.

"I daresay he will be too busy to have much time for study, anyway," Dee prods.

The bookseller looks blank.

"With the Englishwoman?"

The bookseller shakes his head. He has heard of no Englishwoman.

"The cardinal's companion?"

Again, no. Dee hesitates and then uses Walsingham's money to buy a book, a Psalter, bulky enough, and with a brass catch that looks better than it is, which is what he is after. He doesn't bother haggling.

A Spanish fleet. A priest with a newfound interest in cryptography. But no knowledge of Isobel Cochet. His mind is a swarming hive of bees.

As he is walking away, he hears the bookseller call to him.

"Oh sir! She is not an Englishwoman. She is French! From your city, sir. From Paris!"

Dee raises his arm in a good-willed gesture of farewell.

Ahead are the abbé's quarters, and Dee's approach is watched by the bored guards and their intelligent-looking dog. Dee removes his cap. He calls them "masters" and shows them the book he has bought Padre Adán.

"Very fine," he assures them. "Padre Adán is expecting it."

He speaks French with a strong Venetian accent, though it is wasted on the two men and the dog, who stare at him with lifeless eyes. Rust blooms on their helmets and breastplates, and their ungloved hands are raw around their halberds. They must hate it here. The dog barks softly.

"He's at Mass," one of them tells Dee.

"I know, master, it is that I wanted to leave it as a present. As a surprise for his return."

Dee is managing to look very old and hapless. The guards let him through and into the abbé's hall where a servant is rearranging the rushes. There's another small dog asleep in a ball under a low table on which stands a ewer and a mirror. Dee is more upright when he tells the servant the cardinal has asked him to bring the book to the Englishwoman.

"To help her on the path to righteousness," he simpers.

The servant looks blank.

"The Englishwoman? You won't find her here."

"No? I . . . ah. Then there is a mistake. Where is she?"

The servant looks at him as if he is witless.

"Still under lock and key," the servant tells him. "Where she belongs."

Christ, he thinks.

"My apologies, sir."

He backs out.

But the servant is suspicious.

"Wait."

Dee thrusts the book into his hands and turns and is back out and through the guards and scuttling back down the steps before he hears another word. Christ. The dungeons. They are keeping her there.

He meets his pilgrims coming up the slope, and he diverts into the bookseller's again and watches them pass. Up above, the abbé's servant has come out and is talking to the bored guards and their dog. There is much shrugging of the "no-harm-done" variety, and the servant is left with a book, so the matter is let drop. Despite only just arriving, the bookseller has already begun to pack away.

"Looks like rain again, sir," he says. "You never can be sure in this part of the world."

Dee apologizes and buys a poorly produced pamphlet concerning the everlasting nature of the Trinity.

"You know quality when you see it!" the bookseller tells him.

In fact, he knows thick paper when he feels it. He lets the pilgrims pass, then retraces their tracks back down the hill. He passes an open door, from within which he hears that coarse grinding scrape. He cannot resist stepping inside. Two guards sit watching a bare-chested, wild-looking man trapped within a huge treadmill, walking within its center as if against an incoming tide. A winding rope stretches from the treadmill's hub out through a doorway that frames a view of the salt marsh and a clutch of low roofs in the distance. Another guard stands peering out over this doorway's edge, waiting for the sledge to come grinding up its rail. On board is a sheep's carcass and a sack of cabbages.

"What do you want?" one of the sitting guards asks. "A go in the wheel?"

He has an arquebus, which lends him extra swagger.

Dee retreats and continues down the hill until he finds a soldier on the corner, eating a lump of bread from the nearby bakery.

Dee tells him he is looking for the lieutenant.

The guard gestures up the road.

Dee asks if he will accompany him.

After a moment, the guard supposes he must.

They walk together—Dee takes strength from the guard's ignorance—up past the crawling pilgrims. The guard encourages them to crawl faster.

"You will miss Mass!"

In the guardroom, just before the abbé's house, the lieutenant sits at a table eating an onion and is in no mood to listen to Père Whoever complaining that some of his men are drunk and playing dice in a house below.

"And they have a woman with them," Dee tells him.

"A woman?"

Now he is on his feet.

"Show me to her," he says. Dee leads him back down the pathway, to the bottom of those steps. He rolls the pamphlet tightly.

The bell in the abbey begins its ringing for Mass. Seagulls take wing almost as noisily.

"*Putain!*" the man shouts as his shoulder is splashed with bird dropping. It is an easy enough trick. While he is off balance brushing it from his cloak, Dee moves fast. He spins the man into a dark corner and drives the blade of his hand very hard, just below his ear. It hurts like hell, but the man is instantly as if without bones, and Dee must clutch him to himself, chest to chest. He lets him down gently, and then drags his body behind a cistern. He has no idea how long the man will be out. An hour? A day? He pulls off his coat and takes up his hat. Not a bad fit, considering.

A moment later, Lieutenant Dee emerges from the shadows.

The road is crowded now, with men and women hurrying to Mass. The guardsman who'd taken him to the lieutenant salutes him as he passes. He walks up the road following the blood-beaded tracks of the pilgrims and back into the guardroom. There is now only one man there, half asleep on a bench.

Dee stalks across the room and through the far door into the darkness. He slams the door behind him. It takes a moment for his eyes to adjust. There is lamp glow along a corridor. Dee steps out, but instantly staggers. The corridor slopes down, and there is a lamp farther along, in a sconce, smelling strongly of fish oil. He lifts it from its shelf and carries it down with him. He has the lieutenant's sword belted about his middle, but a shorter knife ready, just in case. The smell and the chill rise to meet him. He can feel a putrid draft in his face.

The corridor soon levels out. Gray light sifts through a series of doors set in the weeping rock of the island, all barred in iron. Dee passes along them. Within are men, who shrink from the meager light thrown by his upheld lamp. They are pitifully dressed and the stench is foul. He wishes he had brought the Queen's nosegay of meadowsweet. He feels chilled to the bone, disgusted to his core.

"Mistress Cochet! Mistress Cochet?" he calls.

There are muttered curses and he is foully insulted, but Dee passes on. Hands come at him through one barred door. A woman with no teeth and rat-tails for hair offers him her use for some bread.

He walks on.

At the end of the corridor is one last door, unbarred.

He lifts the lamp and it is nearly extinguished in the draft.

This is it, he thinks, *the cell with the sea view*.

The steps are slick and green with weed, and very treacherous. An iron rail is affixed to the wall. He takes it.

"Mistress Cochet?"

He holds the lamp high. Another step. His breath is a cloud before him, even on a late summer's day. He feels racked in cold and fear, and the walls press in on him. Seaweed covers their lower half and he is still only a short way down the steps. Down he goes, to the last step. Ahead is another iron door. The line of seaweed reaches up the wall to within a hand's span of the dungeon roof. Put a man in here, and in a high tide, he will drown. What horror would go through his mind when the water started in over the sill? It is effortlessly cruel.

"Mistress Cochet?"

No answer.

Dee clutches the still damp, much-rusted iron bars.

"Mistress—"

The door swings open and he is forced to cling to its bars. The window to the sea is likewise barred against escape, but Dr. Dee sees the dungeon is empty.

He retraces his steps back up the corridor where the prisoners implore him for release. It is like being in London, he thinks, when old soldiers beg for coins, and a man must admit he has none.

"No keys," he tells them, clutching his empty purse. "Sorry."

The wailing is pitiful, but Dee must hurry away from the stink. He feels as if he is coming up from the darkness in search of air and light. He replaces the lamp in a sconce and marches through the guardroom where the same guard now stares at him openmouthed.

He walks out and turns left.

The lieutenant is not yet awake, obviously.

But where then is Mistress Cochet?

He will have to find this Father Adán and follow him. Where will he be? At Mass. Dee reclaims his persona of M'sieur Dee and sets off toward the abbey back at the top of the Mont, where bells are still ringing. His steps take him out onto the castle walls. To the north the view of the sea is framed by a series of forelands. Funny to think that far away, beyond even the Spanish fleet that might—or might not—be beating toward them across the Bay of Biscay, elemental forces are gathering, shifting their powers to send the seawater rolling back over the mud, breaking the causeway and cutting the isle off from the land. He supposes he must have been on the island for an hour.

He quickly becomes lost in a maze. Some stairways lead only to locked doors, and when he retraces his steps he finds himself somewhere he has never been before. The streets seem to narrow, and he loses his bearings.

More guards are gathered along the walkway. Dee holds his nerve and passes them with a polite greeting. Now he cannot come back that way. The streets close in on him, filling with pilgrims, shopkeepers, and guides, but also soldiers, priests, and friars in their black.

Dee finds himself in a cloister, and then back outside, and here finally is the abbey precinct. The rain is coming in hard now, on the edge of a blustering wind, and a line of raindrops cling quivering from the brim of his hat. Over the wall he can see the gray sea is etched in the distance with lines of white surf. He has a while yet, he thinks.

The doors of the abbey are closed but a latecomer might be forgiven for creeping apologetically and silently in. The smell of incense and wet wool grip him by the throat.

It is a childhood memory, of terrifying times, when the Mass was one thing one day, and another the next, when what you believed one day might have you burned on a pyre the next—a time of terrible fear among the adults when all certainties were no longer so.

A creeping shudder passes through his body and he must bite a finger to stop himself giving voice to the old fears.

Instead he looks around: it is a high-vaulted church, sparsely decorated, with columns that soar unadorned to a plain roof. He finds a hidden part of him regretting that it is not filled with the ornate iconography of the papist rite.

But he has no time for this. He is in search of Father Adán, or, better still, Isobel Cochet herself, for surely they would let her celebrate Mass?

He moves around his pillar and begins up the south aisle. The abbey is crowded, and he cannot see the altar, but he works his way down, assuming the cardinal will be at the front, and his Spanish priest nearby. He sees his pilgrims, still on their knees, along with many others besides, and there are a hundred friars and priests of every color. At the front is the cardinal: elderly and sallow, but there is something intensely lively about his face, and Dee is reminded that Walsingham calls him Minister of Mischief. He wears red silk, with a white chasuble and a red zucchetto, and his expression—perhaps Dee imagines it—is that of a man on the cusp of winning a long, long game of chess against an evenly matched opponent.

Next to him is the abbé, in burgundy silks, frail and silvery, perhaps a simpleton from a good family. Both are surrounded with men in mustard and plum velvet, but there is no sign of Father Adán or Isobel Cochet.

Dee plans his next move. He will have to wait until the Mass is finished, he thinks, and then follow the cardinal, but the service is at least moving quickly: it must be because the pilgrims need to get back down the hill to their donkeys and the trip back to the mainland before the tide comes in.

Time seems to stretch and yaw. It always does in Mass. But then he feels it. Or hears it. Or tastes it. Something at odds with an abbey. An atmosphere. Dee is silent and still, every sense alert. He has ever been open to this form of communication, though he has yet to formulate the terminology to describe it. It is not unlike his lucid dreaming, but it is more than that: it is an engagement with the world in four dimensions. It is the perception of a message from beyond the usual twenty senses. Dee is yet to fully understand it, but has long been certain such a thing is possible.

Now he knows what to do.

The crypt, of course.

He waits until Mass concludes, and the blessing is given, and the congregation hurries about their business and the choir members troop out after them while the priest and his acolytes snuff the candles and clear the altar. All through this, Dee remains hidden, kneeling in his own private prayers, and when it is done, and the last of the echoing footfall fades, he leaves it for the length of sixty heartbeats, and then rises on soft feet, and slips into the south transept.

At a staircase, he descends. Candles are lit below and their warmth greets him. As does a man: small, dark-eyed, not expecting him. Dee rushes him in a few steps. He repeats his attack on the lieutenant, but this time he cannot catch him, and the man drops backward, down the steps, and cracks his head on the stones with the sound of a sparrow's egg on a brick floor. Dee feels his own pulse in his teeth; he might vomit. There is something very dreadful about ending a man's life, whomsoever it may be. But look, there: the man has a gun—one of the short, one-handed sorts that assassins favor—crammed in his sash. He would have killed Dee had Dee not killed him. It is true that the fuse is not lit, nor likely to be, but still: it is the principle. He who deals in death must buy as well as sell.

But . . . wait. He is a priest. So. Father Adán then.

The candles flicker in their sconces, as if to mark the departure of his immortal soul, and the communication Dee had felt in the nave halts, but there is still something. Some emanation, as if from the stones themselves. He stands still, looking around. Nothing. Only the candles in their sconces. Huge pillars of well-dressed stone. What masons these men were!

Was it the dead man talking to him? Summoning him down here? He thinks not. He hears a creak, from beyond the pillars, in the gloom. It reminds him of being aboard ship. Rope. Above his head. He slips to the shadowed side. Behind a pillar. His breath comes fast. There is not much air down here. Then he hears a voice.

"Well, come on then."

A woman. Slightly strangulated, again from above. He steps around the pillar, ready for what he cannot begin to guess.

Nothing.

"Up here."

Above is a tall cube, hanging in midair about a man's height off the ground. It is too dark to see what it really is. Dee returns for a candle and brings it over. Hot wax on his fingers is nothing: the cube is a lattice of iron bars, hanging from the roof, and within: a woman. Isobel Cochet.

CHAPTER EIGHT

Mont Saint-Michel, September 9, 1572

"My God," she says, "you took your time."

He stares. The cage. The guide mentioned it: the iron cage the size of which can be changed to fit any man. Only now Dee sees what he meant: its size can be changed to *un*fit any man. Too short to stand in upright, too narrow to sit or lie, the cage holds Isobel Cochet crouching with her knees and neck bent. It might be tolerable for the length of time it takes to say the Our Father, but longer than that and it would drive you mad. The sea coming in through your window every day, which he endured, would be bad enough, but this?

"Who are you?" she asks.

"John Dee," he tells her. "Dr. John Dee."

He holds the candle up to light her face. Her eyes are sunken and feverish. Her dress—the color of dried sage leaves—is ragged and filthy, her linens gray and ringed with stains, and her nails are like talons. He can feel the heat of desperation coming off her.

"Walsingham sent you?" she asks. She does not seem quite as pleased to see him as he had supposed.

He studies the cage. Six sheets of iron bars, each edge stitched together with a fat iron chain ending in a lock as large as a man's fist. He reaches up to rattle it. It might hold back an elephant.

"Why do they keep you in this?" he asks.

"Because I have only given them half of what they want."

Dee wonders if he is missing something. Then he sees it.

"And you will not let them have the other half until you see your daughter safe."

"Exactly."

"What have you given them so far?" he wonders.

"The first of the two pages," she tells him. "It is nothing but a strange geometrical drawing, square, like this, with circles within."

"Who has it?"

"Father Adán," she says. "He keeps it locked in there." She gestures at what might be a sacristy door. "He asked me questions about it all day. Most nights, too."

"And the page you did not give him?"

"Burned. Ashes in a sluice."

Dee is alarmed.

"Christ," he says. "What was it?"

"A list of numbers. Some letters."

"That is all? Not a map? Do you recall any of the numbers? The letters?"

She looks at him.

"Do you know anything about me, Dr. Dee?"

"I know Walsingham values you more highly than anyone else in his employ."

Isobel laughs bitterly.

"Why do you think that was? Because I am able to suck on a man's pizzle until he falls faint for lack of strength?"

Dee hesitates. "Can you?"

She sighs. "It was because, among other things, I need only look at a thing once to memorize it forever."

"That is useful," Dee concedes.

She is silent, waiting.

"So?" she asks.

"So I am here, to retrieve the document."

"Ah," she says. "A dilemma."

A dilemma of her own device: now she is become the document he must rescue.

They smile at each other.

"If you were to give me the figures?" he suggests, pointlessly.

She just laughs. "It is a little more complicated than that."

"In what way?"

"My daughter."

Dee stands as if on a threshold. He knew this would happen. He had come to no decision what he would say when she asked. Now he does.

"Mistress Cochet," he says. "That is why I am sent: the Queen has Rose in her care."

There is a long silence. Dee feels the world bending to look at him. Even the abbey's stones. He can hear their screams. He has committed an outrage against God. Isobel Cochet looks at him, too, and she should scream in bloody horror, but she wants to believe him. She wants to believe her child is safe. She does not want to believe she has just been condemned to death.

"How do you know?" she asks. A residue of suspicion.

"She told me before I set out."

"Have you seen her with your own eyes?"

"No," Dee admits.

"But she told you? The Queen?"

"Yes."

"Why?"

"Walsingham believed it was the only thing that would make you kill his intelligencer in Paris."

Cochet closes her eyes.

"He is right," she says. "May God defend me, I had no choice."

She tells him how she was taken in the Louvre.

"Or, not taken, just spoken to, in one of those rooms they have there, with a huge fire, and mirrors instead of wainscoting. One of the cardinal's men, this man, Father Adán, he caught me unawares. He had a doll of hers. Of Rose's. A little thing my husband had once given her."

"So you never spoke to the cardinal?"

She shakes her head. "Not until later. Until they brought me here."

"How did Adán put it?"

"He told me Rose was safe. That she was being well cared for, by a good family. He wished I could see her, even, for she was so enjoying herself. Only if I ever did want to see her again, then I needed to find something that Adán had heard had just come into the English ambassador's possession."

"And you were to bring it to him?"

"Yes. Bring it here. Paris was impossible at the time, even for the king. All that blood. All those bodies. And the people: still maddened by it all. Anyway. I thought to find Rose here, but no. And when I did not see her, I would not give them what they wanted."

"So here you are."

"So here I am. But tell me about Rose. The Queen found her? The *Queen*?"

"Well. Francis Walsingham. Once they had heard what had happened to Oliver Fellowes. Because of it, he rode to your father's house. In Kent. And finding the girl, your daughter, missing, he sealed the ports. She was picked up off a cog of smoked mackerel loaded for Antwerp."

"And she is safe? She is with Her Majesty? Where?"

"In Nonsuch." He is silent for a moment. Gripped with rage at his own riskiness. Why not Greenwich or Hampton Court? Why Nonsuch? Why put even the slightest hint in her mind?

But Isobel Cochet is in no mood to be swayed by such indicators.

She sobs with relief.

"Oh thank God."

Her head hangs low, hidden by hanks of loose hair and she weeps quietly for a few moments while Dee curses himself. *Christ, this is a dirty business.* He imagines that outside the afternoon will be wearing on. The tide: it will be coming in, and coming in fast. He has spent nights in worse places, of course, but as soon as the lieutenant wakes, he will sound the alarm. They will come looking for Father Adán.

After a while Mistress Cochet wipes her nose on her soiled sleeve.

"So now there remains me," she says, "stuck in this thing."

He does not know how she can bear it.

"Get me out, get me to England, and reunite me with my girl, and those numbers will be yours."

He will cross each hurdle as it comes, he thinks.

And getting her out of the cage is the first.

But the truth is: he cannot.

Had he a set of jeweler's tools, or even a blacksmith's tool, or—wait.

He steps away, back over the body of the dead Spaniard, Father Adán. He takes out the handgun and studies it a moment. It is a well-worked thing, though simple enough: a small powder pan covered by a sliding silver disk, a length of fuse poised above. If the disk is slid back, and the lever below the barrel is squeezed to the body of the gun, the fuse will come down into the powder, and if the fuse is lit, the powder will catch fire, and, through a small aperture at the sealed end of the barrel, it will ignite the main charge within the barrel, which will then explode. The force of this explosion will propel the ball in the barrel out of the barrel's end at astonishing force.

Or so Dee is given to understand.

"Have you ever done this before, Dee?" Cochet asks.

"I have seen it done," he lies.

"Show me," she tells him.

He slides the steel catch off the powder pan and shows her it is full.

"Is there a ball in the barrel?"

He doesn't know, but it's still worth a try. Both cringe from the gun as he holds its barrel against the chain lock and squeezes the trigger to lower the fuse. There is a crack and a blinding flash. The gun bucks in his hand, tearing the skin of his palm. Smoke fills the air. Something hits the stones and flies away into the darkness.

"Yes," he answers her question. "Are you all right?"

"God, Dee."

"Sorry."

"Has it worked?"

The lock is too hot to hold. It has a large silver pock in the corner of its face.

"You couldn't even hit it from an inch!"

"I am not a markman," he agrees.

It looks more solidly locked than before. He hits it with the gun. Nothing happens. It is still locked.

God's truth.

Another ball might do it?

"Did you try Adán's purse?" Cochet asks.

"What for?"

"The key."

Ah.

Dee turns the dead priest over and there is not one key in his purse, but two. Both are as long and as fat as a lady's forefinger.

The second one he tries fits in the keyhole, but the lock is made a great deal stiffer for having been shot. Miraculously, though, it opens. He laughs. She laughs. Then she collapses with relief and the cage sways. He starts to unweave the fat chain through the fat iron bars.

"Come on, come on," she urges. She pulls at the chain from the other end.

"It won't help," he tells her.

"It might."

After a long frustrating moment, they have the chain rattling through the final bars and the cage crashes apart. Dee leaps back as the heavy iron lattices hammer to the ground around him. Cochet grabs the top rail and hangs.

"Help me," she bleats, for she is very weak and racked with cramps. He grips her legs. She is unpleasant smelling. He hardly cares. She lets go of the bars and he carries her a few paces and then places her on the ground, just managing to catch her before she collapses.

He helps her to a bench by a lectern on which papers are pinned.

"The other key," she says. "It will be for the sacristy."

Dee hurries to the oak door at which she points. It is plated in parts, and the key seems almost too delicate to open such a thing, but it does, revealing a storeroom into which Dee can walk. On one side are shelves holding a great many books—Bibles and Psalters and nothing of any interest to him, though obviously valuable—as well as various shrouded shapes he assumes will be monstrances, chalices, candleholders, and the various dishes associated with the rites of Mass. On the other, wardrobes for the abbé's vestments. He holds up a candle and searches the shelves. Everything is thick with dust, except there: a leather folder stuffed with loose papers. Dee takes it down.

"That's it," Cochet tells him. "In there. It might only be a copy."

Is that good enough? Probably, if they do not have DaSilva's second page. He takes it but cannot resist looking at it. It is an astrological chart, he is sure of it. Whose? He cannot say. No wonder Walsingham was puzzled. He takes the rest of the papers and folds them into his doublet, wherein he keeps his passport, along with his notes of ponderings jotted down. Even up here, things get covered in grit from the beach. He drags Father Adán over to the sacristy, and once in, he locks the door behind.

Isobel Cochet tells him to break the key in the lock.

"So he'll ripen, and smell the place out for a month or two. It'll remind them of their corruption."

He does so, snapping it off and sending its broken end skittering into the shadows.

That is when the church bell starts its ringing. Not a summons, or a peal, but an urgent booming alarm. The lieutenant is awake. Dee senses the rustle of running feet all over the island as men answer its call.

"Come on."

He helps her up the steps and into the nave. She bangs her

head and winces. She tries to grip him, to share her weight, but she is very weak. He wonders aloud if he should have brought the handgun?

"You'd've hit me before anyone else."

Now everybody is astir. Dee carries Isobel down the south aisle, hurrying from the shadow of one pillar to the next. A young friar steps out in front of them.

"Master?"

"He nearly killed her!" Dee says, nodding back the way he had come.

The friar hurries past: if there is tumult on the island, he wants to be there to bear witness. Out through the door and into the clearing where the bookseller had his stall. Isobel gasps as the rain hits her. A bugle sounds in the distance. Over the edge Dee catches sight of lines of white horses coming charging across the sands. They are much closer now, and the wind is a force off the sea too.

They do not have much longer.

He picks Isobel up again and carries her back down the steps to the wheel room.

The door is closed. Locked? No. He shoves it open. Deserted. He thanks God.

He lowers her onto the filthy mat and finds a breaking wedge to jam the wheel-room door. Then he takes a sled from the rack and maneuvers it into its grooves on the floor. Isobel watches in silence.

"Isobel," he says, "lie on this."

There comes the first shove on the jammed door.

Isobel calms her doubts and crawls across and levers herself aboard the sled.

"What is it?"

Dee hooks the sled to the end of the rope that is wound around the wheel's spit. There is a net, and a line of hooks on the edge of the sled and he draws the net up over Isobel as he would were he tucking a child into bed. She has not yet seen his plan, because he has not opened the door to the outside yet. When he does, she shouts.

"No."

But it is too late. He is quickly behind the sled and he shunts it out over the edge so that if she struggled free, she'd only fall the hundred or so feet to her death. She clings on, cursing at him in language he did not know women of her kind used.

Dee takes one last look at the wheel, and the path the rope takes through a series of pulleys that he hopes will at least slow the sled's descent. He wrote a short treatise on the use of pulleys while he was in the Tower—being so close to the brake does concentrate a man's mind—and their landing will still be quite a bang, he thinks. He looks up. It is growing dark early. The wind is strong and the rain hits like pebbles against his skin. It lashes his hair, pulls at his hems.

And now there are shouts from the other side of the door. Someone is pounding on it. An ax is brought to bear. The wedge is holding but soon the door will be mere shards.

He has no time to linger, or doubt.

Below him Isobel is clinging to the sled, mewling like a fawn in a fox net.

"Here we go," he says.

He clambers down onto the sled and lifts the knot from its crook. The sled drops. Isobel gasps. The rope stretches.

"Dee, you fool!"

Dee grips tight. His feet come away from the sled. He feels very exposed. He tries to press himself to the sled and to the rope, but it flows freely through the pulleys above and the sled picks up speed. It grinds down the side of the castle, rattling on the dressed stones of the ramp. Dee's vision quakes. His teeth are rattling free. Isobel is shouting his name.

The sled hits the buffers at the foot of the hill. His fingers are torn from the rope and he is launched into the air and hurled to the ground. His ribs stretch, his brain is shaken loose, and all the air is driven from his lungs. He drags himself a few paces, scrabbling at the tufts of rough grass. Isobel is half off the end of the sled, bagged in the net but alive and coughing.

He is about to say something when the rope tightens.

They are dragging her back up to the wheel room.

He fumbles for his knife.

The rope is thick, and every slash he makes at it, it pulls away from him. He cuts the net instead. Freeing her and holding her arms as the sled pulls away.

"Come on," he urges.

"Stop saying that."

He carries her limp in his arms toward the stables. They are empty with the pilgrims gone home. The gate beyond is open still. The guards are all looking up at the abbey where the bell still rings. Dee straightens his cloak, and resumes his cap, and once more he is M'sieur Dee, pilgrim, come to offer prayers at the shrine of Saint Michael. With his wife.

"Who is taken ill, masters."

The guards look at her doubtfully, but she coughs. Instantly they step back. There have been outbreaks of plague in Italy already this year. It explains why no one tries to stop them leaving, although one guard, so fresh-faced this might be his first day on duty, tells them they will have to rush.

"It is going to be a high one today," he shouts above the wind.

This Dee has anticipated.

Through the gate, the wind is now stronger still. Dee can hardly hear the bell clanging in the belfry, or the gate booming shut behind them. He puts an arm under Isobel and they set off back along the causeway.

"Soon be there," he tells her.

He knows he must time this absolutely perfectly.

The sand under their feet has taken on an oily shimmer. The water is rising. Away to his right, he can see the white lines of surf converging. They are tall and tumble over one another in a tossing froth of surf. For the first time, he feels the clutch of fear.

On they go.

"You only need to get yourself beyond halfway," he tells her.

She is shivering, almost unable to stand.

"Don't tell me to come on," she mutters.

He doesn't. He is looking back over his shoulder.

The gate! It is opening again.

Soldiers spill out onto the causeway. He hears the pop of a gun. So does she.

"They'll have to be better shots than you if they are to hit us in this wind," she says.

"I have already admitted I am no markman," he says. "I am a scientist, a geographer, and an astrologer."

"And an espial for Walsingham."

"Not if I can help it. Come, save your breath."

The soldiers are still shooting.

They will never—

"Ach!" Isobel cries out.

She staggers in his grasp and claps a hand to her hip. She writhes and grunts percussively. Again she curses. She shows him her hand, pink with rain-diluted blood. In her dress, above her right buttock, it is as if someone has stitched a red poppy, with a black center. He might almost see the ball.

"Can you walk?"

She is looking back at the soldiers as if they have wronged her.

"I will have to," she says.

They can hear the waves falling now.

Dee changes sides and she uses him as a crutch. She swears pungently: Walsingham is a coxcomb and a whoreson whelped in a ditch. The sand under their feet is changing character. It stretches and gives, like well-kneaded dough. He looks to her to see what she thinks. She is in pain with every step. Soon he will have to carry her.

Another pop. Closer this time, and something plucks at his cloak hem. The ball skuffs across the sand, bouncing once, twice. Behind him the soldiers come running.

He scoops Isobel up.

She screams with pain.

He ignores her.

In the sand, his feet seem caught in a slow bounce.

Another pop.

"Put me down," she tells him. "I can walk."

"Just a bit farther!"

He forces himself on. His arms and legs and shoulders burn with the effort. He looks over his shoulder. Ha! The soldiers have come too far and they know it. The tide is come in, and they are caught. They are throwing away their guns and their weapons, discarding their armor and helmets as they run, not to be weighed down.

But they are too late. He sees them struggling in the sand, suddenly wading as the earth changes from solid to liquid. Then the waves break around them.

"Put me down," she tells him.

He has to. He takes her hand and drags her along, moving faster now.

The danger is no longer the men; it is the sand and the sea, and the thing they form together.

She stumbles and falls. He goes to pick her up. He will have to carry her after all. He throws her over his shoulder. He sinks in to the sand. The waves crash twenty paces away, the first tails of froth washing about his shins. He unsticks his foot. The next one sinks all the deeper.

"Dee!" she calls. "Dee! Leave me! We will both die!"

"No!"

"Dee, you bloody fool!"

"I won't!"

Suddenly he feels a rough edge across his throat. She has taken his knife and holds it there.

"Leave me! Leave me!"

Another step.

The blade presses.

"For the love of God, Mistress Cochet!"

"Leave. Me."

One more step.

He feels his skin part under the blade. He stops. He is sinking. He tries to throw her, but he can get no purchase and drops her. She sits with his knife pointing at his testicles.

"We can do it!" he shouts.

"No," she shouts back at him. The first wave froths across her legs. She's bleeding heavily.

He has to flex his legs to keep himself from sinking.

It is only another bowshot to safety.

But he knows she is right.

He can't carry her. She can't walk.

"Oh Christ, Mistress Cochet."

"Don't mourn me, Dee. I go to a happier place. But look to my daughter, Dee! See to her! Make sure she has all she needs. Tell her her mother died out of love for her. No. Tell her—her mother loved her."

There are tears in both their eyes.

There is no sign of the soldiers.

Dee extracts one foot. Then another. A moment later he stands five paces from her and the waves are breaking about her shoulders. She manages to stand. She turns to him.

"Dee! Dee!"

He faces her.

"Don't you want to know the numbers?"

The numbers! The numbers. The thing he most needed. The reason he is there. He stands looking at her. The waves are up to her waist, his knees.

She holds his gaze while she shouts them out. There are seventeen of them. Five letters, too. She shouts the sequence twice.

He repeats them back to her.

She laughs. She can't move now. She is anchored, and knows it, finally, as a fact.

"Not much by way of my last words!" she shouts.

"What?" he calls.

"I said, look after Rose! Cherish her!"

This he does hear.

"I will!" he lies.

"Go now, Dee. I don't want you to watch."

He himself can hardly move. He plucks his leg from the sucking sand.

She raises a hand.

He raises his—and turns away just as the first wave engulfs her.

CHAPTER NINE

Auderville, Normandy, Eve of the Feast of the Exaltation of the Holy Cross, September 13, 1572

The churches in this part of Normandy do not have spires. They are solid and squat, and largely unadorned, much like the people hereabouts, but when their bells ring, they are very intimate, and close, and rouse a man from his deepest sleep. Dr. John Dee is not asleep though. He has slept very little in the last four days, not since he left Isobel Cochet to drown on the sands below Mont Saint-Michel.

Since then he has ridden a horse half to death, and wept a great deal, which surprised him, for he did not believe himself the sort given to tears, especially for a woman he hardly knew, and now he sits at this table in this inn in Auderville—a stone-built cottage, barely, with a thatched roof and branch hanging above the door to signal its offer—tormented with guilt at having left her so.

He shakes so badly with the ague that he can hardly read what he has written, but he carries on working through night, lighting each fresh candle from the stump of the last, his shivering body and wretched soul fueled by warm cider laced with butter. The innkeeper-cum-fisherman has covered the fire and rolled out his bed and sleeps on the rushes below with four greyhounds, the dogs' three-quarter-closed eyes occasionally catching the firelight, soft and companionable. The wind is in the chimney and the fisherman whimpers, dreaming perhaps of the perils of the sea, while Dee tries to make sense of the document retrieved from the sacristy of the Abbey of Mont Saint-Michel, and of the numbers Isobel Cochet gave him before she died.

He owes her that, at least.

The chart is as she described: a series of circles, some infilled with letters and numbers. Dee had recognized it as being an unusual astrological chart, round rather than square, with its twelve houses of the heavens, and true node signs. Some of the chart is filled in with signs that Dee recognizes—Leo, Libra, Capricorn, as well as the familiar exaltation and triplicity points and so on, though for some reason Neptune in Aquarius is emboldened in red—but certain key pieces of information are missing.

Obviously these must be the numbers that Isobel Cochet gave him before she died. Once those are entered, then a skillful caster might read the chart backward: to take from what is written here not, as would be usual, the chances of a man's success and happiness, and so on, but to find the place of birth of the man whose chart this might be.

When he first divined this was the chart's secret, Dee was gripped by intellectual excitement. He believed that he might imminently gain knowledge of the whereabouts of the mouth of the Straits of Anian.

But it has not been as easy as that.

The numbers—they do not make sense.

He has tried every combination, in every house of the zodiac, and so far has drawn latitudes that range from the very farthest south any man has yet dared to sail, to those very far north, which, if he can believe it, would put the mouth of the strait somewhere very far to the north, where the ice is so extensive and the cold so deep that no man could suffer it. Where Admiral Willoughby and his expedition had vanished, eaten up by the ice.

This cannot be the opening of the Straits of Anian.

Admiral DaSilva cannot have sailed so far north and returned alive.

It is just not possible.

After trying every permutation of the numbers in the chart with no more plausible results, he began to wonder if DaSilva has further encrypted the numbers. So he has tried to decrypt them, subjecting them to every process he knows—which is every one yet devised by man, from the simple letter frequency analysis technique as described by the Arab mathematician Alkindus, up to the tabula recta system devised by Johannes Trithemius, as well as various polyalphabetic ciphers as have been devised by Blaise de Vigenère in Paris and Leon Alberti in Genoa—but with numbers, and so very few of them, it is impossible to be certain.

And even then, each time he puts his decryptions into the chart and attempts to interpret the result in this strange backward fashion, he still comes up with nothing that is remotely plausible, and he is left wondering if the numbers are either in a cipher of which he has never heard tell—which he cannot believe for surely Baltazar DaSilva is a navigator, not a cryptographer?—or, worse, that Isobel Cochet got the numbers wrong.

And so he sits thinking about this, reliving those last terrible moments on the sands below Mont Saint-Michel, and the more he does so, the more certain he is that she was not wrong. She did not make a mistake. She repeated the numbers perfectly. Twice.

Nor did he make a mistake either. He has a mnemonic system he developed with Petrus Ramus—may God assoil his soul—and even now, days after the event, he is able to rattle the numbers off just as if he had heard them but moments ago.

And yet . . . and yet. He holds Mercator's globe in his palm and he studies the lines of latitude so carefully scribed through its continents, so much of it still terra incognita, and at the top, almost at the pole, is the line of latitude that DaSilva has identified.

Can it be DaSilva who has gotten it wrong?

That is possible. But very improbable. An admiral's logbook is a sacred thing. This page will have been a fair copy of a fair copy, held almost as a reliquary on board the ship.

So where was the mistake introduced?

On he goes, around and around, a dog chasing its own tail.

He will try one last process, he thinks, of which he very recently heard tell by a Neapolitan (the same who showed him the secret mix of plant dyes and alum needed to write on the shell of an egg, so that when it is boiled, the message becomes invisible on the outside, but transfers itself to the hard-boiled yolk). It is a form of the digraphic substitution cipher, applied to the numbers once they are rotated by seven, the number of the chart's emboldened Neptune, first into Latin, and then into Hebrew.

Dee works solidly for a candle's length, and at the end of it, it still makes no sense, and he is about to give up, when he decides to rotate the letters once more, again by seven, this time back into Latin, which he will turn back into numbers to put into the chart.

Before he can complete this final step, though, before he can turn the Latin back into numbers, he finally sees something. Something that leaps out at him amid the jumble of nonsense.

Something no one else in the world would ever find: a message. He freezes. He sits back. The shock of discovery shortens his breath. His hair stirs as if someone has just breathed upon his neck.

But what is it? A communication. A communication from someone, or something, at many stages removed.

My God, he thinks. *My God.*

Ecce Cardan. Here is Cardan.

Jerome Cardan. The great horoscope caster of the late King Edward, forced to flee the country. And to where? Paris.

Dee lays his hands on the table.

The midnight bell rings.

It is the Catholic Feast of the Exaltation of the Holy Cross, and by dawn he must be on the headland with a muffled lamp, ready to answer a signal from out at sea.

But for a further candle's length of time he sits in frozen silence.

Yes. He sees it now. Oh yes. He sees it now.

He knows only what Walsingham has told him as to how the document ended up in Isobel Cochet's hands, and she confirmed that she had killed Walsingham's espial, Oliver Fellowes, but Dee also knows Walsingham of old. Walsingham is a man who weighs every word. He knows its value, not just on the mouth, but to the ear, too. He knows how much a man hears what he wants to hear. And so Dee must go back and analyze every word said, and what was meant, and what Walsingham intended that Dee should think it meant.

As he is in this state of lucid dreaming, thinking about Walsingham and his various machinations that see within the scheme of things, a further possibility, a deeper layer emerges. It makes sense of everything that has happened and makes sense of the chart and of Isobel Cochet's numbers and of her death.

He stands.

He looks down at his papers.

Yes, he thinks, *yes*. Now he sees it. And he finds he has clenched his fists so hard he must unstick his nails from the palms of his hands.

Bloody goddamned bloody butcher Walsingham.

Dee gathers his papers, all the various versions of the horoscope wheel with the numbers applied, and he picks out the one that suggests the mouth of the straits is in the very far frozen north. This is the version in which the numbers are unencrypted. He lays this on his table, held down with his mug and inkpot, and takes the others in a pile and steps around his table, over the innkeeper-fisherman, to the fire. He uses his sleeve to lift the fire cover and sets it aside. Then, one by one, he feeds the slips of paper into the embers and holds them while they burn. He thinks of Isobel Cochet as he does it, how she must have burned the numbers in just such a fashion, and then, when they are burned, properly, he stirs the ashes with the poker and replaces the cover.

He wipes the soot from his fingers on his breeches and shakes the innkeeper-fisherman awake.

"Where is the Nez Bayard?" he asks.

The man is confused. Dee repeats himself twice. Finally, the man understands and tells him.

"North," he says, gesturing. "A thousand paces. Maybe more."

Dee leaves him and returns to his seat at the table and his long-cooled cider, and he sits looking at the single paper—the original stolen from the abbey—and dark tendrils of blackest thought twist up through his body and soul. They wrap themselves about his mind, and they pull tight. But still he does not move for a long moment, and then, when he does, it is to remove his hands from the document, and he leaves it there, with his pen and his bag, and his extra candles.

He waits.

It will not be long now, he thinks. *They will be here soon.*

A moment later all four greyhound heads rise as one.

Dee pinches the candle wick.

In the dark he reaches for Mercator's globe.

He crosses to the door on soft feet. He knows the innkeeper has a crossbow in the rafters, but is it nocked? Probably not. The bolt though. Dee stretches up and finds it and plucks the bolt from its groove. Thick as his finger, long as his hand, a rough iron spike on one end, stubby fletches the other. He slips it up his left sleeve and presses his ear to the planks of the door.

A thin whistle of wind at the cracks. Can he hear the sea? He's not sure. He stands there a good long while. He supposes his eyes would be used to the dark now, if it wasn't so absolute. He steps back to let the door sigh open on the breeze. Gray starlight falls through the opening and he is quickly through and out into the recondite yard.

Overhead, stars. He is facing west.

Ahead is the stable, but a horse snickers to his left, to the south.

Then a voice, a man's in a low murmur, ahead, by the stable.

Dee ducks below the stone course so that his shape is not obvious against the whitewashed wattle, and he moves softly north. The sea is half a league beyond the scrubby trees, and he can hear it now, breaking on the rocks, but Walsingham's instructions were very specific: ask for, find, stand on, and send signal from Nez Bayard at first light on the morning of the Feast of the Exaltation of the Holy Cross.

How he will do that without a lamp is another matter.

First, though, he needs to be out of the trap of the house.

There is a midden to be negotiated, filled with mussel shells, and then he is into untilled pasture where he stops by the sheepfold filled with pale shapes. He thinks, for a moment, of wolves. Then he turns to watch the house. The night is blue black, and inky shapes writhe in his imagination. Or do they? He needs to look twice. Two men, coming around the north end of the house. A moment earlier and he would have met them head-on.

He crouches and waits a moment. He can smell the sheep, but they are very quiet. Are there wolves in this part of France?

How long has he got?

Dee moves around the fold. He sees into the courtyard from here but cannot be seen. A lamp is lit at the third attempt and lights up five figures. Its yellow light catches on steel plate and sharp-edged weapons. Mustard and plum. They gather at the door to smash it open and they vanish within. The dogs go mad, but they are greyhounds, nothing more. There is a period of confused bellowing from inside. Dee can't hear what is said over the barking. At least two men are shouting at someone: he supposes it will be the fisherman.

He waits a little longer. Another lamp is lit. The fire uncovered. The dogs hushed. Things calm down. They must know Dee is gone, but how long has he been gone? He hopes someone knows what they are doing. Yes. Horses. Four or five of them, coming slowly into the courtyard now. It means a commander of sorts. He will have been told what to look out for.

Dee smiles in the darkness.

But there is another role these men must play.

He watches the commander's party dismount and enter the inn. A single man is left holding the horses. Dee unhitches the gate of the sheepfold, takes a stone from the wall, and lobs it over into the midden. There is a slithering crash of empty shells and the dogs start barking again. Men charge from the hall. The sheep react in panic: they spill out of the fold and fill the yard, blocking it perfectly.

Dee sets off northward, toward the sea, toward Nez Bayard.

The others curse the sheep as they set off after him in pursuit. The dogs are on him in moments, but they are still just greyhounds, and nothing more, and they know him from before. They are, Dee thinks, companionable.

The ground here is rocky, covered in springy turf, unlike the sand and mud of Mont Saint-Michel. He is pleased. He stops a moment to make sure they are following him. They are. Five men perhaps. No horses yet. But they are bringing the lamp! It is almost too good to be true. The dogs race back to their masters.

Dee stumbles on. Someone is growing cabbages and onions, but he can smell the tang of woodsmoke; horses and the playful dogs, also the sea, clean and cleansing. He feels his head clearing of the fug induced by trying to interpret the chart and numbers.

And now Dee finds even greater luck: a stream. He ducks low and steps into its cool waters and wades back upstream, shin deep, its waters bracingly cold. He moves as quietly as he can, cutting back south, so that soon he is alongside the cardinal's men on their way to Nez Bayard, unseen in the dark.

He watches the leader carrying the lamp up high.

The men and dogs pass.

Dee waits a moment, until they have crossed the stream, and then he sets off after them. If the fisherman is right, Nez Bayard cannot be much farther.

From the darkness to the left comes a sudden flash of light, then the ragged boom of a gunshot. The man with the lamp goes down with a cry and the lamp falls extinguished.

By Christ!

There is much barking and shouting. The cardinal's men did not expect Dee to have a gun, so they have not brought any, either, and now, with their leader wounded—Dee can hear his cries—

they do not know what to do. Then there is another gunshot from another spot. Too soon after the first to be the same gun loaded. Two guns.

Whose? Dee remains stock-still, his night sight ruined by the flash, his mind reeling in horror: Can these newcomers really have been shooting at the man they thought was him?

The cardinal's men come running back, leaving their leader wounded in the grass. There is yet a third gunshot.

Three gunmen? Dear Christ! They really wanted him dead!

The third bullet hits a dog. Its yelp cuts through Dee more than the man's. The dog rolls in a curl and whimpers piteously.

Dee breathes hard and waits in the shadow of a wind-twisted tree. The wounded man is calling out to his mother and his God, and he can hear the dog dragging itself after its fleeing master, but he cannot hear the gunmen. He needs to know who they are, and what tongue they speak.

He starts his careful steps toward them, keeping low in the stream's course. The wounded man is still calling out, though his voice is fading as the light grows. Dee sees that they are on a headland, and the sea is almost all around them. This must be Nez Bayard.

The stream peters out, vanishing into the scrubland before the beach. A small boat is drawn up, a pinnace, watched over by a boy. Dee lies flat.

The men with guns are approaching now, talking to one another.

Dutch. The knowledge turns Dee's blood to ice.

Someone holds the lamp over the wounded Frenchman.

"Is it him?" one of them asks.

"He signaled, didn't he?"

"Are you Doctor Dee?" one of them asks the man in French.

The Frenchman moans something. It is not clear if it is a denial.

"Must be him," one of the Dutchmen says.

There is a fourth gunshot.

The wounded man is killed.

"Just didn't expect him to have a dog."

A fifth gunshot.

"He doesn't now."

There is some rueful laughter. No one likes to shoot a dog.

"Search him," the leader says. "Captain says he should have some papers."

There is a rustling. A grunt of effort as they turn him over.

"Nothing."

"Well, bring him then. Come on. Wind is getting up."

They carry the dead body down toward the pinnace. They pass quite close to Dee, and he cowers from the lamplight. He can smell the sailors' usual stench of rotting teeth and unwashed bodies. They must have been at sea a fair while, Dee supposes. Come up from trying to break the blockade of the Huguenot city of La Rochelle, perhaps? The dead man has lost his hat, and his head hangs low enough to graze the rocks on the beach. The sailors fling him in the pinnace.

"What are you looking at?" one of them asks the boy by the boat.

Dee watches them through some thrift and a clump of sea kale. They put their guns on top of the dead man, then push the boat down the beach and into the sea. The boy holds the boat's bow while the men clamber in. They ship their oars and the boy pushes them out farther, and then, nimble as a cat, he is up over the bow and in after them. They begin rowing, smooth and easy, out to sea, where Dee sees there is a light, hanging in the skeleton masts of a ship.

Dee lies dead still and waits. Unfamiliar birds are greeting the dawn. He still holds Mercator's globe. After a while he looks up again. The boat is quite far out to sea now.

Dee crawls backward, never taking his eyes from the ship's sails, making sure, and then, when he is, he gets up and begins to run, gripped with the rage of one who has been falsely betrayed.

CHAPTER TEN

Greenwich Palace, September 17, 1572

Greenwich Palace is a few miles downriver from the city of London. It is where the Queen spent the very few happy months of childhood, when she was allowed to play in the hollow oak behind the palace and escape the oppressive loom of her father's affairs that dominated those terrible years. It is the place she is happiest even now, the place to which she repairs when vexed, or confused or frightened, as she is this day.

A new star has been seen in the heavens. It sits above Schedar and Caph, in the constellation of Cassiopeia, and burns as bright as Venus and can be seen during the day, even through thin cloud.

It is a portent, of course, but of what?

No one knows.

"If only we had Dr. Dee to tell us."

No one is talking of Dr. Dee though. Not today, with news of Admiral Quesada's fleet entering the Western Approaches.

"We have reports of militia numbers for Kent and Sussex," Burghley tells the Queen. "Very low."

And:

"Hawkins has sent word to say that if we are to see a single one of his new ships before the year is out he needs more iron, more oak, and more skilled wrights. He says he needs reliable supplies of pitch and canvas, too, and pine trees that can only be found in Sweden."

And:

"The master of the Cinque Ports tells us Her Majesty's castles at Sandown and Walmer are in so parlous a state he doubts either will stand the breath of a cannon for but a single day."

And:

"There is still no sign of Your Majesty's great traitor, James Hamilton."

But:

"Your Majesty's cousin of Scotland remains safe under lock and key in Sheffield."

Her Privy councillors—Lords Burghley, Leicester, and Derby; Sir Thomas Smith also; and plain Master Walsingham—look at one another from the tails of their eyes.

Surely with this great threat bearing down on them, this is the moment to have Mary of Scotland put to death?

Her going out of this world would remove the cause and point of Quesada's invasion.

But the Queen—in mulberry silks, with a collar so stiff with pearls an axman's blade might bounce from them—sits so clenched and pale that none among her Privy councillors dare suggest the obvious.

There is a quavering bleat from Derby.

"Her Majesty cannot in good conscience order the death of a queen likewise anointed by God," he reminds them.

They've heard all this before. Mary of Scotland has perhaps a greater claim to the throne of England than its current occupant, but she is a Catholic, and a whore, and to all intents is French, and if not French then she is Scottish, which is as bad, if not worse. Whichever way you look at it, she is England's and Elizabeth's Great Enemy, of whom Walsingham and Lord Burghley before him have been conspiring to be rid for a long while.

But because she does not wish to set a precedent, Queen Elizabeth of England will not have another divinely anointed queen put to death.

Yet.

After a moment, Walsingham can resist it no longer. He goes to the window. The panes in this room are removed for the day, though there is scarce a breath of wind, and there is only the garden between him and the broad winding snake of the river. The tide is coming in. Across its oozing breadth is the Isle of Dogs: two trees and a cow. Walsingham tries to look downstream, but his view is blocked by a willow tree.

"Are you looking for something, Master Walsingham?" the Queen asks.

"No, Your Majesty," he lies, and he turns back to the room.

"If only we had some money," Derby is bleating still.

"Yes, Walsingham," Sir Thomas Smith reminds all present. "The last time we were gathered together you'd just lost us the location of the Northwest Passage in one of your sky-brained schemes and left us with this fleet of Spanish galleons on their way to unseat Her Majesty."

Walsingham nods, for, in truth, that is what he had done.

"You promised you would reclaim the page from Admiral DaSilva's logbook, Master Walsingham," Derby continues, "and decode it for us, too, so that we might find some way to resist the

Spanish might. So that we might find some way to preserve not only Her Majesty, you, me, and everyone you see here, but also this our nation, and the faith you profess to hold so dear."

The Queen waits. Does he begin his defense now? Or let the thing run its course?

"Your Majesty," Walsingham begins. "My lords, I—"

And it is then, at that precise point, they hear the dull rap of a gunshot.

All flinch. Their heads whip to the open window, whence the sound comes. The doors crash open and suddenly the room is filled with bulky inconsiderate men with weapons. Her Majesty's halberdiers. Master Beale, too, sword drawn. Leicester leaps to his feet and places himself before the Queen along with the halberdiers, protecting her. Leicester wears a vest of steel against assassination attempts, Walsingham remembers, so feels safe enough.

Every man holds his breath. For a long moment nothing happens.

"Is it him? Is it Hamilton?"

Beale is at the window, peering out around its edge.

"A ship," he says.

"Stay back, Your Majesty!" the captain of the guard instructs.

"No," Beale says. "Look."

He gestures and Walsingham joins him.

On the river: a ship, a smudge of smoke over her bows, her sail dipping to join the gunshot in salute.

"What ship is that?" Smith asks.

He squints for his eyes are becoming bad.

"She's a *fluyt*," Beale tells them. "A Sea Beggar, but my God! Look at her. She's knocked about."

"Seen better days," Walsingham agrees.

The ship is very low in the water. Her mast is jury-rigged and her mainsail ragged and smoke smutted.

"What is she doing here?" Smith asks.

Dutch ships such as this are recently forbidden in English waters.

Walsingham turns to Beale.

"Let us see what her captain has to say before we send to have her impounded," Walsingham tells him.

The Queen steps from behind her human shield, thanking those who would save her life, and she demands the captain of the vessel is brought to her presence. Her color is up. An attempt on your life will do that for you, Walsingham supposes.

After that it is impossible to settle down.

Burghley sends for more wine, and there is the suspicion that Stanley has lost control of his bladder, so the Queen wants air, and they follow her out to the shade of a cedar tree in the palace's formal garden, where ice is brought, along with the first of this year's apples from Kent, and the captain of the Dutch ship.

"Is this really necessary, Walsingham?" Smith demands. "Really? A Sea Beggar before our Queen?"

But the Queen is intrigued. Smith reluctantly sends his secretary, amiable Nicholas Gethyn, to fetch the man.

Gethyn! In among the comings and goings, Walsingham remembers that when last they met Gethyn had something to tell him but was too diffident to spit it out. He was going to ask Beale to look into it. He makes a note of it.

He wonders if his wife has given birth to that eleventh child yet? Or is it about Ireland? Walsingham has already heard that Smith's venture to colonize the north with Englishmen is not going according to plan. It has cost many lives and much money and will continue to do so for how long? Years, at least.

When Gethyn returns, coughing with a kerchief to his lips, he is escorting the Dutch sea captain, *Meneer* Willem van Treslong. Unlike his ship, Van Treslong looks very fine, as if he has had time to visit a tailor, or planned for such an entrance. He wears a light almost silvery doublet and airy rose-colored breeches quite as large as any of them have ever seen.

"He might have used them to patch his sails," Beale jokes.

Up close his collar and cuffs are bright and starchy white, but his eyes are rimmed red and made Walsingham want to rub his own.

Van Treslong bows very low when he makes his obeisance to the Queen.

She greets him with some familiarity, and ambiguity, for it was she who had evicted him and his kind from English ports to placate King Philip of Spain, whose life they made a misery. It was a lesson in being careful of what you wish for, though, because the Dutchmen sailed across the North Sea to seize from the Spanish their ports of Den Brill and of Flushing, from where they still sail to harass their erstwhile masters.

"I dare say King Philip wishes you were still our guests?" The Queen laughs, removing her hand from Van Treslong's grip.

"What is the meaning of this, Master van Treslong?" Smith demands. He is very discontented, for Van Treslong is everything he is not: small, dapper, and Dutch, while Smith is baggy, saggy, and English. He further remains furious that the Dutchman's arrival has allowed Walsingham to wriggle from the Queen's hook.

"Ach, Your Majesty, gents, lords, sirs, I bring news," Van Treslong says. He speaks wonderfully mangled English, slicing across his words as if he held in his mouth a cupful of wet pebbles. "I have just sailed the Western Approaches, from La Rochelle, and I tell you we sighted your Spanish fleet. Quesada's fleet. That sailed out of Bilbao this last month."

"You saw her?" Burghley asks.

"Sure. Fifteen ships, sir, galleons and carracks, all well-armed. As you see."

He indicates his battered ship.

"She caught us off Ushant three days ago. Wind died, then veered. Long story. Anyway. We get away by skin of teeth. Two dead, including Piet the pilot. We think, my God, us next, but then, before we reach Guernsey, they veer southeast, and leave us to beat northeast. Prayers answered I'm saying. I think, sure, they putting into Saint-Malo. Maybe not enough fodder for horses, eh?

"So we wait off Alderney. Repairs, you know. Cut the mast away, put in a spar, and got the rudder answering. But always, with eyes out, you know?"

He points at his eyes.

"Two days. No sign of fleet, day or night. We start to think maybe she slipped by in the dark? But then, third day, we see her. Sailing . . ."

He holds up a finger and smiles.

". . . west!"

The others—Smith, Leicester, Burghley—are confused, but Walsingham almost laughs. West! West! He feels a great weight lifted. Suddenly he can hear birds sing.

"West," he repeats.

It means Quesada is heading out into the Atlantic.

The Privy councillors look at one another in confusion.

"Then we are—saved?" Burghley wonders with a dawning smile.

"For the moment," Leicester cautions.

Derby, Walsingham notes, very nearly crosses himself before remembering where he is.

"Why?" Smith wants to know. "Why has he sailed west?"

"Why?" Van Treslong repeats. "How should I know?"

"Ireland?" Burghley wonders.

That is always a risk: that the Spanish would land troops in Waterford, or Wexford, and so have a base from which to attack England at their leisure.

Van Treslong thinks not. "West," he says, cutting the blade of his palm down. "Out into the ocean, to catch the trade winds."

"To New Spain?"

"Sure. Maybe. Why not?"

But his venture in Ireland excepted, Smith is no fool.

"It is not New Spain he is heading for! It is the Northwest Passage! That's where he is sailing to! They've decrypted DaSilva's pages! They know where it is! By Christ, Walsingham, you have put us out of the pan and into a fire that will roast us for a very long time!"

Walsingham opens and closes his mouth. At some point he knows he is going to have to tell them: that the DaSilva documents were elaborate forgeries of his own device, made with the help of an old exile, Jerome Cardan, whom he recruited in Paris, and who claimed—with some justification, clearly—to know his way around a natal chart. But he will not tell them yet. Not until this scheme has run its course. Not perhaps until Quesada's fleet is wrecked upon the shores of Newfoundland or gripped fast in the ice farther north.

Van Treslong looks incredulous.

"The Northwest Passage?" he wonders. "You found it?"

Smith will not share the tale with a mere Dutch Sea Beggar.

"We almost did," he snaps. "Until Master Walsingham here lost it in one of his foolhardy schemes of espial."

Gratitude does not last long, Walsingham thinks.

"Pity," is Van Treslong's opinion.

"If what you say of the state of our defenses is true," the Queen says, "then it is a blessing that Quesada has been diverted, even if it is to find the Northwest Passage. It will allow us time to make reparations. To recruit men. To fetch masts from Sweden. Bend your energies that way, Sir Thomas, rather than waste time in fruitless recrimination."

Smith is incandescent but can say nothing further.

"But *Meneer* van Treslong," the Queen continues. "What of the other task with which we entrusted you? What news of our most trusted and entirely beloved Dr. Dee?"

Later, Francis Walsingham will think about this moment, and think that Willem van Treslong was panicking, but at the time, when the Dutchman stands about to say something, only to stop and close his mouth with a snap, he thinks only that Willem van Treslong is regretful. He is stoppered up, Walsingham believes. He wishes himself elsewhere so that he need not be the one to pass on bad news. Only his eyes move as his gaze roves about the glade, looking for safe berth.

It dawns on Walsingham what Van Treslong cannot bring himself to say.

"He is dead?" Walsingham asks.

Van Treslong nods once, very slowly.

Walsingham cannot believe it. Dee—dead? Another soul to stain his conscience. But then he thinks, if Dee is dead, then how did Quesada come to decrypt the chart, or so they believed? And what is Van Treslong even doing here? Can he wish to bring the good news so dearly? Ah no: his ship. He wants the Queen to offer use of the dry dock.

Meanwhile all look to the Queen, who has shut her eyes, and tilted her head back to prevent the tears leaking down her powdered cheeks. She is utterly, unexpectedly grief-stricken.

"Oh, John," she says. "Whatever will I do without my eyes?"

Her eyes. It is the nickname she had for Dee, Walsingham recalls, from some silly symbol Dee'd once scratched on the wall of his cell when they were both in the Tower together. He—Walsingham—has the report somewhere. A monad? Something like that. It was one of the many things that had spurred Leicester to act—without her knowledge, of course—to separate the two, so that she did not fall further under Dee's influence and succumb to his more outlandish theories.

"Well, good riddance," Smith says. "I never liked him. Too clever by half."

There is a moment's surprise, for this is disloyal in the extreme, but Smith is actually beaming with pleasure, and might even dance a jig, while the others, Walsingham notes, the others think more or less the same thing.

"The bastard punched me once," Leicester says. "I have never forgotten that, though . . ."

He seems of two minds.

"Nevertheless, gentlemen," Walsingham says, "he has performed a most valuable service for his Queen and his country, and . . . and . . ."

He indicates the Queen, who is still sitting with her eyes shut.

The others mumble their reluctant acceptance of his point. Gethyn coughs softly and looks at his kerchief as if for traces of something. Smith shoots him a strange, gloating look. Walsingham tries to recall why Smith so hates Dee.

It was something to do with his infernal colony in Ireland, he remembers now, and how Dee suggested the Queen invest what little money she had elsewhere in the New World rather than in Smith's scheme in Ulster. Smith had taken it very badly.

"With Your Majesty's permission," Walsingham starts, "I will show *Meneer* Van Treslong to our kitchens. Perhaps give him a bun."

The Queen opens her eyes.

"Yes," she approves.

But Van Treslong hesitates and simpers a little. He indicates his ship, out at anchor in the river.

"I was hoping," he says. "My ship . . . We've made some repairs, but . . ."

He trails off. It is not an unreasonable request, but the Queen is ever prudent with money. This time, though, she honors her debts.

"*Meneer* van Treslong has taken pains on our behalf," she says, "and in recompense for his efforts, especially in regard to our beloved John Dee, I am more than happy to offer him such assistance as he needs to furnish his good ship anew."

Van Treslong straightens the tips of his mustache and bows in gratitude.

Walsingham leads him in retreat through the garden, on which the Dutchman has some thoughts.

"Absurd, these strange patterns of hedges and beds."

"Celtic knots," Walsingham tells him.

"*Pffft.*"

When they are beyond earshot, Walsingham speaks.

"What happened with Dr. Dee?" he asks.

Van Treslong's smile falters, and he pulls a face. He shakes his head.

"I did as the Queen instructed," he says, "but when we got there, it was crawling with soldiers—we thought the cardinal's."

He trails off. He is wearing strong perfume, Walsingham notices. Ambergris. But the smell of his body is beginning to emerge in the warmth of this late sun. It is the truth, behind the lies.

"So?" Walsingham asks. "You saw the body?"

Van Treslong nods tightly.

"Took it off, as instructed, and then—overboard. At sea."

Walsingham never liked Dr. Dee, but this—is not what he wanted.

"He will be with his precious angels, I suppose," he says.

"Sure," Van Treslong says. "And he served his purpose, no?"

Walsingham agrees.

But then he wonders when he ever told Van Treslong what that purpose was.

"Do you believe Quesada is sailing for the Northwest Passage?" he asks.

Van Treslong is unsure.

"At this time of year," he says, "no, but he might cross the ocean to be ready to sail north when the ice melts in spring?"

In his wildest dreams, Walsingham sometimes hoped that Quesada would be foolhardy enough to follow DaSilva's directions there and then and find himself trapped by ice and freeze to death, but no one is such a fool as to set off into the northern latitudes in September.

"Though we can live in hope, eh, Francis?" Van Treslong laughs.

"Have you told anyone else about Quesada?" Walsingham wonders.

"Only you, and . . ."

He gestures at the Queen and the members of the Privy Council gathered in the shade of the cedar tree. They are trying to console her. Did she really feel so strongly about Dee? Walsingham feels a further twist of the blade of guilt. Burghley, in his red, looks rotten, and Smith is still jeering, and it is only Gethyn who looks to the Queen's person and comfort.

"Good," Walsingham says. "Will you keep it to yourself, Willem?"

Van Treslong looks at him carefully.

"Controlling the flow?"

"Something like that," Walsingham agrees.

An hour later Walsingham is at Seething Lane, and Beale wonders at his boss.

"You do not seem so very pleased?" he asks.

"I am," Walsingham tells him.

"But?"

"But it is a mere reprieve. They will be back to set her free next year, or the year after. So long as she is alive. They will be back. And each time, stronger than ever."

He means Mary of Scotland, of course, and the Spanish, or the French. He is forcibly stuffing linens in a saddlebag.

"Pack your stuff, will you, Master Beale," he says.

"Where are we going, Master Walsingham?"

"Up t'North," he says. "To t'Sheffield to see if we cannot once and for all declaw the bitch."

The road north is long, but they travel it swiftly, lightly encumbered on good horses, and without drawing overmuch attention to themselves they aim to be in Sheffield within five days. A courier might have overtaken them, in the night, say, or by a different road, so they ride fast and far each day, doing as much as they might to forestall word of Quesada's change of tack from reaching Sheffield before they do, and most especially the castle's royal prisoner.

Beale had broached the subject of Dr. Dee on that first day.

"So he did not manage to retrieve the DaSilva document?"

Walsingham had shrugged.

"Perhaps we will never know," he said, which had struck Beale as strange, but Walsingham was deep in thoughts elsewhere.

"Talbot knows to expect us," he had told his secretary, "the others, too."

"The others?"

"The watchers, in the castle."

They ride in silence after that, both thinking, and Beale divines the scheme before they reach Oakham. Or at least identifies its possibilities.

"How can you be certain that Queen Mary knew Quesada was coming to rescue her?" Beale asks.

Walsingham, never comfortable on a horse, gives him a look.

Of course, Beale thinks, *he told her so himself.*

"I had to explain why her guard was doubled," Walsingham admits.

Beale laughs.

"So how will she hear that Quesada has changed course?" he wonders.

Another, different look from Walsingham.

"Ah," Beale says. "That remains to be seen?"

They ride in silence for a bit. Walsingham's eyebrow is cocked, waiting for the next bit, waiting for Beale to say: "And when she does, if she does, she will be utterly dejected and will send desperate messages to Hamilton, forgetting all precaution of secrecy!"

Et voilà!

"That is very neat," Beale has to admit.

Walsingham almost smiles as they ride.

He thinks so too.

There is, though, one thing, or perhaps two, that bother him still.

The first is *Meneer* van Treslong.

The second is also *Meneer* van Treslong.

PART | TWO

CHAPTER ELEVEN

Sheffield, September 22, 1572

The town is of gray stone, handsome, with a marketplace in which to buy strong cloth and cheap pies. The dogs are lean, the tongues are sharp, and the scent of burning coal hangs thick in the air. At its heart: the castle, of the same gray stone, and of the old sort that has stood three hundred years or more but might now be knocked down in an afternoon by a single cannon. Moat and ditches to the south and a lively brown river—the Don—under its northern wall.

In rising dusk and falling rain, Masters Walsingham and Beale leave their horses at the stable and cross the drawbridge, but they linger in the gatehouse and do not enter the cobbled bailey.

"One of her household will see us," Walsingham says.

Instead a servant is sent to find George Talbot, Earl of Shrewsbury, who will meet them in the guardroom of the gatehouse. When Talbot comes he is about forty, forty-five perhaps, with a spreading beard and sad, wise eyes. How does he feel about his charge? Does he see her in the round, as a person? Or does he, like every other man, see her as a threat, or a means to an end? Beale cannot guess. But there is another dimension of course: should Queen Elizabeth die without issue, then Queen Mary of Scotland will take her throne. How would she then repay a gaoler who mistreated her now?

"She is at prayer," Talbot tells them. "Up there."

He points through a door to the limestone tower in the south-western corner of the castle. It is three stories high, with windows from which light filters through thick panes. The rain still comes down, and a fire would be nice, Beale thinks.

"Anyway, this way," Talbot tells them, and he leads them through a long kitchen in which a boy sits staring at an empty pot, and a deserted bake house that smells of mold. They pass through a very thick oak door and find themselves in the tower, the ground floor of which is given over to a hall, from which lead two doors, and a spiraling flight of closed steps up into the darkness above.

Talbot knocks very gently on one of the doors and a moment later a bolt is drawn back. The door swings open on oiled hinges to reveal a tired-looking man with his shirtsleeves rolled up, despite the cold.

No one says anything about the strong smell of shit.

Walsingham doesn't introduce him. "Wouldn't be his real name anyway."

"Arthur Gregory," the man says, catching Beale's eye, but not offering to shake his hand.

Walsingham grunts good-naturedly. "As I say, not his real name."

On the table is what might be a chamber pot covered in a linen cloth.

"That hers?" Walsingham asks, just as if he has spoken to Gregory not five minutes earlier.

Gregory grunts affirmatively.

"Anything?"

Gregory lifts the linen cover of the chamber pot. The stinking mess within sits in a bath of purple liquid.

Beale is shocked. Walsingham is unsurprised.

"Porphyria," he tells him.

Then he turns back to Gregory: "Who's upstairs?"

"John Wilkins."

"And with Mary?"

"Lord and Lady Livingston, Mary Seton, the priest they've got pretending to be her usher, and Margaret Formby."

Walsingham nods.

"Come this way," he tells Beale, "but take off your boots."

Beale does so. He has been wearing the same socks for five days. Walsingham leads him up the steps and along a short corridor, the boards powdered so they do not creak, past a door through which they can hear the burble of a man's voice, and on to another, smaller door, iron battened, and seemingly made for a dwarf. Walsingham has a key. He opens it on more oiled hinges and crouches to enter. Beale follows. Inside it is absolutely dark save for one tiny spec of light that comes in about waist height. There is another man within, sitting on a stool. The room smells rank.

No word is spoken.

They can hear the man's voice more clearly. He's chanting the Latin Mass. The hair on Beale's arms stands on end: this is enough to get them all hanged.

The man on the stool moves to let Walsingham press his eye to the hole. After a moment he lets Beale take his turn. The hole is drilled through the plaster, through a knot in the wainscoting, and there is little enough to see: a chair covered above with a purple cloth of state; the heels of three kneeling women. That's it.

Despite his own socks, Beale can smell the man next to him, John Wilkins. It is like gaol scent, and he is pleased when Walsingham taps him on the shoulder and they are able to leave him to it.

Talbot is waiting in the kitchens.

"There is one more thing," he tells them. "The Queen has sent permission for Her Majesty to go hawking this week."

Walsingham is surprised.

"When did this come?"

"Today. In the hand of Sir Thomas Smith."

Beale calculates that this means the Queen must have granted permission five days earlier, probably longer, when, to all intents and purposes, Quesada was on his way to attack England, burn London down, and set Queen Mary free. The last thing they would have wanted was for her to be out in the countryside, on a horse, with a hawk. A spasm of irritation crosses Walsingham's face.

"And you've told her? Queen Mary?"

Talbot nods, as why should he not have?

"I will have Beale ride along," Walsingham decides. "You like hawking, don't you, Robert? You can borrow one of Sir George's birds."

They leave the castle through the postern gate and make their way back up to an inn—the White Hart—that Walsingham knows. It is thatch and timber-built, overlooking two fish ponds, and prey to damp.

"You will concentrate on Margaret Formby, won't you, Robert?" Walsingham says.

Beale knows what he must do.

Walsingham hardly drinks a thing. He is rapt, and his eyes are glossy and fierce, Beale thinks, like one of those hunting birds; his whole self is honed but for one purpose. And that purpose? To catch Queen Mary in the act, to find proof that she is plotting the death of her cousin Elizabeth of England; to find incontrovertible proof of it, that he may, at last, and once and for all, lay before his mistress and force her hand in the matter. He wants to bring about the death of that woman.

Sleep that night comes hard, and Walsingham wakes Beale long before dawn to tell him that it is raining.

No hawking.

Walsingham paces all day. He is a ball of heat, twitching in frustrated fury.

"God damn it! God damn her!"

He writes messages then won't send them. He scraps the page or burns it. Once he laughs very bitterly.

"Dr. Dee," he says, "he always swore there was a way of communicating instantly over very long distances. He said there was a book—one he couldn't find—that described how it was done. Something to do with angels."

Beale notices Walsingham talks of Dee in the past.

The next day Beale is once again woken by Walsingham, his pacing this time. Up and down the end of the mattress they have shared. Beale lies in bed. He can hear the rain on the roof. Still no hawking.

"We have but six months' grace, Robert," Walsingham tells him more than twice that day. "Six months before the Spanish equip and send another fleet. We'll still be as poor as we ever were, and *that devilish woman* will still be alive, sending out her treacherous messages, like some terrible spider, pulling men into her web of treasonous deceit. I will not have it! I will not have it! I cannot be thwarted by this accursed rain. I cannot."

The day after that, it dawns bright and clear, as if the rain has washed the air. It will be good for hawking.

"Thank God," Beale says softly. He would not have been able to stand another day of Walsingham's impatient fretting.

Beale is to pass as a member of Talbot's household, and he presents himself at the castle in riding clothes. The ostlers and stable lads have the horses ready in the bailey, and though there may be thirty or so riders in the party, Queen Mary is instantly the center of attention. It is the first proper sight Beale has of her, and he feels as he did when as a child he was taken to his first bear-baiting: he could not then believe such an animal as a bear might exist, and yet there it was. When he saw it in the pit, he could not take his eyes from it. It is the same with Mary, Queen of Scots: human and yet not. She is veiled in the French manner, aloof and isolated, and she looks sickly, moving as if in pain, and Beale recalls the purple contents of her chamber pot.

He has to tear his gaze from her, for he has been told to look for Lord and Lady Livingston, whom he identifies as the nervy man and his anxious wife; and Mary Seton, the last of the queen's longtime companions, all four of whom were also called Mary. She is fraught and fussing impatiently with points and buckles. Beale wonders what it might be like to have your fortunes depend so much on one person. Beale's eye is then drawn to the girl trailing behind: Margaret Formby. She looks cowed, he thinks, as if straining under a mental load. No. She looks guilty. That is it.

He looks forward to telling Walsingham his divination. He can imagine him now: utterly restive, pacing up and down, waiting; waiting for Beale to come back with his report; waiting to get on with the next part of his plan. The thought makes Beale smile, though it should not. It is the death of a queen they are talking about.

After a while during which pewter cups of warm wine are passed around, and the birds are brought from their mews and cautiously admired, the queen is anxious to be off. Beale lingers at the back, almost with the servants, while at the head of the party Queen Mary rides with unexpected ease. Behind her comes George Talbot, hunched in his saddle as if going to a funeral, and Beale realizes that far from being the usual happy hunting party, there is a strange nervous tension to this one, as if everyone is primed for a disappointment.

They pass through the furlongs and market gardens that surround the town, and everything is at the peak of harvest. Men and women come to the wayside smiling and offering a taste of their produce: apples, pears, strawberries even, and it should be a sight to gladden any heart, but the hunting party seems immune to its pleasures.

When they emerge onto sheep-cropped pastures at the top of the hill, they look down into the town below as if into a plate: the castle, the church, the marketplace, and the houses all packed within its walls and rivers. On the other side of the hill is a stretch of moorland, and beyond, deep oak and beech woods where the huntsman says the beaters are ready.

It is perfect.

There follows the usual fussing about with the birds: their hoods, their jesses. The huntsman signals his men in the nearby wood, who start beating the trees and soon the sky is filled with the alarm calls of various fleeing birds. This is when the hawks should be launched, but the hunting party remains stationary in their saddles, waiting for the queen to remove the hood of the bird she has been passed.

"Come on," Beale finds himself murmuring. "What is she waiting for?"

But she will not do it. He can hear the sigh suppressed in every chest. Here we go again.

The huntsman looks desperate.

A long, long moment passes.

The beaters are still beating but the wood is emptying of birds. The sky likewise.

Beale has slowly maneuvered himself to be alongside Margaret Formby.

"Shame," he murmurs.

She glances at him. Under her veils she is very pale. She seems on the verge of tears.

When at last nothing seems to be about to happen, there is one last bird, a pigeon of some sort, that comes flapping up out of the margins of the wood. How the beaters can have missed it, Beale cannot guess.

And only now does Queen Mary remove the hood of her falcon and, when its eyes are right, and it has seen the pigeon, she sets it free. It drops and hurtles through the air and it brings its prey down with precise ease. The pigeon tumbles to the ground and the dogs bound down through the bracken after it. The falcon circles back and kills it but is put to flight by the dogs.

He comes circling back to Mary's glove and lands with a thump. There is polite applause. Mary seems not quite indifferent to the bird, but she is watching the huntsman extract the pigeon's little body from the jaws of the dog, and the way he gives the dog a treat of sorts.

"May I have it?" she asks.

It is the first time Beale has heard her speak. Her accent is neither French nor Scottish, but somewhere in between. He'd like to hear her speak more. The huntsman brings her the bird. It is not an everyday pigeon, Beale sees, but a dove of some sort. Probably escaped from a nearby cote.

"Won't do that again," he jokes.

Margaret Formby glances at him again. She looks terrified.

"Are you quite well, my lady?"

She nods tightly. She will hardly look at him. Instead she watches Queen Mary with a feverish intent.

Beale is rebuffed.

Meanwhile Mary holds up the dove for her falcon to take sharp pecks at and returns it to the huntsman to do with it as he will.

There is a settling sense of unsurprised disappointment among the hunting party when Mary summons Lord Livingston to her side and tells him something none can hear. He announces that Her Majesty is tired and wishes to return to her chamber.

Hoods are put back on birds, and jesses are tightened.

Beale knows better than to suppose the rest of them might stay to enjoy the rest of their day.

The party turns and winds back down the hill after the queen, the day done.

He returns his horse to the stable and tips the ostler and finds himself back in the hall of the White Hart before noon.

"Well?" Walsingham asks almost before he is through the door.

He tells him all he saw. Walsingham writes down all he says.

"What did you make of Margaret?"

"She is very unsettled."

Walsingham is pleased. He senses a stress point. A possible fracture.

That night Walsingham sends Beale to the castle to relieve Wilkins in Queen Mary's tower. Wilkins open the door.

"Just in time," he says.

Her Majesty's chamber pot is still warm and in its puddle of purple urine is a sizable turd.

"What do you want me to do with that?" Beale asks.

"You have to go through it," Wilkins tells him.

"Why?"

"Two years ago we found a note tied in a length of sheep's gut. They'd paid the dong farmer to tip it to one side."

Christ.

"It is the only way she can get anything out," he goes on. "So. We do what we must. I've got everything ready."

There's a bucket of water and a block of black soap. There's also a spoon.

"You have to kind of . . ."

Wilkins mimes a pressing action with the spoon.

Beale gets to work. He gags constantly.

After a moment there's a thick paste and a little knot of what could be anything.

"Give it a wash," Wilkins tells him when he shows him.

He picks it out with the tip of the spoon. Into the bucket of water and then vigorous stirring. Then he fishes it out and puts it on the table.

He still doesn't want to touch it.

"She's a queen for Christ's sake." Wilkins laughs. "It's an honor to touch her shit."

Eventually he teases the knot apart. A thin strip of silk, that's all. Wilkins whistles.

"So what?" Beale asks.

"Maybe nothing," Wilkins admits, "but how did it get there?"

"She must have eaten it," Beale supposes.

Wilkins agrees. "But why, eh? That's the question."

"We'll have to show it to Master Walsingham," he says. "He'll be pleased."

Beale goes to stand outside, to get some air.

Above, in Cassiopeia, the new star shines as bright as ever.

CHAPTER TWELVE

Sheffield Castle, September 25, 1572

There is not a single thing—ewer, candlestick, book, sample of embroidery, pot of dried flower heads—left atop any surface. All have been swept to the floor, and Margaret Formby has never seen the queen in so foul a fit of rage. Mary Seton strokes the queen's back, whispering to her in French, while the queen stands leaning straight-armed against the window, legs apart and breathing very heavily. It is, Margaret thinks, as if she were giving birth.

She wishes she had never come here. She wishes she had never entered Mistress Seton's service. It had seemed perfect at the time, but as soon as they came south and found the bonds of captivity tightening around the queen's household, something dark and ungodly had entered her life like a canker in a rosebud.

When Margaret was first asked to perform the strange procedures for Queen Mary, she was told they were on the orders of Mary's French physician. It was a way of isolating the malign humors they told her. Margaret had been flattered to be so trusted to tie the knots in just such a way—tight, tight, really tight, but not *too* tight—but when, afterward, when they would summon her back to untie the ropes, she was always shocked to see the queen's body dissected by the welts the cords left in her soft, soft flesh, and the patchy rashes left from the beeswax they melted over her naked body. There were often puckered pinch marks too: once she saw Mary Seton rubbing down the queen with a linen cloth, and her pale, blue-veined breasts were crowned with green bruises.

Soon after that Mistress Seton told Margaret that Her Majesty's health was not improving, despite the time spent in the cords, and the French physicians had sent further instructions that involved more strenuous efforts at soothing Queen Mary, and of removing the malignant humors manually.

"No one must know that Her Majesty is ill," Mary Seton said. "Nobody."

And so it had begun, an almost daily regimen of stroking the queen's nether parts until she shuddered.

"That is good," Mary Seton said. "You are good at this."

Margaret was surprised this was good for the queen's health. She had done it to herself more than once, and afterward always felt drained and a little depressed. Queen Mary seemed to seek what she called "translation" and yet the very moment it was over, she found it repellent, every aspect and even the idea of it. But soon she would demand it once more, as if this time it would end her miseries. It never did. She never felt better.

Meanwhile further orders came from the French physicians—though how, Margaret never knew—to rub harder, faster, and to push her fingers more deeply. The physician said she must bite the queen's breasts, not so hard to draw blood, but to leave the nipples raw.

And then the suppression of the airway started, and she went to Mistress Seton, who had by this time passed onto her all these medical duties, and Margaret told her it frightened her to be half strangling the queen, and of her fears of misjudging it.

"You must do as she commands," Mistress Seton had told her.

"But it feels—against God's command," she'd said.

"You must do as she commands."

And so she had.

Time and time again, until now she has become an almost constant companion and knows the queen's body—not just its outer appearance, but its inner workings—better than her own.

But she is not happy. The queen's morbid neediness for this stimulation sickens her and she has come to dread the summons: "Margaret."

But what is she to do? She was plucked from her family in Scotland and is risen above all other maids, high, yet not so high as Mary Seton, and so there is no one with whom she can talk, share fellowship, or find relief for herself. She finds she craves fresh air, silence, a cool wind in her face, spring sunshine, the chatter of children, anything but this oppressive shared captivity. She could scream.

"Margaret."

Oh God.

This time the queen wishes for rapture for the wrong reasons. She is fixated, almost mad with desire for it, yet is not at all desirous, and is so tense and burningly miserable that rose oil needs to be used, and her breath is hot and foul, and she never relaxes, and so it is almost impossible. No. It *is* impossible. It is dangerous. Margaret panics and loses her touch. The queen will not be delivered.

"Get off me! Get off me! Get out!"

Margaret leaps away as if scalded.

"Mary! Mary!" the queen shouts and Mary Seton comes swiftly to her side to correct her dress. The queen is clench fisted, weeping hot tears of anguish. Mary Seton soothes her as she would a child, and Margaret hurries away, likewise in tears. She cannot stand it. She cannot stand being cooped up all day in this foul atmosphere, performing all these wicked tasks.

She runs down the steps and out into the castle bailey.

Guards in Shrewsbury's colors watch her impassively. She walks and walks, and only occasionally does she glance up at the top floor of the tower, where she sees a face, briefly, like a smear at the window, but what is she to them?

At length Mary Seton sends John Kennedy to fetch her in. He is a boy of about fifteen winters, someone's son, obviously. He runs errands and fetches bottles and so forth. Most of the time he sits by the door of the bailey, whittling spoons and leaving piles of splinters. Ordinarily they hardly speak to each other, though they might be five years apart in age, and from similar families, though his are from Edinburgh, she knows, while hers are of York. He is very pale skinned, with cheeks that flare whenever he speaks to a woman.

"Mistress Seton is after you," he tells her.

Margaret hardly knows what to expect. Will she be sent packing? If she is honest, she does not care.

In fact, it is an errand: to walk with John Kennedy into town and rent him a horse at the White Hart, in Mary Seton's name.

"Her Majesty is very upset, Margaret," Mary Seton tells her in a very low voice. Like Queen Mary she has eyes the color of polished hazelnuts. "And needs this done as it is a matter of grave import, but we are much observed by the Queen's enemies, so keep this close, and make certain you are not seen going to, or coming back from the inn."

It is easier said than done, of course, but Talbot's guards are oafish and care only for Queen Mary's whereabouts.

John Kennedy wears a traveling cloak and carries a bag in which is some awkward shape.

When they are on the street, out of sight of the castle, Margaret asks him what it is.

"Can't tell you," he says.

"Go on."

"A candlestick," he tells her with a shrug.

"Where are you taking it?"

"Back home," he says. "I've got a message writ here for a man, but—"

Another shrug.

She cannot read either. "Will you come back?"

He looks very uncertain.

"I am told I must," he says, "though by God I do not wish it."

Queen Mary watches the flickering shape of Margaret Formby returning across the castle's bailey through the lumpen glass in her windows. The girl has a tendency to stoop, she thinks. It is an unattractive habit.

"The new man was making himself agreeable to her," Queen Mary tells Mary Seton.

"Oh yes?" Mary Seton smiles.

Queen Mary laughs softly. "And do you trust the boy?" she asks.

"I do, Your Majesty."

She is still trying to be soothing. She might stroke her hair were she not wearing a veil.

The queen is still unable to believe what she read in the message received today. Quesada has diverted his fleet, and the prospect of her release is stillborn. She is now stuck here in this miserable castle as a prisoner for all eternity. It would have been better for her if he had not sailed at all! At least then she might still be at Tutbury, or taking the waters at Buxton, which allowed her some freedom. Some air. Here in Sheffield she is overwatched constantly. Not just by the Earl of Shrewsbury, and all his many men and servants, but by Burghley and Walsingham's mice downstairs too. Even if she could not sometimes smell them, she would know they were there, know she was being subjected to this close watch. She has acquired the sense in her years at various courts, first in France, and then in Scotland. There is a tight airlessness to the world about her, as if there are no gaps in anything, no sense of space beyond the walls.

Still, she thinks, she is not done yet.

She watches Margaret Formby until she disappears below, out of sight, and then there is a gentle thud of a door being closed.

How long will it take? she wonders.

A day? Two? A week at the most. Or will they wait until the boy reaches Edinburgh?

But what if it doesn't happen at all?

She has nothing else to do but wait anyway.

She turns away from the window.

"Margaret," she calls.

Wilkins sends word: "Something's afoot."

He saw them coming out of the tower with their heads bowed, Margaret Formby and the boy, John Kennedy. Nothing very odd about that, "save," Wilkins says, "you could just tell."

"She is no good at this kind of thing."

Also, Kennedy had a pack and a riding cloak.

But by then Walsingham already knows. Ill luck—for Margaret and the boy—had sent them to the White Hart, where Mary Seton was well known enough to be trusted to hire a horse. They told the ostler the boy was bound for Doncaster, where he would leave the horse at the Seven Stars.

"After that, who knows?"

Margaret Formby and the boy had walked awhile together, talking, and then he had set off eastward, down the valley toward Doncaster.

Doncaster means the Great North Road, along which the boy will either ride south, toward London, or north, toward, well, God knows where.

Margaret Formby had returned to the castle.

"Not looking too happy," Wilkins told them.

Beale laughs to see how quickly Walsingham's plan has borne fruit: Queen Mary has received word that Quesada is not coming to her aid this season, and lashing out in disappointment, has contacted one of her allies to set some other plan in play. To discover the identity of this unknown ally, all they now need do is follow the boy.

It is genius, and Walsingham looks more hawkish than ever.

"Here we go," he says, rubbing his hands. "Here we go."

But their swift success leaves them with a dilemma: they have only enough men to keep watch on either the boy, or Queen Mary. Which is it to be?

"The queen's not going anywhere, is she?" Wilkins suggests.

Walsingham agrees.

"Get after him, Robert," Walsingham tells him. "Now. This instant. Leave word of which way he's gone at the post station, and I will follow along this night with Wilkins and Gregory."

They find Beale the best horse left in the White Hart's stable and Beale is up in the saddle before the hour is out. Walsingham thrusts a pie in his hand.

"God speed, Robert."

Beale thanks his master and sets off along the road to Doncaster. Twenty miles perhaps.

Francis Walsingham has much to do, much to think about. He must in all haste send word to Lord Burghley: tell him he is in need of more men. Until then he must pull Wilkins and Gregory from the tower and set off after Beale and the boy. Note must be made of where he goes, and of whom he meets, and Queen Mary will not have abandoned all precautions, however distressed she is, so the boy will have been instructed to see at least two decoys before he meets the person he has really come for. Or perhaps not. Either way, all eventualities must be covered, and that takes time, people, and money.

And meanwhile there is that little knot of silk to fret about: What was it? How did it get in to her rooms, and why was it swallowed?

Still there is no time. He will have to come back to that.

Wilkins and Gregory are delighted to be summoned from their tower. They have been incarcerated so long with the queen, and it is not good for a man to sit within all day. They borrow horses from Talbot and set off after Beale and the boy, leaving Sheffield Castle with some relief.

"Ha."

It is not an expression of surprise, nor even of much pleasure. Queen Mary is back at the window. The panes are so thick and watered she cannot be sure, but there is a general rustling in the secret parts of the tower, as if the mice were on the move, as indeed they are.

She feels less hemmed in. The air is clearer, and this morning her breath comes more easily.

"Ha," she says again. This time: slight pleasure.

Her own scheme is likewise beginning to bear fruit.

She will ask George Talbot if she may take a walk in the castle bailey.

The boy John Kennedy passes the night with his bag as a pillow on the floor of the hall of the Seven Stars in Doncaster and is up on his feet well before cockcrow. He drains his ale and finishes his soup while his horse is saddled and fettled and he is already on the dew-soaked road by the time its stones are visible.

Robert Beale watches him from behind the stables, where he spent the night. The boy turns north, toward the estates of all those northern lords who have been ever ready to rise up in favor of a Catholic majesty.

He leaves word of his direction with the innkeeper, climbs back up into his own saddle, and sets out after the boy again. Crows caw in the elms, and he feels the first onset of the autumn to come. Excitement too. The snare is tightening. If Walsingham is right, they will have Queen Mary and perhaps even someone like the assassin Hamilton in their bag by the end of it.

George Talbot wakes and thinks that he cannot see why he should deny Queen Mary her request for the pleasure of a walk within his castle bailey.

Francis Walsingham wakes with a start in the attic of the White Hart and listens to the rain. He thinks of Isobel Cochet, and of Dr. John Dee, and he thinks of Willem van Treslong. He thinks of his queen, Elizabeth, and James Hamilton.

Most of all he thinks of Mary, Queen of Scots.

He gets up very quickly and is at the stables before gray dawn.

Queen Mary is transported on a tide of seething pleasure.

Later, she dismisses Margaret Formby, and the rest of her servants, and Mary Seton, too, and sitting alone in her chamber, she lights a candle, even though it is day. She takes up her Bible, her pen, and the second of the small jars of face powder. She opens her Bible on the book of Lamentations. The date of the month and the day of the week matter. She dips the feathers of her pen into the blue-tinged face powder and strokes it across the face of a small piece of paper she has cut from Margaret Formby's flimsy Bible, which she then covers with the piece of paper on which she has already encrypted her message.

Her hands are shaking and the blue powder scatters across her lectern. Using the blunted point of her fattest needle she goes over the letters and numbers, pressing only hard enough so that the blue powder is transferred to the cheap paper, but not so hard that she indents it. When that is done, she inspects it: blank. She rolls it into a tiny scroll no bigger than a lady's fingernail and places it in the lid of the pot of face powder. She tips the candle so that the wax drips into it, and while it fills and seals the note, she tears all her other writings into shreds, half of which she chews fifty times before swallowing, half of which she will force Margaret Formby to swallow.

When the scrap of paper is submerged in the wax, she straightens the candle, and takes up the soft fat disc of wax. She rolls it into a ball the size of a chickpea, and before it cools too much, she inserts this into a small hole cut in a piece of wood that she had the boy John Kennedy carve for her especially. He had been pleased to be asked and has come up with something that is almost the size of a duck's egg, in pinewood, with a plug to stopper the hole, which can then be sealed in candle wax.

"Will it float?"

He supposes so.

Later, the sun appears, and Mary Seton comes.

"Sir George suggests you might like to take your walk now, Your Majesty?"

They put on their cloaks and hats and old-fashioned pattens, and they walk together, clacking across the cobbles with Margaret Formby trailing miserably behind, along with Father Goole, who is pretending to be an usher. It is hardly scenic, or far, and so they must walk in a circle: right out of the tower door, past the gatehouse with its raised drawbridge and lowered portcullis, then a left turn past the old tower and here, for a few paces at least, the wall is lower, and they have a view down the precipice to the burbling brown waters of the river Don, twenty feet below.

A heron stalks through the rushes at the far side.

"Can you throw a stone?" Queen Mary asks Margaret Formby.

The girl nods. She does not look well. She may be ill. It is a pity, but Mary believes she will soon not have too much need of her anyway. Only a few more weeks perhaps.

"Do so," she instructs. "I should like to see the heron fly."

She wishes them to finish her sentence *for I cannot*.

Margaret finds a stone and tries to throw it. It falls short of the heron, so another is found. Father Goole is more successful. A guard watches them from the battlements of the great tower.

"Throw another," Queen Mary instructs.

He does so. A bit better this time.

"I shall try."

She throws the wooden egg. It sails across the river and lands in the brown waters with a plop. The heron sets off along the valley.

Mary Seton watches the guard.

He doesn't notice the stone is floating.

Off it goes, downstream, where three men, hose rolled up, are "fishing."

The queen laughs. Walsingham would have seen through that. Not Talbot though.

The boy has been brought up with horses and is a steady rider, and, despite the rain, he makes good progress. He rides from dawn to dusk, swapping horses at the post stations, always taking the best, so that in pursuit, Beale is forced onto swaybacked nags, the lame and the halt. Pontefract, Ripon, Darlington, Newcastle, Alnwick. Five hard days in the saddle. By the middle of the sixth, Beale believes there is only one place the boy can now be riding: Berwick, and from there: Scotland.

It is not a surprise. In fact, it is a relief to know that Queen Mary's allies are not, as was most feared, among the nobility of northern England, but across the border in Scotland. These are the sorts of enemy the English are used to. Beale can see that even from every house he passes: stone-built, grimly defensive, studded with arrow loops, and on every horizon another all-but-impregnable castle.

Nevertheless, something must be done about the boy before he gets over the border.

Walsingham is too old for all this, but he so badly wants to know what the boy has, he rides so hard and far that when he catches up with Robert Beale in Berwick, he has lost all strength in his body and must be helped from his saddle. He is sodden from the rain, and his skin is the color of rendered goose fat.

"Where is he?" he gasps.

"Asleep in the hall at the Garter," Beale tells him.

Wilkins and Gregory look better than when Beale last saw them. Fresh air and exercise, but something more than that too.

"Has he seen you at all?" Walsingham asks.

Beale thinks not.

"Better not risk it, though, eh?" Wilkins says. "We'll go."

Beale stands with Walsingham huddling under the eaves of the Angel, south of the river, from where they can see the bridge over the Tweed, and the town's new-built walls against the Scots.

"More than a hundred thousand pounds, they cost," Walsingham tells Beale. He is not sure if they were worth it. Probably though.

They see Wilkins and Gregory crossing the bridge.

"What will they do?" Beale asks.

"Think of something," Walsingham tells him.

Wilkins and Gregory are good at this, though when, at length, long after curfew, they return they both smell of drink.

They seem thoughtful.

"He's just a boy," Gregory says.

"What is in his bag?"

"A candlestick. Silver. Good quality. Worth a bit."

"But only a bit."

He means it is not six hundred gold coins. Not enough to fund a revolution or an invasion. An assassination, though? Perhaps.

"Carrying any message?"

Wilkins pulls out a piece of paper.

"I got most of it down, but—"

He shrugs.

Walsingham, recovered, reads the letter.

"Who is this Hamish Doughty? Have we heard of him? A silversmith? In Edinburgh?"

Walsingham passes the letter to Beale. It is an instruction from Her Majesty, Queen Mary of Scotland, to a Master Hamish Doughty, alderman of the guild of Scottish silversmiths, addressed to his place of work on a certain corner of the Land Market in Edinburgh. It instructs him to melt down the candlestick that is brought to him by the same hand as the letter, and to reconstruct in as close a manner as possible the "certain piece of personal adornment" as was undertaken by himself on behalf of Queen Mary's erstwhile husband, and once his client, James Hepburn, fourth Earl of Bothwell.

"'Save if it pleaseth you to make its girth somewhat more fulsome'? What in God's name can that be about?"

"I copied only what was written," Gregory says.

Walsingham is pulling hard on his beard again.

"A new encryption," he says, "or else—she is supposed to have some powder—some form of brimstone—that pressed into paper is invisible to the naked eye, but once exposed to ammonia becomes legible."

They know not to bother asking how he knows this.

"We'll have to get hold of it then," Wilkins says. "Make a copy to put in his bag, and get to work on the original."

"We will have to move fast in the morning," Walsingham says. "But he's seen you already, so you will have to make the swap, Master Beale, tomorrow night."

The next morning they are once more up and about before dawn. Gregory and Wilkins cross the bridge into town again and return with papers and inks from a bookseller, and wax, too, the color of blood. They sit outside in the best light possible and while Wilkins makes a passable copy of Queen Mary's signet, Gregory re-creates the letter.

When it is done, Beale is up into the saddle, and Master Walsingham passes him the letter, as well as another addressed to Sir Thomas Randolph.

"Our man in Edinburgh," Walsingham tells him. "An introduction. We'll meet at his house tomorrow night, yes?"

Beale rides out across the bridge. He has never been to Scotland. It doesn't feel so very different for a while, and he catches up with the boy as they are approaching the town of Dunbar. The road winds through bracken and heather, and there are black-faced sheep dotted about. A cold wind comes off the North Sea, and already night falls earlier.

"God give you good day, master, you've come far?"

The boy is cautiously polite and tells him the truth. Beale tells him he is a salt merchant from Droitwich. The boy is quite obviously bilious from last night's ale and wishes only to get down off his horse and to sleep. They stop at the Dolphin tavern, in the shadow of the slighted castle, and stable their horses. The language here is impenetrable and Beale expresses his gratitude for the boy's help by buying him beer in the Flemish style. The inn is old-fashioned, and straw pallets are brought out and set up around the fire on which the clay cover ticks as it warms and then, much later in the night, as it cools. By then Beale has already extracted the message the boy was carrying, replaced it with the copy, and both now snore loudly.

The next morning, after a smoked bony fish and more beer,

Beale leaves the letter, enclosed within another letter, for Walsingham and the others to examine at their leisure, and he and the boy set off together along the coast road, toward Edinburgh. The boy does not mind his company, but nor does he beg for any salt-dealing anecdotes, so they ride in easy silence, with the wind at their backs and they raise Edinburgh in the early afternoon.

⌖

Francis Walsingham stares down at the paper in fury. They have tried everything, but none avails.

"Maybe . . . maybe it just is a thing that she wants?" Wilkins asks.

Everything smells very strongly of alum and vinegar, and Walsingham's fingers are stinging from touching one or the other of the solutions.

"But what is the thing she wants?" Gregory wonders. "What did the silversmith make for the Earl of Bothwell?"

Walsingham has a terrible feeling he is doing something he should stop doing, or that he is leaving undone a thing he should do. But what?

"Beale will tell us what steps the silversmith next takes."

They collect up their bottles and jars and brushes and they set off after Beale and the boy.

⌖

Three days later they are all gathered in the solar of Thomas Randolph's house near Holyrood Palace, thinking about Hamish Doughty, the silversmith, who turns out to be . . . a silversmith, and, at first glance, not much more besides. No assassin, at any rate.

"He is just another link in the chain," Walsingham tells them.

He sounds desperate that this should be so, but Wilkins and Gregory, and now Beale, are no longer convinced he is dispassionate. Besides, following Doughty will not be easy. He is moderately active in Edinburgh politics. He comes; he goes; he speaks to many men; he sees many others. It would need ten of them, all of whom knew Edinburgh, just to keep a watch on him, and there are only four of them.

Thomas Randolph is there though; Walsingham's brother-in-law or something. He's a dapper little man, bright-eyed and clean-shaven, with an unsuppressed delight in life, and full of stories of Russia, from where he has just come back, and her tsar, Ivan.

"I do not wish to sound disloyal, Francis," he says, "but in the matter of her cousin of Scotland, Queen Elizabeth might have done better to take a page from Tsar Ivan's book: he'd've had her strangled at birth. Then he'd've had everyone she was ever likely to meet likewise strangled—at birth again—and then he'd've sent his Cossacks to conquer every land she had ever thought to set foot in and they'd've forced the men of those countries to plow salt into their own fields, dig their own graves, and then kill themselves. In Russia they *know* how to make an omelette!"

Meanwhile, they have lost the boy, John Kennedy.

"There is something not right about this," Wilkins murmurs.

It is dark, but Queen Mary is in pain tonight and does not wish for a candle. Instead she summons Father Goole to the solar and tells him she wishes to make her confession.

He looks alarmed.

"Here, Your Majesty?"

"The mice are gone," she says. "They will not hear us."

It had always been her idea to have the portable altar set up in the solar so that the mice could see them saying Mass, because the mice would then think they did not know they were being watched, and, crucially, would not strive to find a peephole into the chamber above.

She lies on the settle while he says the prayers, and then she begins.

James Hamilton of Bothwellhaugh and Woodhouselee is back from service with the French king and now stands over the meager fire in the hall of the keep of Ferniehirst Castle, in the county of Roxburgh, twenty miles from the English border. He fingers his rosary beads while he listens to his host, Lord Kerr, eating the haunch of some animal. The noise reminds him of being in the kennels, and he wishes he had not left Paris.

It is strange to think he would not have been able to do so had Master Francis Walsingham not paid him that angel for having saved his life on that day of vengeance. God works in mysterious ways.

But he has in mind this evening the message that awaited him when he arrived in Ferniehirst this morning, sent from Queen Mary in captivity, which he just spent an hour or more decrypting. He very much wishes to discuss it with someone, for he cannot decide if it is what he has been waiting for all this time, or dreading all this time. He wishes his priest were here, Father Goole, or that his wife were still alive so that he might consult her.

"What ails you?" Kerr asks. He is still in his hunting boots, and in fustian trews the color of blood. He speaks Scots.

Hamilton does not wish to tell Kerr. The man has given him shelter, and with it his life, but he does not wish him further implicated in any plot, should it go awry, and nor, if he is honest, does he trust him completely.

Still.

"Her Majesty has overcome her scruples," he says.

Lord Kerr stops chewing.

"Oh, aye?"

"I am to go to London," Hamilton tells him. "To find Elizabeth Tudor."

Kerr's eyes shrink with pleasure.

"Bang bang," he says.

"That is no sin, Your Majesty," Father Goole says. "Queen Elizabeth is excommunicated these past two years, and in his bull *Regnans in Excelsis* did not our holy father in Rome command all her subjects to seek her end? Indeed, did he not say that those who did not do so were likewise to be included in the sentence of excommunication, likewise to be damned to hell for all eternity!"

"But she is a queen, appointed by God," Queen Mary says.

Father Goole sighs.

"She would not hesitate to have you murdered herself, Your Majesty, were it to suit her, and you are no heretic as she is, nor cut off from the unity of the body of Christ our Savior. You are not excommunicated as she is."

They find the boy John Kennedy not so much by skill, or by chance, but by sitting still, in an inn, diagonally opposite the house of Hamish Doughty, the Edinburgh silversmith, and waiting.

It is three days later.

"That's him."

They don't move for a long moment. They watch the boy knock on the shutters, which open. A few words are exchanged, then the boy is permitted within.

Not very much later he emerges. He is carrying his bag, less bulky this time, and he looks left toward the castle, then right, down the road that will eventually lead him to England.

"He looks heartsore," Wilkins says.

"He looked that way when he went in," Gregory tells them.

"Maybe he doesn't want to go back?"

"How are we going to do this then?" Beale asks.

"Master Walsingham'll have to do it this time."

They watch the boy set off eastward down Land Market.

"Get after him, Robert," Wilkins tells Beale. "If he hires a horse in Leith or somewhere, send word to Master Walsingham at Thomas Randolph's house."

"What will you do?"

Wilkins looks across at the silversmith's.

"I think Master Doughty is due a trip to England."

Beale leaves and tails the boy down the road. The houses get steadily less grand and soon they are among cottages and hovels, and patches of unappetizing vegetables cropped at by ugly sheep. The wind is in his face and a thin rain begins to fall.

He watches the boy enter an inn on the outskirts of the town, and then, a little while later, emerge on a nag that has ideas of its own, which do not include walking to Berwick with this lad on his back. Beale watches the boy plodding eastward: he looks so weary that Beale can only believe he is privy to bad news. He cannot believe he is riding to find Hamilton. He risks returning to Thomas Randolph's house, where Walsingham is deep in thought. Within a few moments they have said good-bye to Randolph and are on the road on hired horses.

They catch sight of the boy within a few miles and Beale leaves Walsingham to ride ahead and befriend him at the same inn in Dunbar.

Wilkins and Gregory catch Hamish Doughty while he is on the privy in the backyard of his workshop. He is a big man who fills the tight space almost completely, and it is a struggle to subdue him without making a lot of noise. Once he is down, he makes a very heavy deadweight. They force him into a couple of sacks, though, and haul him out and up onto the bed of a cart that Thomas Randolph has acquired for their purpose, and they are rolling down the nameless lane that runs parallel to Land Market before he is missed by his assistants and apprentices.

"You didn't even let him finish his business," Wilkins tells Gregory. "That is something you're going to have to clear up, not me."

"A bit of shit'll be the least of it," Gregory says. They have both seen men hanged, drawn, and quartered. Bellies sliced open and guts wound out and held up to the crowd like a master butcher showing a string of prized sausages. That is to see a man bathe in blood.

Ordinarily Master Walsingham would not spare a glance let alone a word for this boy, but here he is, plying him with the Dolphin Inn's best ale and telling him tales of Lincoln's Inn, and jurisprudence, in the hope he will soon be fast asleep and relinquish his grip on the bag at his side. John tells Walsingham he is an apprentice cutler, on his way to Sheffield. It's a good lie, because it is close to the truth. He has a funny view of what travel in Scotland is like, for, he says, this is the third night friendly men have bought him his ale, and so far he has not been robbed, as he feared, "or worse."

He tells Walsingham of the salt merchant, and of the two journeymen hog gelders he met, and how they seemed very decent fellows.

"Noble professions," Walsingham falsely avers.

He pours him another mug from the jug.

Soon the boy's eyes flag, and a little after that the dogs are put out, the mattresses are unrolled, and the fire covered. That is it for the night.

"You have chosen a good spot for it," Walsingham tells the boy, stretching out next to him.

"You are not taking a chamber, master?"

"I have stayed in it before," Walsingham confides. "The mattress is rife with fleas, and there are rats, too."

He offers to show him a bite.

The boy is already asleep.

Walsingham eases the bag from under the boy's head during the short hours. There doesn't seem to be much within: some of his linens, a single shoe, a heft of long-stale bread, a spoon, nicely carved, and a hook for carving more of them. There is no message written as before, and the only oddity seems to be the parcel that must have come from the silversmith. It is heavy, about half a cubit long and tightly wrapped in waxed linen. In the gleam of his covertly lit lamp Walsingham can make neither head nor tail of it. He puts it back and slides it next to the boy's head.

James Hamilton can shoot an arquebus more accurately than any man alive. He can hit a scallop shell at fifty paces, a pumpkin at a hundred, but this new gun is another matter.

"It kicks like a donkey," he tells his host.

Lord Kerr suggests he aim lower to allow for the kick.

Several moments later he tries again.

The ball smashes the shell to pieces.

"Ha."

"The Queen is dead," Lord Kerr smiles. "Long live the Queen."

Queen Mary has been in a good mood for two days now. She seems almost excited by the possibilities of life and has been hard at her needlework with the Countess of Shrewsbury, Bess. Every now and then you can even hear her laugh.

"But it must be hard," Mary Seton tells Margaret Formby.

"What?"

"Being constrained so."

"Yes, I can see that."

"Still," Mary goes on, "it will be over soon after Michaelmas."

Margaret is startled. "Michaelmas?"

But Mary Seton will say no more.

In the end, they arrest the boy in Pontefract.

"It is convenient for the castle," Walsingham admits, "and I could not stand a moment longer not knowing what it is."

When the boy recognizes his captors he glares at them with hot eyes and swears feebly as he is taken away. Robert Beale feels a stab of guilt at his betrayal, for he had actually liked the boy.

"It's a bad business," Walsingham agrees, "but who knows? Perhaps we have saved the Queen's life. Now let's see what this damned thing is."

They are in the guardroom at Pontefract Castle, waiting now for Gregory and Wilkins to bring the Scottish silversmith.

Walsingham slices through the stitches of the linen and parts the various other wrappings to leave a fine silk drawstring bag. He raises and lowers his eyebrows.

"No expense spared," he says. He loosens the ties and lets the contents land with a meaty thump on the table.

It is the candlestick melted down and recast into a six-inch shaft of dimpled silver about the girth of a baby's arm, knotted along its length with irregular bumps and welts. At one end is a loop through which is loosely tied a length of red silk cord.

Walsingham prods it.

"What is it?"

He has no idea.

"Does it open?"

It feels solid. He raps it against the tabletop. It sounds solid. He gives it a twist between his two fists. Nothing.

"Bring the boy up."

The boy is dragged up by two guards. He has obviously cursed them, too, for his lip is split and one eye is swollen shut.

"Fell down the stairs," they tell Walsingham.

"Make sure it doesn't happen again, will you?" Beale asks.

The boy knows nothing about the object.

"Do you know nothing, or admit nothing?"

"I know nothing," the boy promises.

Walsingham looks at him a long time. The boy stares back.

"I have a feeling," Walsingham says, "that you are telling the truth, but you are not telling all the truth. All that you know."

The boy holds out his hands, palms up, as if to say: *I can't tell you* everything *I know, for where would I end?*

"What do you do for Queen Mary?"

"I light the fires in the morning. Bring down the pots. Clean the shoes and boots. Take the laundry to the maids. Help the cook and then the other women in any way they wish. I run any errands she wants."

"You are a useful man to have about," Beale supposes.

"Aye," the boy agrees, but he has forgiven none of them their pretenses on the road to Edinburgh.

Walsingham gives a rare, reassuring smile: John is such a simple, honest hapless youth that they agree, when he is taken away, that it would be wrong to put him to close questioning, even supposing they had license to do so.

Hamish Doughty, on the other hand, is another matter entirely, and when he is brought before them, he is a hot pocket of angry grease, and no one is at all surprised. *But by God, it is fascinating to see someone so fat*, Beale thinks. One of the guards is actually feeling his dimpled flesh. Pushing it and letting it slowly spring back. It is like dough. He stops when he sees he is being watched.

"You've no fucking right to be bringing me here. You've fucking kidnapped me from my own fucking country and brought me to this fucking shithole. You've no right to look at me, let alone ask a question."

Walsingham slaps him. His jowls quiver a long moment later.

"Stop your yammering and listen."

Doughty is, if possible, more enraged.

They will get no sense out of him today.

"Put him in the Gascoigne Tower."

Other than the Tower in London, there is no place in England more likely to bring a man eye to eye with his own mortality than the Gascoigne Tower. Flint-faced, windowless, it is where the Lancastrian kings put men they wanted the world to forget ever lived, including King Richard.

"Do we have license to put him to close questioning?" Gregory asks.

"Yes," Walsingham lies.

It is desperate. *He* is desperate. If he cannot find evidence enough to condemn Queen Mary, then this second part of his plan, the most intricate part, will unravel, and he will be left with what? With only the strange ghost trail of *Meneer* van Treslong's shifting loyalties, and sideways dishonesty to pursue.

They sit for a while, thinking, the silver object on the table between them. All the bright pleasure of the early days of the scheme has contorted into frustration. Walsingham is furious.

"Well," he says. "We will have to confront her ourselves then."

Hamilton should have taken a ship from Berwick, but suffers terrible seasickness, so he takes one of Lord Kerr's palfreys and rides east from Ferniehirst to find the London road. In addition to what might be expected of a traveling man, he carries two medals blessed by the pope himself, an ivory crucifix made in Venice, an earthenware vial of water from the river Jordan.

He rides south, sleeping at the side of the road, wrapped in his traveling cloak. The leaves are turning, and it will soon be autumn. Will he live to see Advent? *Not in this world*, he thinks.

Just before Doncaster he takes the precaution of pulling his horse off the road when he sees a large party of men following him along the road from the north. He stands letting the horse crop the weeds, waiting, and his blood turns to absolute ice and then fire when he recognizes among them Master Francis Walsingham.

He should have shot him in Paris, as he stood against the wall on the day of vengeance. No one would have guessed he had done so deliberately. Instead he'd shot a Frenchman, of his own faith, and saved the devil. It was pride, of course. *Look what I can do.*

There are ten of them: Walsingham; another man, his secretary probably; six men who are obviously soldiers; and a boy who looks panicky. Hamilton watches them go, and he misses that gun now, for with it he could have lodged a bullet in the man's ear. But for fear of attracting attention to himself, and of being caught abroad with it, he has left it with Lord Kerr in Ferniehirst and is riding now to find its twin, sent from Milan especially for his purpose.

He waits until Walsingham's party is out of sight, and then for a long while more before he leads his horse back onto the road, mounts up, and continues south.

Queen Mary cries out with frustration.

"No! No! No! You let it go! I was nearly there, but you let it go!"

Margaret Formby gets up off her knees and wipes her face.

"I am sorry, ma'am, I—"

"I don't care! Get out! Get out! Oh God! Send me Mary!"

Margaret cannot help weeping as she runs past Mary Seton on the steps. She runs out of the tower and into the bailey. There is a conduit across the cobbles, providing clean water for the kitchen and the brewery. She plunges her head under it, letting the thick flow soak her headdress and her face, careless of the guards watching. She wants to scream and cry and fly from here.

When she looks up and wipes her eyes on her apron, she sees the bailey is now filled with men on horses. They look down on her in stern surprise.

One of them speaks. "You are Margaret Formby?"

She bobs in acknowledgment.

He gets down off his horse. He is short, stern, with, when he removes his cap, short-cropped hair.

"I am Francis Walsingham," he says. Her heart seems to engorge with terror. This is the very devil, she knows, and so, God help her, she cannot help but look at his feet, expecting hooves. His gaze seems to peer through a window into her soul, and he smiles to see what she is thinking.

"We are here to see your mistress," he tells her.

Queen Mary sits in her chair under her cloth of state, silent and still. Her face is pallid and swollen, and Beale remembers the purple urine in her chamber pot. Master Walsingham betrays no anxiety. He stands likewise in silence, and equally still, waiting with unfeigned patience.

They are in the gloomy solar of the tower with its thick old windowpanes, and Beale finds himself looking at the back wall for the knot in the wainscoting through which he saw this room, when the man who is now pretending to be an usher was saying Mass. He cannot identify it and wonders if it is filled up when not in use? The room smells of old water, of dead flowers, of pent-up sorrow. He cannot wait to be out, in fresh air, to be able to breathe.

At length the queen sighs.

"Have you come to set me free, Master Walsingham?"

"Oh, you are not in any state from which you need be set free, Your Majesty."

Mary makes a dismissive noise. She is too tired for silly arguments and they all know the truth.

"Then to what or whom do I owe the unexpected pleasure of your company?"

"I am in need of your assistance," Walsingham tells her.

"*My* assistance?"

Beale feels sure she is about to develop some further ironic curlicues, but Walsingham cuts her off.

"We believe we have stumbled upon the strings of some plot that is currently in play designed and directed to bring an early end to the life of our own dear sovereign, Queen Elizabeth. We believe that—unwittingly or no—you may be the focus of this plot, the point about which it revolves."

He includes a small hand gesture to indicate something turning.

Queen Mary looks at him. Her nut brown eyes betray almost nothing.

"Oh yes?"

Walsingham's smile tightens. He hates this woman. A bead of sweat in his hairline betrays his feeling.

"Yes, and in the certain hope that you would not wish to see the life of your cousin of England harmed in any way, I am left wondering if you could enlighten me as to why in the week before last you might have sent your servant—one John Kennedy—to Edinburgh, against explicit embargo to communicate with they whom may indeed be Her Majesty Elizabeth's great rebels?"

Queen Mary makes a show of confusion, but there enters into her eyes and onto her lips the ghost of a smile.

"John Kennedy?" she wonders. She turns to Mary Seton, who stands at her side.

"The boy, Your Majesty."

Queen Mary pretends she did not know before, and Walsingham goes on to describe what the boy has been doing, when and where, and then comes to the subject of Hamish Doughty.

The curious thing is that while Walsingham speaks, Queen Mary seems impassive, or even slightly amused, and it is Mary Seton who cannot hide her feelings. Her eyes are very wide and wet, and she looks strangely beautiful in her anxiety. She betrays her queen in every gesture and every glance, and when, at last, Francis Walsingham calls for Beale to come forward and present the silver object to the queen, Mary Seton gives a small scream.

But Queen Mary merely smiles.

"What is it, Your Majesty?" Walsingham asks. He is burning with rage.

She now looks up at him.

"Are you married, Master Walsingham?"

He is taken aback by this change in tack. "Your Majesty?"

"You have a wife?"

"I do. I do. Yes."

"And do you indulge in coitus?"

"Coitus?"

"Coitus, Master Walsingham. Between a man and a woman. A husband and a wife."

She looks at him dead levelly. She is challenging him. Defying him. Fighting him. Beating him. Walsingham's face is flushed.

"My God, ma'am, I— What are you saying?"

Mary says nothing. She stretches to take the length of silver from Beale. Her fingers wrap around the silver shaft.

And it is then that it all suddenly becomes clear.

Francis Walsingham stands waiting for his horse to be readied in the bailey of Sheffield Castle. His gaze is fixed on the star that is still shining in Cassiopeia but he is not thinking of it, not wondering what it means. His guts, his soul, his mind: all three are turbulent. He cannot yet bring himself to laugh at what has happened, at the fool he has made of himself, though he can see Beale cannot hide his smirk as he sets about altering the stirrup strap on his saddle.

Christ. How could he have been such a fool?

He stands waiting, watching the boy—John Kennedy, blameless John Kennedy, with his black eye and split lip—who now sits on an old log by the door, using his hook to carve a spoon, and Walsingham thinks how he chased him five days up, five days down, all over the country; how he kidnapped the subject of another country—and God knows how that will play out up there, since last night Hamish Doughty died on the rack, without his close questioning being approved by the Privy Council—and how he confronted Queen Mary, all because—because—because of what? His own hubris.

He clenches his eyes shut. He could scream.

Instead though, he controls himself.

He will do the right thing. He will start by apologizing to the boy.

He walks over to him. Beale is there, too, now, probably likewise apologizing.

Yes.

"Hello, John," he says.

John squints up at them, but says nothing. He is rightly furious. With them, but also with Queen Mary.

He carries on working, furiously slicing through the wood.

"What is it you are making?" Beale is asking. He is trying to engage the boy. Make conversation. The boy says nothing. A long peel of wood comes off his knife and falls between their feet on the dew-wet stones.

"It is not a spoon," Beale continues.

The boy grunts.

"Are you—what? Carving an egg?"

The boy holds it in his palm.

"Queen Mary likes them."

Beale and Walsingham lock alarmed gazes. Is this another *thing*?

"No," the boy says, reading their minds.

"Then what?"

The boy shrugs.

Walsingham asks to see it. It is very light, soft wood, pine. There is a little hole in the side.

"Can't be easy, that," Beale suggests.

"Have to do it with an awl," the boy agrees. He mimes the action needed.

"Whatever for?"

The boy shrugs again. Walsingham rubs his thumb over the notch. It reminds him of a dead-letter drop that he once used in Leuven. That was a notch at the base of a wringing post in which one of his agents—was it Willem van Treslong?—placed a note rolled in a wax ball.

The boy is watching him, as is Beale, too. Walsingham tosses the egg into the air like a trainee juggler. It has little heft. He throws it to Beale, who catches it.

The boy holds out his hand for it.

Beale gives it to him.

"Well," Beale says, ready to finish things up.

But Walsingham hears that jangling inner bell again. He feels he is atop something. But what? What is it?

"Can I see it again?" he asks.

The boy passes him the egg.

Walsingham stares at it for a long moment. In the silence, a flight of geese slice through the gray sky not twenty feet above, their wings creaking. Walsingham looks up to watch them pass, across the bailey, and over the low wall, making to land on the river beyond.

My God, he thinks. *My God.*

He walks across the bailey, rests his hands on the wall. Damp gray stone, chest high perhaps, and beyond, haunted by a faint mist, is the choppy broth of the river Don.

He weighs the wooden egg in his hand.

My God.

It comes perfectly natural to him, the obvious thing to do.

He throws the egg into the waters. He loses it for a moment, and then, there it is, bobbing along.

Downstream is what? Fifty miles of nothing, then the sea.

He feels as if he is falling. He struggles to breathe.

My God. My God.

Walsingham turns.

In the thick glass window of the tower, the pale smudge of a face.

Is she laughing at him?

PART | THREE

CHAPTER THIRTEEN

Seething Lane, City of London, October 9, 1572

"Come on! Coming through! Clear the way now!"

The porter at the gate uses the butt of his staff to nudge an old man away from the gates. He's been there a couple of days now, fruitlessly holding out a stained cap, his shaved head abraded with scratches and cuts. A horribly stained bandage over one eye. He smells strongly of fish, as if he sleeps on the Billingsgate steps.

The porter clears enough space to allow Master Walsingham through, with Master Beale by his side, and six of Queen Elizabeth's guards behind. Walsingham looks grim, but Beale at least greets the porter with a nod as they ride into the courtyard.

When he closes the gate, the old beggar is gone, leaving only his cap, in which sits a rotting fish.

Walsingham is slow off his horse. Disgrace, disappointment, and age have stiffened his body, and he can hardly move after the long ride, but he is pleased to be home. His daughter comes running and she throws her arms around him. She knows nothing of this. None of it. Then his wife, too, and the nurse, and there is much fussing over the new baby, and he knows he has done nothing to deserve all this. After a while his wife divines his self-disgust.

"Did it not go according to plan, Francis?"

"I believe she played me for a fool," he says.

Her face falls.

"But Quesada? His fleet is not sighted?"

"No. True. The trick saved England, but at what cost? And for how long?"

He genuinely does not know. With whom did Queen Mary communicate while his attention was misdirected elsewhere? King Philip? The pope? James Hamilton? Or one of her many firebrands? Young men who'd consider it martyrdom to lay down their lives for their Catholic queen, the sort who have pictures of her drawn on a card, and then stitched into their flesh.

He leaves his wife then and goes to his office, springing his three locks, his turbulent thoughts elsewhere.

It is not until he opens the door and closes it behind him that he smells the whiff of burning fuse rope.

By then it is too late.

He stops stock-still.

A man sits in his chair, two glowing fuses and two barrels pointing straight at Walsingham's face. His heart nearly ruptures.

"Dee!" he shouts.

"Don't move, Walsingham," Dr. Dee tells him. "I have discovered I may not be much of a shot, but even I cannot miss from here, and if you move so much as a muscle I will take great pleasure in blowing your bloody head clean off your accursed fucking shoulders."

Walsingham doesn't move.

"Dee?" he says. "How? How did you—"

"Survive?" Dee wonders. "Yes, it must be somewhat of a surprise to see me alive."

"I . . . I admit I had given up some hope."

"*Hope?* You had given up some *hope*?"

"Yes."

"By the blood of Christ, Walsingham, you have nerve."

As he becomes used to the gloom, Walsingham looks at him more carefully.

"Christ, Dee, you look terrible. Why are you dressed like a beggar?"

"Shut up, Walsingham. Don't even speak or so help me God I will put a bullet in your stupid fat brains before I get to the bottom of this. You don't get to ask me questions, do you hear me? Not while I have these. Do you understand?"

He waves the guns. Walsingham can see how dangerous he is, deliberately or not.

"Understood."

Can he reach the alarm wire he has installed under his desk to alert the guards? Dee, as if reading his mind, shakes his head. He gestures one gun at the severed wire. A silence settles between them, as if Dee does not know where to begin. Then he does, but his voice, when it comes, is unmodulated, a croak, a squeak.

"So did Bess know?" he asks.

"Bess?"

"Her Majesty. The Queen."

"Did she know what?"

Dee sighs. Walsingham can see his finger tighten on the trigger.

"About the papers," Dee prompts. "Admiral DaSilva's papers. Did she know they were falsified?"

Walsingham feels the blood rushing in his ears. "How did you know?"

Dee cannot resist it.

"I spent a day with them, in a horrible inn with a fisherman who smelled like a seal sleeping by my feet. I went through every aspect of them, all the figures, every permutation of every encryption I know, and then through them all again in Hebrew, Latin, Greek, English, Scots, Spanish, and French. I tried Dutch and Saxon. I tried Genoese. For a while I supposed—*hoped!*—the admiral had discovered the language known to Adam, for nothing worked. Nothing made sense. All my calculations put the Straits of Anian where they could not possibly be, or where I knew them not to be, or where they cannot have been found by mortal man, and I was almost in despair, but then I saw, buried within, a clue. A mark. A little curlicue you'd never have spotted unless you half expected to find it, because you had begun to suspect you were looking at the work of an old friend who could never resist that sort of thing: Jerome Cardan."

Hearing Cardan's name, Walsingham starts.

"Yes," Dee says, seeing it. "It was his mark that gave it all away: your scheme. If I hadn't seen it, I daresay I'd've been shot as planned."

Walsingham thinks that if he gets out of this alive, he will be paying Jerome Cardan a visit, even if it means another trip to Catholic Paris to winkle the little bastard out of whichever wine shop he is spending his fee for the work.

He says nothing though. Dee continues: "So I thought of Isobel Cochet—"

At the mention of her name Walsingham cries out.

"You found her? You found Isobel? How is she?"

Dee looks at him with nothing but disgust.

"I found her"—he spits out the words—"I found her and I lost her, and she's dead."

Walsingham cannot suppress a mew of horrified shame.

"Yes," Dee says. "That's right. That is on you, Walsingham. Her death. You sent her to die."

"No!" Walsingham shouts. He is passionate about this.

Dee raises the guns. Walsingham subsides.

"As God is my witness," he says. "I did not. I did not know they would take her child! I thought it was Oliver Fellowes the cardinal had turned. I thought Oliver was a Catholic! His father was, and I thought he might be one, too. So I took a risk—one that nearly saw us both killed—to prove to him the faked DaSilva pages were genuine, and I gave him his chance to take them to the cardinal, but . . . but he did not. I admit, I made a mistake. A mistake. I did not know they had taken Isobel's child. I did not know it would be her the cardinal would turn. But I did not send her to die."

"And have you done anything to get the girl back?" he asks. "Isobel's daughter?"

Walsingham is brought up short. Guilt feels like a cold wet eel winding around his innards. It carries the smell of death and decay.

"I have been busy," he says.

Dee stares at him, and he—Walsingham—shares his disgust.

"So tell me this, Walsingham, so that when you're dead I can tell everyone how your mind worked: When you let the Cardinal of Lorraine know you had documents relating to the whereabouts of the Straits of Anian, how did you know he would try to steal them? Then having stolen them, how did you know he would take them to the Spanish?"

Walsingham hates telling anyone anything, but he owes Dr. Dee this, he supposes, or, in fact, if he does not tell him, then Dee will put a ball in his brainpan. He also hopes the longer he talks, the less likely it is that Dee will shoot him.

"It was a risk," he admits. "But I knew the cardinal was in dispute with King Charles of France—the de Guises and the Valois remain mortal enemies—and that he was trying to reach out to King Philip of Spain, so I believed if knowledge of the straits fell into his hands, he would be sure to use that knowledge to buy King Philip's favor. Had the cardinal known Quesada was already at sea, sailing to attack us, he might have sat on his hands, and let it play out, but he did not, thank the Lord, and I was certain that if Philip learned of the whereabouts of the straits, he would move heaven and earth to get this far larger prize before we did, or the French."

"So you let him know you had them?"

Walsingham nods.

"Easy enough," he says. "Paris is—was—full of espials. I half suspected Jerome Cardan himself was in the cardinal's pay."

"But then how to get the papers to him, eh?" Dee muses rhetorically. "In a way that looked as if you had lost them?"

Walsingham looks down at the floor. One of Dee's feet is bare.

"I told you," he says. "I made a mistake. I thought Oliver Fellowes would take them to him, but . . . but he wasn't what I thought he was. He was loyal. And the cardinal devised some lever to get Isobel Cochet to take them. So. Rose. Her daughter. Yes."

The air has seeped out of the room. The twin jewels of the pistols' fuses are dimming too. Dee reinvigorates them.

"But," Dee presses, "that wasn't enough, was it? You needed to prove that the DaSilva papers were genuine, and that you wanted them back, or perhaps the cardinal, or King Philip would think they'd come by them too easily and smell a rat. So you sent me, in the certain hope that I would fail to get them. In fact, you needed me to fail, didn't you? Which was why you sent those Dutch sailors to shoot me dead—"

"Wait— No."

"Yes. So that in the unlikely event I did manage to steal them back, I would never get off that beach but would be killed with them still about my person, there to be found by the cardinal's men."

"No!" Walsingham says. "That much, no. I did not do that."

Christ, he thinks, *why* didn't *I think of that? It is what I* should *have done.*

But then it occurs to him: "But . . . then, if you *did* manage to steal the papers, and you decrypted them, what made Quesada change course for New Spain?"

Dee lets out a long, frustrated sigh.

"Because at the time, Walsingham, what I thought of you was that for all your evil intent, you do not act, as far as I then understood it, for your own benefit, but for the benefit of one whom I love, and for one I thought loved me."

Here Dee falters and his voice cracks a moment, just as Walsingham's had, and a silence follows.

"So what did you do?" Walsingham asks. "With the documents?"

"I left them on the table of that inn, just as if I'd been surprised by the cardinal's men. I left them unencrypted, too, so the cardinal would see only what he wanted to see, and King Philip likewise. And what they wanted to see was a reason to send Quesada beating across the ocean and up into the ice fields from where, God willing, he may never return."

"Dee," Walsingham begins, holding his hands out. "You have saved England, and I can only begin to—"

Dee waves the pistols.

"Stow it, Walsingham. Your thanks are no good to me. Get back over there. At the end of this I am still going to shoot you, you do know that, don't you?"

Walsingham takes his step back.

"Look, Dee," he starts. "It was . . . a bloody shabby business, I agree. But I was desperate, and by Christ, I did not do it lightly. Both Isobel Cochet and Oliver Fellowes were dear to me and their deaths will weigh heavily on me as long as I live—"

"Not very much longer then."

"—But it was all we had against Quesada. It was a gamble: their lives for the lives of countless others; their lives for our country, our Queen, our religion. Surely you understand that?"

Dee kisses his teeth. He blows on one of the fuses to keep it glowing.

"There must have been other ways," Dee mutters. "And to send someone to kill me—"

"I did not do so, Dee. So help me God. I did not send anyone to kill you."

"Then who did? Someone did. Those Dutch copulators didn't just start shooting for fun. They were there for a purpose."

"How do you know?"

"Because they shot the man whom they thought was me."

Walsingham is pulling his beard. He is thinking.

"Do you know a man named Van Treslong?" he asks. "Willem van Treslong. A Dutch Sea Beggar."

"Who helped take Den Brill from the Spanish? I know of him. Why? Was it him? Were they his men?"

"Who knows? Maybe. I hired him to keep an eye on Quesada's fleet, and then to pick you up from Nez Bayard. Apart from you, and me, and Beale, of course, and the Queen, he was the only man who knew you would be there that night."

"You three. I see. And did he . . . what? Misunderstand you? When you said 'pick up John Dee' he heard you say 'shoot John Dee in the head'?"

Walsingham regains a measure of moral composure. He no longer believes Dee will shoot him. He lowers his hands.

"I am still going to shoot you, Walsingham."

Walsingham raises his palms again.

"If confusion arose, it cannot have done so in that way," Walsingham tells Dee, "for I did not speak to him. He was already at sea, off La Rochelle, and so I sent message through the established channels. He will have destroyed the codes but you can ask him yourself."

"He will be somewhere in the Bay of Biscay, I dare say, looking for men to shoot, things to steal."

"No," Walsingham says. "His ship was badly mauled by Quesada's fleet, just before he came to find you. Her Majesty afforded him use of the dry dock at Limehouse to fix the rudder. He is still there."

Dee looks at Walsingham for a long time. His eyes are very brown and steadfast, Walsingham thinks, but they are filled with a benign, forgiving intelligence. At length, Dee lowers just one of the pistols.

"Well then," he says. "We'd best go and find him, hadn't we?"

Walsingham agrees. He would like a word with Van Treslong too.

CHAPTER FOURTEEN

City of London, October 9, 1572

A little after four of the clock, James Hamilton leads his horse through Bishopsgate. It is raining. His collar is turned up, and his brim bent down, and he is careful not to catch the eyes of the watch. He stables his horse at the Bull, with a fat keep with a forked red beard, just south of the gate, and carries his saddlebags over his shoulder and down the road toward Cheapside. He is so long unused to passing among the populace that the crowds make him testy, and he finds himself jostled by men who cannot speak his language, and who have queer colored skin, and dress in outlandish clothes that no true Englishman would ever wear upon their backs, and it is as if he—an Englishman in his own country—counts for nought. He must bite his tongue and restrain his fist and boot.

Still though. It is what he wants. To pass unobserved, unnoticed, down Gracechurch Street to the Church of Saint Magnus the Martyr. The smells intensify as he approaches the river. He has always hated London. There is no sky, no earth, nothing but the river that is not made by man. Its rich fetid air stops up his nose and mouth.

He stands in the agreed place and after a moment a man takes his elbow.

"Walk with me, sir," he says.

This is he, the Roman priest, who will pray with him, and hear his confession, and bless him for the task that lies ahead. He is as tall as Hamilton, but cadaverous. His cap hangs around his ears and his teeth are jumbled like tombstones.

They walk eastward, away from the bridge, along Billingsgate, past Wool Wharf, through a maze of piled wool sarplers waiting to be weighed on the tron, with the river glimpsed between the houses on their right.

But Hamilton only has eyes for the edifice that looms ahead: the Tower.

He is suddenly terrified. This is where his journey will end. In a welter of blood, viscera, pain. The faces of the men he passes seem to loom up at him, as if from under water, each uglier than the next, contorted, scarred, fissured by age and debauchery. They know. They know. They are waiting. He is in a circle of hell.

They walk toward it.

They are about to cross a road running down to the river when the priest sees something to his left. He flinches and turns. He snatches at Hamilton's elbow. His fingers are pincers Hamilton cannot shake off.

"He comes," he says, hissing the words. "Master Walsingham."

The priest jerks him into the shadows on the corner of Seething Lane and Tower Street.

"Keep walking," he tells him.

They do, retracing their steps toward the bridge.

"Don't let him see your face. Once he has seen it he will never forget it."

Yet Hamilton cannot help it. He turns and looks and there he is again: Master Francis Walsingham, marching swiftly down the street toward the river with a crowd of others and some armed guards.

Hamilton wonders what it means, that their paths should so nearly cross so often? First in Paris, and then twice in this week: on the London Road, and now here in Seething Lane. It is a sign, he thinks, sent from above. If God did not wish his mission to succeed, he would have engineered those meetings to end very differently.

Now Hamilton feels himself swell with ecclesiastic fervor.

God wills it. *Deus Vult*.

When they return to the street, they pause again. Stepping out into its various ruts and potholes feels a terrible risk, but they do, and cross it unmolested. Then they feel safer, in the warren of darkened alleys north of the Tower, an area of leatherworkers, where the upper stories are so close a man might lean from his own window to shake the hand of his neighbor opposite. Within, it smells of rats and of rotting leather. They climb a ladder in the dark, and Hamilton must feel his way. His heart pounds, his breathing uneven. It is very close and noisome. Like breathing ancient cloth.

The priest strikes a light. They are surrounded by cured leather skins, as if in a bed at home, save the stench is so powerful. There is a crucifix on a low table, covered in a cloth, and what looks like a very small tabernacle. In one corner is a chamber pot.

The priest takes off his hat. His skull is shaved and dented with old scars, small pox, and worse.

"I am called Father Simon," he says.

He moves as if to take Hamilton in his arms.

Hamilton thrusts him back. "Do you have it?" he asks.

"All in good time, my child."

"No. No. Now."

The priest's eyes catch the rushlight's glow. He looks like no one Hamilton has ever seen before. A fervor rises from him, like a miasma. He has a perverted zealotry of purpose. Every fiber of Hamilton's body revolts against him.

But he is a priest.

"Father," he adds.

The priest's breath is cold, as if from a crypt.

"Very well," he says.

He turns and is gone for some little while. When he comes back, he carries a long tube of waxed linen. Hamilton takes it, feeling the familiar heft of the gun, muffled by padding and sackcloth. He cuts through the bindings to reveal the gun within, a sister to that he spent so many days shooting in Ferniehirst. With her he could shoot the head off a wren at fifty paces. A woman's from a hundred will be easy.

A woman's from two hundred remains to be seen.

It is an object of great beauty, longer than any ordinary arquebus by a cubit or so, slender where she can be, beefy where she need be, the work of the finest smiths in Lombardy. In its stock, an ivory lozenge with a verse from the book of Numbers: "The Avenger of Blood shall put the Murderer to Death."

There is fine black powder and there are balls, each blessed by the pope himself, with words from the Old Testament engraved by the best Venetian craftsmen upon their silken surfaces. He runs his fingers through the powder, searching for larger crumbs that will blow with too much force, and then he rolls each ball between finger and thumb. Even the slightest irregularity will send it awry.

The priest watches him, his stare disquieting.

"We must go to Greenwich," Hamilton tells him hurriedly.

"Tomorrow, my child. It is too dangerous now: she will have guards in numbers. Ushers. Agents. Poursuivants."

His voice hisses like a snake. *Usshherssss, agentssss, pourssssuivantssss.*

"I will need to see the lay of the land."

"Put your faith in God, my child, for He is the wise father and will guide you in all things."

His hand crawls out of its long greasy sleeve to cup Hamilton by the cods.

Queen Mary has been ill these last few days, but now she is up, out of bed, on her feet, in blood-red grosgrain and ostrich feathers, pacing by her window.

"Where is she?"

Mary Seton does not know and cannot explain it.

"Gone, Your Majesty. The boy John says she left with her bag, two days ago, but he did not think to tell me."

"Why? Why would she leave me? Why would she abandon me?"

"I am certain it is a misunderstanding, Your Majesty."

"When I am queen, I will have her winkled out and I will repay her disloyalty."

Mary Seton looks around to see that they are not overheard.

"Oh, the mice are not yet back behind their wainscoting," Queen Mary says. "And even were they I should not care to curb my tongue, for I shall be queen long before they are able to bleat their nothings into the ear of my dear cousin of England."

John Kennedy sits on a log within the Tower's doorway, barely sheltered from the thin rain, and he strokes the knife away from him. A very thin peel rises from the spoon's handle to fall to join the others beneath his feet, and he thinks his mother will like it.

In Waltham Cross, in Hertfordshire, nearly 170 miles to the south, Margaret Formby is offered a ride for the last twenty miles to London by a dark-skinned sumpterman, whose cart holds three sacks of unmilled grain and a sad-eyed cockerel in a cage.

"There is no need for this, Dee," Walsingham tells him. "I am as anxious to talk to *Meneer* van Treslong as you are."

But Dee keeps the barrel of his pistol pointing at Walsingham's nethers.

"Walsingham," he explains again. "I trust you only so far as a man might spit a rat, so sit tight and let us pray Master van Treslong has not yet weighed anchor."

They are in the stern of a ferryman's humble riverboat, the ferryman pulling on his oars, anxiously eyeing the gun that smokes in Dee's hands. Behind them, following along in his official boat, sit the rest of Walsingham's guards, halberdsmen, and so not much help in this situation. Dee feels their contemptuous gaze on his back. But he has the upper hand here.

Evening is falling. Gray clouds scud overhead, and the tide is on the wane. Their passage downstream to Limekiln is swift.

"Over there," Walsingham points, and the oarsman slushes his oar and the boat noses toward the northern bank where it is lined with wharves and cranes and forested with the masts of many ships. Somewhere in among them all they hope to find Master van Treslong's *fluyt*, the *Swan*.

When they do, squeezed in between a carrack and an old-fashioned caravel, its repairs seem nearly complete, and its deck smells of pitch and resin and new-sawn wood. Van Treslong sits under a spread of rust-red sailcloth, talking to a man in a bearskin hat, a mug of beer at each of their elbows. Gone are the voluminous breeches, on are patched sailor's slops.

"Eh!" he greets them. "I was about to set off to Southwark!"

His little eyes darken when he sees Dee's pistol.

"*Meneer*, please, no firespark."

Dee ignores him.

"This is Dr. Dee," Walsingham introduces them.

"Dr. Dee?"

Van Treslong stills, but his eyes are lively, flitting from one to the other for a long moment before he gets to his feet and extends his hand to shake Dee's. Dee curtly greets Van Treslong in his native language, then they slip into English.

"It's an honor, Dr. Dee," Van Treslong says, "to meet you alive."

He catches the eye of the man in the bearskin cap. Broken nose, scarred knuckles. He gives a sort of a shrug. Both are looking at the gun. Only one ball, but who'd they rather take it?

Walsingham does not waste time. "Willem, Dr. Dee has some questions for you about what happened off Nez Bayard a few weeks ago."

Van Treslong turns his questioning gaze on Walsingham.

"Sure," he says, slowly. "But . . . you want me to tell him everything? I mean, it is your choice, Francis."

Walsingham is puzzled.

"If you please, Willem."

Van Treslong shrugs. His logbook sits on the table. For God and Profit. He opens it and finds the right page.

"So," he starts, "I got your first note—the ciphered one—delivered twenty-first day of August. Off La Rochelle."

He proffers the book so that they may see the mark he has made. There are plenty of them on the page, each signifying a certain event, probably entered by men who cannot read, let alone write. It forms, Dee supposes, a little code of its own based on shared knowledge. He would like to see more, at another time, but Van Treslong is going on.

"That message was about Quesada's fleet. Shadowing it. To let you know when it entered the Narrow Sea. Yes?"

Walsingham agrees.

Van Treslong flips a page and runs his finger over the various further squiggles.

"Then, second message. Not coded. Brought by hand of Master Raleigh aboard the *Pelican*. This one I kept. Not every day Queen of England writes a man a letter, *hein*?"

He actually has it, still, kept safe in the back of the book. It is a single sheet of paper folded in thirds, with a hard disk of brittle wax, carefully preserved when the letter was cut open. He takes it out and passes it to Walsingham.

Walsingham reads out the letter. It is addressed to Willem van Treslong, Master of the ship the *Swan*, from Elizabeth, by Grace of God, Queen of England, France, and Ireland, Defender of the Faith, delivered this day by hand of Master Raleigh of the *Pelican*. She requests and requires that in addition to the task entrusted to said Master van Treslong by Her Majesty's most loyal and well-loved servant Master Francis Walsingham—to wit: the providing of information as to the whereabouts and disposition of his Catholic Majesty King Philip of Spain's fleet, newly sent out of Bilbao to cajole, threaten, and menace the said queen and her peoples of England, as well as all those peoples of the Reformed faith—the said Master van Treslong is required to proceed henceforth with as much dispatch as is deemed necessary to stand off the promontory known as Nez Bayard, at sunup on the eighth day of September to wait for communication from another of Her Majesty the Queen's servant, Dr. John Dee, who, should he, by the grace of God, find himself on said promontory, will request and require of Master van Treslong safe passage back to Her Majesty's kingdom of England.

In consideration of such endeavorments thereby involved, and likewise conveyed by the hand of said Master Raleigh, Her Majesty's treasury is able to advance to Master van Treslong the sum thirty ryals, cash, in addition to such moneys as agreed by Master Francis Walsingham, with another thirty ryals payable on delivery of said Dr. Dee to a port of his choosing.

"It says nothing about shooting me," Dee says.

"No," Van Treslong says, slightly shamefaced. "That instruction came a day later."

"Another note? Who brought this one?"

Van Treslong refers back to his log once more.

"Master Peter Bone of the *Foresight.* Very stupid man. Bad sailor, too. Lovely boat though. Fast, you know?"

"We must ask him," Dee says.

"He's trying to make himself a second Hawkins," Walsingham tells them, "trafficking souls along the Guinea coast."

He means there will be nothing heard from him for months, if not years, if ever.

"You have that letter, too? The one that instructs I should be killed," Dee prods.

Van Treslong does, but for various reasons Walsingham needs to persuade him to pass it over. When he does, it is on similar paper to the first, though smaller in dimension, and the seal hangs by its ribbon from one side of the paper, rather than from its center. Walsingham reads it through in silence, then passes it to Dee.

It is in the same hand as the first letter, intended as an addendum to that letter, which—it says—had been written earlier and sent before certain diverse and shocking details had been brought unto Her Majesty's attention. This letter tells Van Treslong that Dr. Dee is this day disclosed as a notorious papist, heretic, and traitor sent by the pope in Rome to countenance the destruction of the life of Her Majesty, Queen Elizabeth. It requests that should *Meneer* van Treslong ensure Dr. John Dee does not reach England to carry out his entirely wicked act then he—Van Treslong—will find the nation accordingly grateful, to wit: a further seventy ryals, delivered by hand of said Master Bone of the *Foresight*, in cash.

"She sent the money there and then?" Walsingham demands. "In cash?"

"Yes," Van Treslong admits.

The writer of the letter goes on to explain, owing to the secret and sensitive manner in which the information as to Dee's culpability was revealed, the matters herein contained are in no wise to be discussed, mentioned, or disclosed to any person, or persons, whatsoever, on pain of the direst consequences. The writer concludes by asking Van Treslong to burn the letter after reading.

"Oh, yes," Van Treslong says vaguely, as if that were something he meant to do.

Dee is not listening. He is looking at the signature.

It is signed Elizabeth R.

It is his own death warrant, signed by Bess. His Bess.

He drops the letter. The seal lands with a clunk. His body is made of ice, and ash, and something very tender. The horror of his betrayal almost chokes him.

Van Treslong pushes his mug of beer his way. Dee drinks, hardly noticing the bitterness of the hops, hardly noticing the beer on his doublet. Seagulls wheel overhead, screaming like the souls of the damned.

"Well, that at least explains that," Walsingham says. He takes the pistol from Dee and pinches the fuse between beer-wet fingers.

Dee puts down the empty mug.

"No, it doesn't," he says. "It doesn't at all. Why would Bess wish me dead? She cannot believe I am some papist firebrand sent to kill her! By the blood of Christ, Walsingham, you have to help me."

Dee is now suddenly unmanned and utterly desperate.

And there is something strange about all this, Walsingham thinks. He remembers Van Treslong's appearance at the Privy Council meeting in Greenwich, after he had fired his gun from the river; and how the Queen had wept to hear of Dr. Dee's death.

"One moment, Willem," he says. "You told us Dr. Dee was dead."

Van Treslong laughs awkwardly.

"Well," he says. "We shot someone."

"But not Dr. Dee."

"Seems not."

"Why?" Walsingham presses.

"Why did I tell you he was dead? Or why did I shoot someone? Why do you think, Francis? You see a plot? You are too long in your espial game, I think."

"So it was just the money? Just the seventy ryals?"

Van Treslong shrugs. "There's a reason we're called Sea Beggars."

He is right, of course, but there is not much money filling up the coffers of England, and the Queen is notoriously tight with it. It was a surprise, even, when she offered to foot the bill for repairs to the *Swan*. She would not, surely, give money away, the whole sum *in advance*?

"And why seventy ryals?" he wonders aloud.

"Ten more than bringing me home," Dee supposes.

Van Treslong smiles in confirmation. He is missing only one tooth. That is good for a sailor. That money must explain those new breeches, Walsingham supposes.

And just then a boy appears from the cabin holding those self-same breeches over his arm, with that same doublet. He holds them out to show they are clean, as requested, ready for Van Treslong's night out in Southwark. The Dutchman collects the two letters for his logbook and stands to bring the meeting to a close.

"*Verdammt!*" he cries. Seagull shit lands with a splatch on the doublet. Van Treslong cuffs the boy and seizes the jacket and starts brushing at the cloth.

Walsingham notices Dee's hand move like a snake. A moment later, the letters are gone, and they stand to go.

"Thank you, Willem," Walsingham says. "God give you a good evening."

"Sure you don't want to come?" he asks. "They are going to set the dogs on an ape tied to the back of a horse!"

CHAPTER FIFTEEN

London, October 10, 1572

Robert Beale is summoned from his office just before curfew.

"Some bint with a funny accent," the porter tells him. "After Master Walsingham and will not take no for answer."

Beale sets aside his work on the accounts of their recent action with something like relief and follows the porter into the yard, where, standing behind the gates, is a road-weary Margaret Formby.

When she sees him, she starts to weep.

He summons bread, ale, an apple for the love of God, and with her mute permission he takes her elbow and guides her to the fireside in Master Walsingham's outer office.

After a little while she gathers herself.

"I am sorry; I did not know who to come to."

"What is it?" he asks.

"Is there . . . a woman I might talk to? I have much to say that I cannot . . ."

She trails off and Master Beale understands. He calls for Mistress Walsingham to the outer office and introduces the two women, then he leaves them to it, though only so far as the doorway, where he stands out of sight and listens to what is being said.

At first the girl is nervous, suspicious even of Mistress Walsingham, but Mistress Walsingham is a good listener, and the girl soon plucks up courage, and her tale pours out.

At first it is heartrending, and Mistress Walsingham clucks maternally, shocked at Queen Mary's devilish treatment of the girl.

"You poor soul, no Christian should be made to practice such a thing!"

But then she starts on the ruse with the candlestick, and what was done while Francis Walsingham was looking elsewhere, and it becomes very alarming.

Queen Elizabeth sets out to Greenwich from Windsor. It is not yet cool enough for the blue cloak lined with marten fur, but she shivers uncontrollably tonight and starts at every sound—the barking of the dogs, the slop of the river against the pontoon, the distant laugh of the bargemaster's boy. She has had more days like this recently, of the sort when she will stand at her window and look out over the horizon and sense it: the massed malignance that is gathering there. So much hatred, gathered up from all over Christendom, and it is pointed at her, at her tiny fluttering heart, which she can feel beating like a finch in a cage. It is fear. Fear for her life, for her country, for everything she knows.

And so she shivers like a greyhound.

Accompanying her are three ladies-in-waiting and Lord Burghley. Burghley wants passage only to his house on the Strand, for he is ailing of some complaint and wishes to consult his own physician from the comfort of his own bed.

Her Majesty's barge is a luxurious craft: a sharp prow, eighteen oarsmen, a small deck on which a chair may be placed so that she may be seen by the city's populace. Then: a cabin with glazed sides in which she may retreat should the miasma on the river prove too much, screened by dense velvet curtains the color of blood, and aft, a deck for the helmsman and bargemaster.

Her bargemaster sends word that he aims to pass under the bridge just as the tide is on the slack.

Above them, she believes the star in Cassiopeia is brighter than ever.

As Francis Walsingham and Dr. John Dee make their way back up Seething Lane there comes the hue and cry.

"What is it?"

"A murder!" a bedel tells them. "Some fucker's been slit from bollocks to chops."

It is not a matter for them, but for the various watchmen, bailiffs, and bedels such as this one, who are gathered on corners threatening passersby with their clubs and their questions, looking for someone to blame.

"He'll be fucking covered in blood," the bedel tells them once Walsingham has identified himself. "He's made a right mess in there. Gralloched the fucker he has, begging your pardon, sirs, like a butcher."

They are looking for a tall man with a long parcel, the bedel tells them, "like a longbow, but heavier." Neither Walsingham nor Dee have noticed a man fitting that description, so they leave him to it.

As they walk Dee feels he may faint.

"By Christ, Walsingham, I have not eaten for three days."

They stop at the Angel. Once seated, Walsingham orders them ale and a greasy pigeon pie to share and they find a corner with only one dog. Dee has stolen both Van Treslong's letters and he produces them now. He looks down at them with head-hung, sorrowful incredulity. Walsingham thinks he says, "Bess, how could you?," but he hopes not.

After a moment Dee looks up. He has stumbled on something.

"Look at the edges," he says, passing Walsingham the smaller of the two, the second one instructing Van Treslong to kill Dee. When Walsingham looks at it, he sees what Dee means: the cuts of the four edges of the document do not match; two are old, blurred by time and touch, two are new, still pale.

"It is a corner," Walsingham says. "Cut from a larger letter."

Which explains the off-set seal. But so what? Saving paper is only prudent, and the Queen is nothing if not that. But then, the more he looks at it, the more he sees the disconnect between this matter of saving paper on one hand, and an unconditional offer of seventy ryals on the other, in advance—and with no mechanism for refund should Van Treslong fail to kill Dr. Dee. He would expect the first of Her Majesty, but the second is entirely out of character.

"Put them together," Walsingham tells Dee. "Side by side."

They study the handwriting. There is one less ornate underlining of the word *Elizabeth* in the second one, but that might easily be explained by the limitations of space. And it is the same with the date. *Written on this day the first day of September, in this the year of our Lord, 1572.* The second is dated the day after.

"Both are in the same hand," he says.

Walsingham nods.

"Where was she when she wrote these letters?" Dee asks.

"What difference does it make?"

"Someone must have slandered me," Dee says.

That makes sense, Walsingham supposes. He has heard many accusations leveled against Dee—he has been the author of some himself—but never that Dee is an agent of Rome, sent to kill the Queen. That is a new one.

"It was whoever the Queen listened to between writing that first letter, and the second letter; they must have told her I was a . . . a papist and so on."

Again, Walsingham agrees.

"Then who was it? Where was she? Surely you keep her diary, Walsingham?"

Walsingham nods. Of course there's a diary of the Queen's movements. It'll be there in black-and-white, secretary hand.

"Well, where is it?"

"Whitehall," Walsingham tells him. "Or wherever she is."

"Let's go there now then."

He shakes his head.

"Dee," he says, "I have been on the road for two weeks. I hardly had chance to say hello to my wife before you pointed your guns at me. Can I just have one night's sleep in my own bed?"

"Walsingham! This is important!"

"I know, Dee. Believe me, I know. But the diary will still be there in the morning. It is safe under lock and key, and there are any number of copies that can be found. I do not happen to have one to hand, that is all."

"Back at your house?"

"No, Dee. You go back to Mortlake. I will send for you tomorrow when I have the diary."

Dee has no choice. He sighs loudly again.

They can hear running feet and much shouting in the street outside.

"Have they caught him?" Walsingham wonders.

"Doesn't sound like it," Dee says. "Listen, shall we get something stronger?"

A bottle of French brandy, the best in the inn, appears before them.

"So I suppose you have to wonder if she still wants you dead?" Walsingham asks.

Dee drinks very deeply and shudders. "Can we talk about something else?"

Walsingham tells him about Mary Queen of Scots, and how she saw through the second part of Walsingham's plan to lure her into disclosing her means of communication, and perhaps even the whereabouts of Hamilton. He tells him how she turned it to her own advantage. Dee laughs the bitter laugh of a man who hardly cares anymore. He drinks more brandy, listening to Walsingham's story of his wild-goose chase up to Scotland, and about the silver shaft. Dee spits brandy onto the table and laughs as if brought back to life.

"But who was she communicating with?" Walsingham wonders to himself. "And what was she saying?"

"You think she was tipped over into something . . . what? Rash? When she learned Quesada wasn't coming?"

"Of course, but what?"

Dee shrugs. They both know what.

"That's it? A shrug? Christ, Dee, we are talking about someone trying to kill the Queen!"

"Well, she has just tried to have me killed, Walsingham, so I hope you will pardon me when I tell you I am not too bothered by what happens to her now."

Walsingham is shocked, though he does not altogether blame Dee for thinking that, at the moment. He hopes it will pass though.

"What will you do?" he asks.

"I will finish this bottle of brandy—*hup!*—and then I will go home, as you suggest, to my mother, my books, my instruments. You will have noticed the new star in Cassiopeia. I should like to have a moment to myself to study that."

Dee downs the rest of the brandy and bangs his cup on the table.

"Come on then," he says.

But outside they are met with a great shout.

"There you are!"

It is a guard made up of the Queen's troop, sent by Robert Beale to find Master Walsingham and bring him home.

By now Dee is very drunk, Walsingham less so. Dee reels off into the night, about his own business, and Walsingham bids him a good night.

At home Beale takes him to see Margaret Formby, still tear-heavy in Mistress Walsingham's arms. His arrival starts her sobbing again, and he does his best to be soft-footed and patient, but he needs to know what he is up against, and he needs to know now.

"With whom was Queen Mary communicating?"

The girl is reluctant to spit it out, and he sees he frightens her. What must she have heard about him? That he breathes fire? Has a forked tongue? His wife gives him a stern look.

He sees her lips forming the start of words that do not come, and he is not sure what he expects.

Eventually, she speaks.

The Queen's bargemaster orders his men on the starboard side to lift their oars, and the barge buffs against the lamp-lit dock with a gentle bump that flutters cloth, but sends no one staggering.

Elizabeth gives thanks to God and pays the bargemaster a small coin to share among his men (he won't) (and nor does she expect him to) and she walks with her ladies up the gangplank and across the gravel path where the dew is already falling.

Sir Thomas Smith is there to meet her with a deep bow, pleased to have her to himself. He will want money, she thinks tiredly.

The star in Cassiopeia is now very bright.

"Whatever can it mean?" she asks.

Smith has no idea. He thinks only of himself and of his scheme in Ireland.

How she misses John Dee.

James Hamilton props his sackcloth-wrapped gun against a wall and washes the blood from his hands and face in the horse trough behind Limehouse wharves. He thrusts his arms deep into the cold water, then splashes his doublet, breeches, and boots clean of blood. He smells it, feels it stiff in the wool and in his linens, between his toes in his right boot. For such a desiccated stick of a man, Father Simon gave up much blood, and Hamilton had had to clamp his mouth ghastly shut for fear his girlish screams would summon the neighborhood.

When he is done, he collects the gun, and moves swiftly into the shadows before the night watch guards come stamping around the corner.

While the boatman pulls hard against the running river, Dr. John Dee sits athwart the skiff and allows himself to slip into lucid dreams of Rose Cochet, Isobel's girl. He sees her playing a game in which she wears a blindfold, with other children running around her, and she must touch them all to win the game. Everyone laughs, including Rose, and her little teeth are like seed pearls. She has dimpled cheeks and pretty clothes. She is happy, and in another time, the sight would be one to bring a tear of joy to any man's eye.

But the image starts Dee awake, for it is false. It cannot be. He knows it cannot be: on his way back from France, the boat on which he had stowed away—a single-masted trader in all-sorts from the port of Damme—had docked in Sandwich, and Dee had walked to the house of Sir John Pinkney, Isobel Cochet's father. He found the old man hollowed out with grief at his missing granddaughter, like an oak tree in a field struck by lightning. News of his daughter's death would have killed him. So Dee lied and played the part of a traveling minstrel, down on his luck, and the old man gave him a penny, but he was too sad to hear him play.

"Smith? Sir *Thomas* Smith?"

"It is what she says."

Beale and Walsingham are back on Seething Lane, striding ahead of the nightwatchman with his swinging lantern, followed by five of the Queen's yeomen. The hue and cry has been successful, and some Italian tailor with a cast in his eye has proved to be what was needed and is now unlikely to live to see sunset next. Walsingham cannot concern himself with that sort of injustice. He cannot rid himself of the heat that thrums through his body since hearing Margaret Formby confess.

Smith?

Walsingham thinks of the efforts he has gone to, the risks he has taken, the lives he has sacrificed, only to find out that it is Smith, Sir Thomas Smith, Privy councillor and Queen Elizabeth's close confidant, who provides the conduit between Queen Mary and the outside world! Smith who is feeding her all she needs to know, who takes her messages to England's enemies abroad.

"What messages did they send to each other?" Beale asks.

The girl did not have all the details, of course.

"Queen Mary sent her away whenever she was at her secrets, so she never saw what was written, and Margaret only heard the odd word when Mary spoke to her priest, or sometimes Mary Seton."

"What in particular?"

"She heard Queen Mary tell Mistress Seton that Smith had begged her to remember his services when she came to be Queen of England. Mistress Seton asked her what she thought he had in mind, and Mary told her that Smith was in need of money to save Ireland."

To save Ireland. My God. Smith's colony in Ireland. A constant thorn in everyone's side, not just the Ulstermen's. How much money can he have sunk in it to be so desperate as to conspire with a foreign power against his own Queen!

"Fucking Smith," Beale mutters.

He does not usually use farmyard language in front of Walsingham, but there is sometimes a time and a place for this sort of thing.

"Yes," Walsingham agrees, "but that's not the worst of it. The girl overheard Queen Mary laughing—a rare enough event apparently—saying that she'll not have need of Smith much longer, and that soon after Michaelmas she will be able to talk to her uncle directly."

"Her uncle? Which one? Cardinal de Guise?"

"I suppose."

"And she used the word 'directly'?" Beale asks.

"Well, she said, 'to his face, as befits a Christian prince,'" Walsingham tells Beale. It is this detail that confirms—to Walsingham's mind—that Smith is Mary's conduit to the outside world in general, and to de Guise in particular. But it takes a moment before Beale sees that is not the most important thing about what was said.

"'Soon after Michaelmas'?" he asks. "Michaelmas was two weeks ago."

"Exactly."

"Did she believe Quesada would be the one to set her free?"

"That is the thing," Walsingham says. "Mary said this *after* she had learned we'd diverted Quesada's fleet."

Beale looks away.

"My God," he says. "You mean, whatever she set in motion, it is still in motion?"

It is.

Tears cling like diamonds on Queen Elizabeth's eyelashes as she listens to the Children of the Chapel Royal bring Master Tallis's exquisitely sorrowful "Lamentations of Jeremiah" to its haunting, ethereal conclusion. Ordinarily, such beauty is a great consolation, but today it leaves her aflutter. It is more than this new star in Cassiopeia, she thinks. She feels on the verge of some great change, one that has been ushered in by the death of Dr. Dee, whom she misses with greater intensity with the passing of each day.

It is not supposed to be that way.

"Walk with us, Sir Thomas," she tells her Privy councillor, "and tell us such things that will reassure us of God's love, for this evening we feel atremble at the world, as if we were on the threshold of some new and awful design."

Sir Thomas Smith holds his arm out for Her Majesty to take should she wish it, but he is out of words, and so they pass out of the chapel and along the corridor in candlelit silence.

It is gone midnight when Dee walks with sober purpose down through the apple trees toward the river. He carries the largest of his cross-staffs and is accompanied by Thomas Digges, a boy of fourteen winters the son of his late neighbor, Leonard Digges, who is passed out of this world. The boy carries a bull's-eye lamp and has an acute scientific mind, being much interested in mirrors and in glass lenses, with which, when placed in certain ways, he can make the sun, moon, and stars descend to here below.

"I am pleased you are back, Doctor," the boy tells him. "I have been trying to measure it myself but lack your expertise."

He indicates a ruler as tall as a man that he has placed in an apple tree.

"I am sure you lack only a good-size cross-staff," Dee says with a laugh.

The night is cold and clear, but a mist has risen from the river. Dee has been looking forward to this moment since he first saw the star, in Picardy, what seems like months ago now.

"What do you think it can mean?" the boy asks.

"We must first discover if it is fixed," Dee tells him, "or if it moves in relation to the other stars about it. If that is the case, then it is a comet, with a tail so small we cannot see it, and . . . well. Who knows? They portend many things."

"I heard a woman in Putney gave birth to a child with the feet of a goose," the boy tells him.

"Did she now?"

They set up the cross-staff and spend the next hour in pleasurable contemplation of what they come to believe is a star. Thomas reminds Dee there are only two well-known appearances of stars: one that caused much commotion among the Jews of Hipparchus's day and the star of Bethlehem.

"It is a sign of great change," Dee supposes. "Remember the words of Tiburtina: 'the firmament of Heaven shall be dissolved, and the planets be opposed on contrary courses; the spheres shall justle one another, and the fixed stars move faster than the planets.' "

They are both silent for a good long while. At length the eastern sky brightens, and the stars dim, and Dee and the boy return, dew soaked and shivering now, to their separate houses to sleep, and to dream.

CHAPTER SIXTEEN

London, October 11, 1572

It is not yet dawn, and still quiet in Limehouse, when he kills the widow. Her lips tremble and turn blue, and she soils herself. When it is done, he rolls her body into a corner. Her hovel sits on stilts above the mud of the river, a few stinking yards downriver from where the river Lea meets the Thames. It smells of rot and fish guts, and there is a privy hole in the floor that sticks out over the river when it is at high tide. He opens up another hole the size of his fist in the sodden daub of the wall that gives out onto the river. It is at its narrowest here, and through the hole he can see all the way across it to Rotherhithe, on the southern bank, perhaps a hundred yards away. It is perfect, just as he knew it would be.

He jams the door shut and settles down to wait.

Francis Walsingham has not slept all night, and now, as gray dawn breaks, he walks into the Queen's newly planted garden in Greenwich, among a lattice of hedges as high as his shins, watching the skeins of mist drift across the placid surface of the Thames.

He had not expected Sir Thomas Smith to be with the Queen at Greenwich, and the night before, when he and Beale had debouched from his barge to find it so, his heart had sunk. Without the explicit support of Lord Burghley and the Earl of Leicester, he cannot hope to bring any sort of accusation against Smith, but without doing so—without revealing that he knows Smith to be a traitor—he cannot admit the origins of his information about the threat to the Queen's life.

He had asked that she be moved to the Tower that very night.

"It is the safest stronghold we have," he'd told Smith.

"How dare you come here, Walsingham," Smith had shouted, "upsetting Her Majesty with your absurd scare stories."

"Please let me see the Queen, Sir Thomas," he'd asked.

"No, Walsingham, I will not, for I do not trust you."

There was nothing Walsingham could do save keep close and remain vigilant. He and Beale had passed the night in the guardroom, doing what could be done: sending word to Burghley and to Leicester, summoning them to come urgently with as many troops of their own as was possible.

"Before then we have to move her to the Tower," he tells Beale.

Beale nods. It is the thing they have most feared about the Queen passing time in Greenwich: a few ships filled with Spanish troops landing on the river's bank, and bringing bloody murder to the palace.

"You saw how easily Van Treslong made his way upriver," Walsingham says. "What if four hundred well-trained troops mobilized in Greenwich at dawn tomorrow? What would we do? Shout for the yeomen of the guard? There are a hundred of them, and the only fighting they are trained for is for their ale, and their pensions. The Queen's household—all her gallant gentlemen, with all their gallant talk—would take flight at the first whiff of powder and be in Blackheath before the Spanish stepped ashore."

It was an exaggeration, but not by much.

Beale has a worse fear though. Of a single assassin, a man with one of the new guns from the Italian city of Milan that can shoot accurately over a hundred paces. He supposes if he were the pope, and he wanted the Queen dead, then that is what he would do: send a battalion of such men to come over here and lie in wait. Why haven't other princes done so? He puts it down to the fact they believe one another anointed by God, and to plot to kill one is a plot to kill them all. It is why Queen Elizabeth will not have Queen Mary put to death. Such things are contagious.

He had opened his mouth to say something to Master Walsingham, but he had refrained. It is dangerous to be overheard even countenancing the death of the Queen.

So they had returned to their letter writing.

At dawn Walsingham rises and goes outside, heedless of the night miasma that rises from the river and from the meager fields and broad marshes beyond. He ordered the Queen's barge to be made ready earlier and now she is tied up against the jetty, and the bargemaster's boys are busy about polishing the glass of her windows. A handful of Her Majesty's yeomen prowl the foreshore in the dawn, at least, but they are more familiar with bullying beggars and river gypsies.

A bell rings.

The mist slowly lifts. Eight geese land on the water. From the river's north bank a merchant's ship is foresail up, just getting under way. Walsingham wonders where she is bound. Antwerp?

Le Havre? Cádiz? He thinks of Dr. John Dee again, poor Dr. John Dee, and he wonders why the Queen would ever want him dead in the first place.

One day he will have to ask her.

When she is awake.

In the meantime, there is still Sir Thomas Smith.

In Mortlake, John Dee wakes with the word *Bess* on his lips. He has dreamt of a dirty river snaking by under a dipping gray mist; of a dead woman with no teeth lying in a filth of fine fish bones and human mud; of a rotting hovel with its footings in the water; and of the flash of black powder.

He walks down to the orchard to relieve himself in the river.

Thomas Digges is there, likewise engaged.

When they are finished and dressed again, Digges shows him his perspective glass.

"What can you see through it?" Dee asks.

"Nothing much."

It is a fat tube of smooth bark with a polished lens at one end. Dee holds it up and looks through it. It is not that he can see nothing much, only that there is nothing much to be seen. A stretch of riverbank, a few houses to the north. A boat under a murky green sail, a boy in the bow, approaching the dock. It is all within touching distance.

He lowers the perspective glass, and suddenly he is filled with a terrible, fateful certainty.

"Come with me, Thomas, now."

"Why? Where?"

"To see Master Walsingham," Dee tells him. "The world depends on it."

The black powder cannot be even slightly damp, or it will clump and explode with unpredictable force, even destroying the barrel, and likely to be more dangerous to the marksman than his target. So Hamilton lights a fire of damp wattle on the stone and tips a fat pinch of the powder into as clean an oyster shell as can be found, and he places that as close to the meager flames as he dares. Smoke fills the hovel, sifting out through the many gaps in the walls and the ceiling.

He takes the gun out of the oiled linen. It is a thing of great elegance and beauty, made all the more so in these surroundings. He places it on its stand, with its barrel through the hole in the wall. He has a perfect view of the river, here at its narrowest point, and he can with no difficulty imagine the Queen's barge coming upriver toward him, two perfect banks of oars: dipping, pulling, dipping, pulling. Then the boat will turn through the course of the river, exposing one long length to this bank for a stretch of perhaps one hundred yards.

That is where he will shoot her.

"What do you want?"

It is the porter on Francis Walsingham's gate, looking Dr. Dee up and down, trying to remember where he has seen him before. But Dee is properly dressed this time, washed, even, and with what looks like a servant, and no eye patch.

Dee tells him who he is and what his business is.

"Well, you're out of luck, Doctor, for he is gone to Greenwich with Master Beale."

Damn.

As he is walking away, Dee is hailed by a rough voice.

"Why, Dr. Dee! Fancy seeing you around these parts. Thought you'd still be in the tun?"

It is, of all people, Chidiock Tunstall, the keeper of the Bull on Bishopsgate, leading a very fine horse.

Dee shakes his hand and apologizes for leaving him with the debt collectors breaking up his inn. It feels a very long time ago now.

"Water under the bridge, Master Dee," Chidiock tells him. "And I made them pay handsome like, so no harm done. Did I just see you knocking up Master Walsingham?"

"I was, though I am told he is in Greenwich."

"Christ on his cross," Chidiock swears. "I am in search of him, too."

"Well, we are on our way there, if we can help?"

"Mebbe you can," Chidiock says. "A gent stabled this horse two, three days ago, but only paid for the day. My lad went through the saddlebags to see if there were anything that'd cover what's owed."

Dee is thinking: *I have no time for this*. But Chidiock is untying the bag and delving within.

"And the lad found this, just a letter like, I thought, only when I got an old bloke what used to be a friar to cast it over it and—"

Dee claps a hand on his arm.

"By Christ, Chidiock! Put it away."

It is a copy of the papal bull *Regnans in Excelsis*. Mere possession of it will lead a man to his death on a pyre.

"There was more; look." He holds out a very small crucifix designed to be secreted within some other thing, but also: small clumps of black powder and there, sitting in the folds of the innkeeper's calloused palm, is a ball of lead.

Christ.

"Walsingham likes to pay us to keep a bit of an eye out for this kind of thing, see?" Chidiock is saying. "And I reckon this looks quite interesting."

There is a gleam of greed in his eye.

"Come with us, Chidiock," Dee tells him.

"What about the horse?"

"Forget the bloody horse."

"I can't just leave it, and besides, I ain't got time for going to no Greenwich. I'll just take it back and wait for him another day."

In the end he decides he trusts Dee to give Walsingham a full and fair account of the matter, and he passes him over the bag, complete with the papal bull, black powder, and ball. The leather is good, and the bags are well made, clearly expensive, and within are linens far finer than those worn by Dee or the boy Thomas. On the inside of the flap is a small imprint of a sun in splendor. A heraldic device used by—well, any number of families.

But a well-known family, nonetheless, and alongside the obvious quality of the horse, this means whoever left it there did not do so because they could not afford to return and collect it. They meant to do so, or, rather, they did not care that they had done so. Which means, what? That they did not expect to have use for the horse in future?

Which leaves what?

Someone, with a gun, on an errand for the pope from which they do not expect to return alive.

Dear God.

"Come, Thomas," Dee says. "To Greenwich."

Sir Thomas Smith controls access to the Queen, and so despite the urgency, Francis Walsingham must stand with all other suitors in the great hall of Greenwich Palace and watch Sir Thomas Smith carefully serving Queen Elizabeth her breakfast: a loaf of the finest white bread; three baked herring; a dish of sprats, as well as a cup of beer and another of wine, each poured from a silver ewer. Smith performs his task at an aching, tortuous pace, no less grave than he had been at her coronation, save that every now and then he will glance up at Walsingham and catch his gaze.

He seems to think what he does is amusing.

Walsingham does not react. He counts almost every pace—there and back again—between here and Lord Burghley's house on the Strand; every pace—there and back again—between here and the Midlands, where it is believed the Earl of Leicester is overseeing some improvements to his castle of Kenilworth.

He has given up hope of the latter coming in time, but surely the former will rouse himself from his sickbed?

Finally, the meal is ended and the Queen stands to have her hands washed in warm rose water, then dried on snow-white linen. When this is done, her whole household—ten gentlemen of various ranks, none of whom are of the slightest interest to Walsingham, and perhaps fifteen women-in-waiting, likewise of no import—proceed very slowly toward the great mirrored library.

But even then Walsingham must wait his turn to address Her Majesty, and still he has no idea how to couch it without directly accusing Sir Thomas Smith—who will be standing at her side—of treason. So he waits, lingering by that same window through which he saw Van Treslong's *Swan* what seems like months ago now.

Below him, in that garden, he has at least managed to prod Her Majesty's yeomen into some action, and they are gathered there in what their captain—a boy of about twenty whose cheeks flush when he speaks—calls "warlike array." Walsingham cranes his neck to look eastward, downriver, whence he fears the Spanish will come, when they come. Then he peers westward, upriver, whence he hopes Burghley will come, if he comes.

He can hear murmurings and the occasional forced laugh from the throne to his right as the business of the court proceeds.

"Come on, come on."

Eventually his hopes are answered before his fears are confirmed.

Burghley's barge makes its way through the river traffic coming down from the city. Five oars on each side, but its flags are not raised. *Odd*, he thinks. He slips away from his place by the window. He needs to intercept the Lord High Treasurer before he speaks to the Queen or most especially Smith, so he is out into the garden before Burghley's bargemaster gives the order to up oars and a boy in the barge's bow tosses a rope ashore. Walsingham notices a slight slackness among the bargemen, though, and the reason soon becomes clear: their passenger is not Lord Burghley, but another man, and a boy.

"Dee, what in God's name are you doing here?"

"Couldn't find a regular ferryman," Dee tells him, "but listen, Walsingham, I have had a dream."

"Oh Christ, Dee! I don't have time for this."

But then he thinks: *The Queen will wish to see Dee. Sir Thomas Smith will not be able to prevent that.*

"Come on," he says, without asking what Dee's dream might be.

The Queen remains in her great mirrored library, with Sir Thomas Smith, and a small audience of the loose affiliation of lords and ladies from her court. She wears russet silks today, in keeping with the slight autumnal chill.

"Where is Master Walsingham?" she asks. "He was much agitated earlier."

Smith laughs dismissively. "There is always something to agitate Master Walsingham."

"But he is gone?"

"He will be back, Your Majesty, I have no doubt."

She thinks Smith would like to keep her in aspic. But he is sweating, she notes, and forever dithering on the cusp of asking some favor he fears she will only decline. His colony in Ireland—he tries to hide the reports that come in, but the others in her council talk of the disasters quite freely. She wonders how much money he has lost, and what personal costs he bears too.

An usher in plum velvets comes and stands before both, looking ruffled, and seems, for that moment, unable to find his words. It is Sir John Ivesy.

"Sir John?" she prompts.

"Dr. Dee, Your Majesty, he is arrived this minute, in Lord Burghley's barge, and seeks—"

Elizabeth cannot believe it. She gets to her feet.

"Dr. *Dee*? Our Dr. Dee? *Dr.* John Dee?"

"No!" Smith shouts.

The Queen finally glares at him and Sir John looks from one to the other in mute confusion.

"Send for him," the Queen says.

When the man has gone, she turns to Sir Thomas.

"You forget yourself," she says.

He can only bow his head.

She lacks the heart to scold him further, for she is too taken up with the idea that Dee lives. She crosses to the window. Sure enough: Lord Burghley's barge is moored against the bank, and her yeoman, too, are astir about something.

She turns as she hears the footsteps and the grounding of her guardsmen's halberds. The doors open, and in comes first Francis Walsingham, and then her own, entirely beloved, John Dee.

She almost runs to him, but she sees his face. His expression is cold and haggard, entirely and actively repelling any friendship between them. She cannot even stifle a gasp. She returns, stunned, to sit in her throne under her cloth of state. She feels as if staring down from a height. The floor moves of its own accord, and she is fraught at her lack of control, at her inability to predict what will happen next.

Dee bows without looking at her.

"Dr. Dee," she says.

"Your Majesty."

"We believed you dead," she says. "We heard rumors."

"Premature, I am afraid, your Majesty."

Walsingham is hopping up and down, anxious to unburden himself. She turns to him.

"But Master van Treslong—" she starts. "He told us. He told us you were dead?"

"Your Majesty," Walsingham interjects, "we can discuss the whys and wherefores at some later date."

"Hold your tongue, Walsingham!" Smith barks.

"What is amiss, Master Walsingham?" the Queen overrules.

"Your Majesty, I believe your life is in immediate and grave danger if you remain here in Greenwich. You should prepare to move to the safety of the Tower."

"What nonsense is this, Walsingham?" Smith demands.

"Sir Thomas, please, silence, we pray."

She stands and comes down the steps. She wishes to stand close and look Dee in the eye.

"John," she says.

"Your Majesty," he replies.

His voice is cold, and his face is closed, like a gripped fist.

Walsingham speaks, low and urgent. "Please, Your Majesty, we can discuss this matter later. I have reliable information that Spanish troops will land—in the garden, not a hundred paces from here—today. We need to move your person to the safety of the Tower."

It is an exaggeration, perhaps, a lie, but intended for good effect. It snaps the Queen from her intense concentration on Dee and brings her up short.

"How do you know this?" she asks.

"Again, Your Majesty, I will tell you all, but we need to move you, and move you now."

"No," Dee cuts across, addressing Walsingham. "That is not right. That is what they want you to do. They *want* you to take to the river, Your Majesty. They will shoot you in your barge."

Smith scoffs.

"With a gun? Impossible."

Dee holds up the ball.

"Look at this," he says.

The Queen takes it.

"It is very beautiful," she says, for it is: almost black, silken smooth, and perfectly round. It has a lovely, heavy feel in her palm, but it feels utterly deadly, and it makes her shudder.

Dee summons Thomas Digges from the shadows.

"What is it now, Dee?" Smith asks.

"Show Her Majesty your lens, please, Thomas."

Thomas takes the small lens from the back of his perspective glass and passes it to the Queen. She holds it as one might a coin.

"Hold it like so," Dee instructs, "and look through it, at the ball."

She does so, and then takes a second look.

"What does it say?" she asks.

Engraved in the ball, in letters so minute they are not visible to the naked eye, are the words "The punishment of your iniquity is completed, daughter of Zion."

"From the book of Lamentations," the Queen murmurs.

"What sorcery is this?" Smith demands.

"It was found in the saddlebag of a man come to town, two days ago, along with some black powder, and this."

Dee shows them the copy of the papal bull.

The Queen blanches.

"Burn that thing," she mutters, looking away.

"I believe there is an assassin sent to kill you, Your Majesty," he says. "Someone gifted with a gun."

She places her hand on her throat. This is utterly chilling. Kings and Queens have always been prey to assassins' blades, of course, and so have always taken care to surround themselves with loyal bodyguards. The invention, and improvement in accuracy, of the gun brings with it a terrible new threat, which no one yet knows how to counter, including Francis Walsingham.

Walsingham shakes his head. "All the more reason to get Her Majesty's person safely to the Tower."

"You can say it again," Dee argues, "but if you put Her Majesty on the boat, you will be signing her death warrant."

"Dee! You do not understand! If the Queen stays here, she will be killed! We cannot risk it!"

There is a rising hubbub of voices raised against his.

Dee turns to the Queen, who stares at him with tears in her eyes.

"What is it, John?"

"Your Majesty," he says, quietly. She lifts her hand for silence from the other men. It is instant.

He tells them of his dream: of the dead woman lying in fish

bones; of the rotting warehouse with its footings in the water; of the explosive flash of black powder.

Walsingham is exasperated. "It's just a dream!" he says.

"You remember how I knew that Isobel Cochet was on Mont Saint-Michel?"

Walsingham opens then closes his mouth. He catches Beale's eye over Dee's shoulder. He does not have to be able to read minds to know what Beale is thinking: Hamilton.

"What is it?" the Queen asks.

Walsingham tells her his fears about her great enemy, James Hamilton, well known for his gift with the gun.

After a long moment's silence, the Queen turns to Dee.

"You are my eyes," she says.

Dee notes Walsingham's wince.

But the Queen goes on.

"And so what would you have me do?" she asks him.

She is placing all her trust in him, publicly, and so everyone must follow suit and do likewise.

Dee takes a long deep breath. He is struggling, struggling to resist her. Still he says nothing, but he cannot. He looks around the library, at all the books he will never own, most of them useless, and at the paintings, and at the myriad images of the Queen, of himself, Walsingham, Smith, and all the others reflected almost endlessly in the polished glass of all the Venetian mirrors.

They wait his word, his decision.

"You must get in the boat," he says.

Everyone starts shouting at him all at once.

It does not take the workmen long. Two of them have the mirror down from the wall within the hour, and they carry it—two foot by three foot of polished glass and metal that is worth more than them and their entire families put together—out to the master carpenter's workshop.

"Are you certain about this, Dee?" Walsingham nags.

Dee can see how it might go wrong, but he says nothing.

"Fetch two more," he tells the workmen. "The next largest there."

The workmen go back to bring another mirror.

"What are you up to, Dee?"

"We need a diptych," he tells Walsingham. "Two mirrors, braced upright and placed at an angle, just so."

He indicates with his hands.

Walsingham is hardly any the wiser, but the master carpenter is at work with his mallet and chisel, creating a mortise and tenon in a frame of wood.

"Like this?"

"Perfect. Now one more, identical."

While the work goes on, the only sign of the Queen is a glimpse of her in the window, and Walsingham is drawn back to that painful afternoon in Sheffield when he was taught a lesson by Queen Mary. If Dee is right, the lessons have not stopped there. Christ.

When the frames are done to his satisfaction, the workmen carry them out to the Queen's barge and place them behind the cabin.

"No. Move it to the front of the cabin."

Then they bring the mirrors and the master carpenter attaches them to the frame with a series of leather straps.

"Proper job," he says, though he has no idea what the job is.

The curtains in the cabin are drawn to one side, rich red velvet, while the windowpanes are removed on both sides, and good beeswax candles are lit and placed on the deck, with smaller mirrors positioned behind them to magnify the light, and throw it into the cabin.

"I hope you know what you are doing, Dee," Walsingham says again.

Dee tells him that while he was a student at Cambridge he once made the audience of a theater believe a golden scarab beetle the size of a man could fly.

"How?"

"Just wait, can't you, Walsingham?"

"We do not have time, Dee!"

"We do this, now," Dee says, "and we catch our gunman. And the Queen can live in peace for some little while. Or we run and hide, stick her in the Tower. And she is there forever."

The oarsmen, all eighteen of them, sit in the barge and stare back, bewildered as anyone, as Dee makes young Thomas Digges sit in Her Majesty's chair in the cabin. Their view is obscured by one of the mirrors, so they cannot see it, but Dee has turned the chair to one side, so that instead of facing forward, as it might usually, it faces the port side of the boat.

"Stand behind the mirror, will you, Walsingham, and do as I say."

Walsingham stands behind them, watching Dee walk up the pathway to the palace, about fifty paces away. Once reaching the walls of the palace, he turns and stares back at the barge.

"Move the one in the cabin a little to the left," he calls.

"For Christ's sake, Dee."

When it is in position, Dee comes over. He has a chalk stone in his pocket, and with it he marks the positions of the frames, and then replica marks on the other side of the boat.

"Dee! What are you doing?" Walsingham demands as Dee shifts the mirror frames around.

"Go to where I was standing, and look back."

As Walsingham clambers out of the boat he hears Dee tell Thomas Digges to look queenly.

Walsingham walks, seeing the Queen in her window once more, until he is where Dee was. He turns and stares back at the barge.

"My God," he says. "My God."

James Hamilton kneels in the filth of the old woman's hovel. He clasps his hands hard and offers up his final prayer, his final amen, and he gets to his feet. He has been praying since the first pink ray of dawn probed through the hole he has made in the wall, and he now approaches it and looks out over the choppy green brew of the Thames.

It is a beautiful day. On the river are numerous small craft, and one caravel, laden with cloth perhaps, anchored against the waning tide. On the far bank is a small church with a spire, where once the Mass was said; a windmill; a stone wall; three muddy cows in the river; and a boy on a cart. There are some fishermen, too, though, Christ, what would they catch in this soup of human filth?

He turns to his gun on the ground, kept from the damp and dirt by its sackcloth wrappings, lustrous with rose oil. Alongside it is the ball he will use. He has lost one, he knows, and believes he must have left it with the horse when he panicked and bolted from the inn.

He knows he will never live to reclaim it.

He has returned the powder to the horn, the powder in its oyster shell. It flows fine as sand in a timer. He has the tow wads, too, likewise steeped in rose oil.

The ramming rod, and the stand, are propped against the wall.

He stands. His heart is beating wildly but when he holds out his hands, they are steady.

He will eat.

And then he will be ready.

They say their prayers as a household, as a nation, kneeling where the night before the Queen heard Tallis's "Lamentations," and when it is over, they stand in silence and gather themselves.

The Queen says her farewells, and her courtiers stand pale-faced. Some of the women weep, as if she were mounting the scaffold just as her mother did all those years ago.

Smith glares, his hands clenching, unclenching.

There is no sign of Burghley or Leicester.

Helped by her bargemaster, the Queen steps aboard her barge.

"I am to sit here? Facing this way?"

"Yes, Your Majesty."

There is not a lot of room, for gone are her usual ladies-in-waiting, and in their place, crammed into the gloom of the curtained cabin, behind the second mirror, are eight yeomen of the guard, harquebusiers, each nursing the fuse of a gun. Among them sits little Thomas Digges, with his perspective glass ready, and there, too, is Francis Walsingham, as pale and anxious as she has ever seen him.

"And where is John Dee?" the Queen asks.

"Here, Your Majesty."

He is hidden behind the first mirror, with his back to the oarsmen, roughly in the middle of the boat.

"Are you certain about this?" she asks.

There is a long pause while he tries to think clearly.

"Some of it, Your Majesty."

She manages a laugh that stirs up a memory of her in the Tower, when things were at their most precarious for both of them, and he cannot soften a fraction. She is the woman who wanted him dead, and yet, and yet—

The bargemaster stands by the tiller at the back of the cabin. He looks quizzically at Dr. Dee: *Are you sure?* Dee is not. Everybody is looking to him, though: those on the boat, and those gathered on the shore.

Dee looks to the Queen: *Ready?* She nods. He turns to the bargemaster and nods in turn. The bargemaster sounds his whistle and the boys on the bank let go the ropes while three men with boat poles push the boat out into the river.

"Ship oars!"

There is a chorus of moans from the bank as the boat shudders underfoot, as if this is a funeral barque, and the barge drifts for a moment until the oarsmen set about their work. The barge gathers itself and slides forward into the current.

"Smooth!" the bargemaster calls and a moment later the oarsmen are into their rhythm, pulling the boat through the water northward. The Isle of Dogs is on their right, which the harquebusiers face, though cannot see for the curtains are down, and Deptford on the left, which the Queen faces, and which she can see, for her curtains are up.

There is a gentle breeze, seagulls screech high above, and it is turning into a day of the sort that tricks you into believing it will be like this all winter. The water thrums on the underside of the hull. The air is freshish, only slightly tinged with rot and spoil.

No one says anything until at last the Queen speaks.

"John," she says. "Why are you so angry with me?"

For a moment Dee is stunned. Then he laughs. "Because you tried to have me killed?"

The Queen turns to him.

"Please, Your Majesty, you must look straight ahead."

They are in the middle of the Thames now, fifty paces from each bank. The oarsmen must work hard, for the river is flowing fast against them, but they are strong and well-nourished, unlike most ferrymen, and the creak of their oars in the rowlocks is steady.

"What did you mean, that I tried to have you killed?"

"Well, didn't you?"

"No."

The Queen shakes her head as if to clear her thoughts. What a conversation to be having.

"Why would I wish you dead?" she asks.

"You wrote—to that absurd Dutchman—that I was a notorious papist. That I was a heretic and a traitor sent by the pope to kill you. And that you wanted him—the Dutchman—to ensure that I did not survive the voyage home from France to do so. Please! You must keep looking at the southern bank."

"But, John, I never wrote such a thing."

"I have it. I have the letter."

"I don't care, for the love of God, John. I would never—why would I wish that?"

"If you believed it?"

"If I believed it? If I believed you were a papist sent to kill me, then I suppose I should wish you dead before me, yes. But I do not believe it. And even if I did, I should never have you . . . what? Put over the side of a ship, or murdered on some beach in France."

The oarsmen are warming up, and the barge has begun its sweep northward toward the city. Walsingham stands tense. He has his ears on the conversation, his eyes on the right-hand bank of the river. Thomas Digges is likewise peering through his perspective glass. They pass a boat coming the other way, dipping its sail in salute, its crew removing their caps and cheering.

But the Queen sits stony faced. She is right, Dee supposes. She would have him dragged through the streets, half hanged, then taken down and eviscerated. She'd have his innards and his nethers burned on a fire so he could smell them roast; and then she'd have him beheaded, and his head placed on a pike atop the bridge, while his body would be cut in grisly quarters to be nailed to gate posts in and around Mortlake to warn others off his path. And she'd be right to do that.

"But I have both letters," he tells her again.

"If you do, John, it is a forgery, for it is not in my hand."

"It is in the same hand as the other letter you sent him, Van Treslong."

"I did not write to Van Treslong."

"You sent him word that I was to be picked up from that beach. Then that I was to be killed."

"For the love of Jesus, Dee," Walsingham snaps, "let us sort this out at another time."

The Queen is hidden from his view by the mirror in the cabin, but he can see over this and around it and is afforded glimpses of the north shore in the mirror out on deck: blank-sided warehouses and tumbledown hovels, the beaks of cranes, ships' masts and spars, spools of rope hanging from their hooks. A few men—porters—stop to watch and wave as Her Majesty's barge goes by.

The sun is behind now, throwing pale shadows toward the bow, but these are inching around as the barge follows the curve of the river.

"Keep her in midstream, master," Dee calls to the helmsman. They are about to turn west in the pool of London. Apart from under the bridge itself, this is where the river is at its narrowest.

"I have both letters," he tells the Queen. "I have them here."

"I should like to see them."

"Coming up Limehouse on starboard!" the bargemaster calls.

First: a disk of oily tow, pushed into the barrel's end by the clinking rod of steel. Then: the powder, tipped into the eye of the barrel through a loading horn. Then: another disk of tow. This he slides down slowly, gathering all the powder in the barrel into a charge, tamped firm under the tow. Then: the ball. He cannot read the inscription, but he knows it to be from Jeremiah: "The Lord is a God of Retribution." He palms it into the barrel and it rolls down the barrel in one smooth glide. He follows it with the third and final disk of oiled tow. He tamps the charge and ball together and sets the rod aside.

Next he uses a horn to fill the hole between the pan and charge with more powder, and last he taps a little powder into the pan. He sets the gun aside and takes up his tinderbox. It consists of a flint, and steel, and a scrap of linen, baked black. A few scrapes of flint on steel, and the linen is aflame. With it, he lights the gun's fuse. He waves them both in the air: one to extinguish; one to get going.

The smell of the burning cloth and fuse rope covers that of the belching corpse.

When that is done, he attaches the fuse to the lever of the gun, and he stands for a few moments, breathing very deeply.

The barge turns slowly through the river.

Dee passes the Queen both letters.

But she must not look down, he tells her.

"Please, Your Majesty, ahead."

She does so and unfolds the first of the letters on her lap without looking.

No one speaks. No one breathes. No one knows what to expect.

The guards in the cabin are looking to Dee for guidance, while little Thomas Digges uses his perspective glass to examine every shadow on the river's bank. Walsingham ignores them. He is tensed, eyes closed, pinching the bridge of his nose. Dee waits crouched in the hull, his eyes on the mirror, calculating the turn of the river in relation to the jumbled rooflines of the buildings on the north bank. They are approaching Limehouse, the creek where the river Lea flows into the Thames. The Queen sits in her chair, her shoulders hunched, her eyes clenched tight shut.

Christ. What if he's wrong?

The Queen glances down at the letter. A frown crosses her face.

The shadows are beginning to bleed off the starboard bow as the barge turns to follow the river westward.

"Dee?"

But Dee is elsewhere. He is thinking: *I was wrong.*

He has misinterpreted his dream.

And he is just about to look over to say something, to apologize to them all for disturbing them, and for having them tear apart the Palace of Placentia, and the Queen's barge, to make this absurd frame for the mirror, when—*plock!*—a hole appears in the mirror above. The Queen gasps and claps a hand over her cheek, and a fraction of a moment later there comes a dull thump from the shore.

"There!" Thomas Digges shouts, pointing. But the harquebusiers have seen the flash, or the smoke, and now the curtains are drawn aside and they squeeze their levers and apply their fuses. The Queen clamps her hands over her ears as the cabin resounds to the flash and boom of the arquebuses. The noise is tremendous. The boat seems to stagger. The cabin fills with dense smoke. Everybody seems to be shouting. Across the water a small wooden cabin splinters in numerous places as the balls hit.

Dee and Walsingham collide as they rush to cover the Queen in case of any more shots.

"Take us in!" Walsingham shouts to the bargemaster. He is deafened by the gunshots and cannot hear his own voice, but the bargemaster leans on the tiller. The barge slews toward the ships moored against the north bank. The bargemaster shouts something and the oarsmen on the starboard lift their oars as the boat thumps against a low-sided fishing vessel with a deadening boom that throws the fishing boat's boy to his knees. Strong arms clamp the gunwale and hold the barge fast.

The harquebusiers discard their guns and spill out of the back of the cabin. They jump out of the Queen's barge and scramble across the fishing boat, careless of the fishermen, and vanish over its far side. Walsingham stands and bends over the Queen. She is hunched in her seat. He hesitates to touch her.

"Your Majesty?"

She lifts her head.

There is blood on her hands.

Walsingham gasps.

"It's a scratch. A scratch from the glass. The others will guard me. Go! Go and get him!"

Dee and Walsingham need no second word. They scramble over the gunwale and up onto the fishing boat where the fisherman stands openmouthed.

"Stand by to push off!" Dee hears the bargemaster call.

Dee jumps down from the boat. The mud is gritty and gray. It stinks of shit and butchers' spoil. He sees the house, the one he saw in his dreams, a hole in its daub, its patchwork of planks shattered by gunshots. It's the other side of the creek.

Damn.

He scrambles back up to the dockside, up a great midden of discarded oyster shells and onto the cobbled dockside above.

"Dee!"

Walsingham slips and slides behind him. Dee stops and offers him a hand, hauling him up. There is a dark badge of blood amid the mud.

"Quick! Come on!"

They run along the dockside, looping around to the bridge where they see the harquebusiers storming ahead with their swords drawn. Men, women, children, geese, and even pigs move quickly out of their way. Dee and Walsingham cross the bridge over the Lea and are now on the lane at the end of which is the hut they shot at. The harquebusiers arrive as a phalanx and smash the door down.

Dee and Walsingham keep running.

The hut is so small it hardly fits the harquebusiers, and by the time Dee and Walsingham reach the step up, they are stepping back out onto the lane again.

"Go that way!" Walsingham points down the lane, to the east. "Search every building! Everywhere! Find him! He mustn't get away."

Dee steps into the darkness of the stinking hut.

It is empty, save for a cooking stone, and the dead woman. Flies hum and slice through the beams of light streaming through the various holes that are scattered over the wall.

Walsingham comes in and gags.

Dee crosses to the wall. Under the larger hole is a smaller one. On the ground, a scatter of blood.

He sees the gun's rest, lying where it has fallen, but there is no sign of the gun, or the ramming rod. Or its owner/master.

Hamilton moves softly through the water. The soldiers are gone, but there are two men up there yet, slow moving, more considered sorts. Perhaps it is Walsingham himself? *By the blood of Mary*, he thinks, *imagine killing both Elizabeth and her chief devil incarnate in one day?* His thoughts are broken by a terrible rack of pain in his gut. He knows he is dying. But he has done what he set out to do. He saw the ball strike the Queen, just above her ear. A killing shot, for certain. He was surprised she did not seem to flinch, but that thought was taken no further. It was overtaken by astonishment at the volley of gunshots that sprang from the cabin. The other bullets sprayed everywhere, as you'd expect, and that one of them caught him in the groin was punishment sent down by God upon His imperfect servant.

To spite the pain, he grips the stock of the gun. He needs to load it. If he cannot, he might as well consign it to the mud.

"Come on, Dee," Walsingham says. "He will be miles away by now."

But Dee remains still.

The tide is up, and he can hear its slop against the hut's footings, but it is the smell that bothers him. He bends over the firestone: cold. And yet, even above the spicy sweetness of the woman's decaying body, there is the smell of burning.

He is about to use Walsingham's name but stops himself.

Instead he gestures. They leave the hut.

"What are you up to, Dee?"

"Come with me."

The two men skirt back to the creek.

"By Jesus, Dee, I am not going back down there."

Below is the stinking green-gray mud. Walsingham's leg is bleeding heavily.

"All right," Dee says. "Listen to me carefully, Walsingham. Here is what I want you to do. Count to sixty, slowly, and then walk into the hut again."

"Why?"

It is best not to tell him. This is different from the Queen, since Walsingham will not be an image in a mirror.

"Just do as I say, Walsingham. Sixty, and then back in there."

Despite his doubts, Walsingham will do it.

Dee drops down into the mud. It is glazed with what might be tanners' spoil, and the cold grip of the mud reminds him powerfully of Mont Saint-Michel. He drags each leg from the slurry's grip and wades, thigh high in it, along the creek below the dockside wall. Ahead is the open water of the Thames. He rounds the wall and finds himself amid the jumble of the huts' footings and stilts. They are treacherous with green weed and there is what looks like a dead dog caught in a crook between two beams. Stinking rushes are strewn everywhere and Dee is certain he can hear the constant and close squeak of rats. He presses on. He is counting under his breath.

Twenty.

Here the water is deeper, and the mud below scoured away by the Thames's stronger current. He peers around the stilts. There. Twenty yards away: a fine gauze of fuse smoke. Just as he thought. He lowers himself into the water, up to his chin. It is bracing, not too bad. But Christ! What a stench.

Thirty.

He strokes through the water.

It has a cold, dipping green, clammy grip.

He sees the bulk of the man, his left shoulder, linen shirt. He is conducting some operation. Loading his gun! A leather bag over his shoulder. The man hesitates a moment. He's looking for somewhere to put the ramming rod where it won't sink.

Forty.

Dee slithers through a lattice of stilts. Above are latrine holes, as why wouldn't you? Dee sees the man twist the strap of his bag over his shoulder. His gun is held upright. He's waiting. Head tipped back, eyes raised. He has good teeth. Waiting.

Fifty.

It is a long-barreled gun, and its muzzle must be nearly touching the floor above. No wonder his shot at the Queen was so good. Dee can see him clearly now: tall, very strong, his arms corded with muscle.

Fifty-five.

But now the man feels something. He glances down to where Dee was a moment ago. A frown. But then: up above. Some disturbance at the door of the hut. A scrape. He looks back up. He grips the gun, his thumb over the powder pan.

Sixty.

Walsingham enters the hut above.

The man moves the gun to follow his steps, turns his back on Dee, but then—last moment—he glances down, and around, and as if preordained, he and Dee lock gazes. Dee lunges.

He catches the man from behind, both arms around him as he holds the gun up. The man pulls the trigger. The fuse connects. The powder in the pan flashes. The gun explodes as the damp powder bursts its barrel. Dee presses his face to the back of the man's neck. Dee's head is enveloped in a ball of sound and fire. The man's head cracks back into Dee's face, sending him against the rails of the footings. He nearly goes under. The man is still upright, still clutching the stock of the ruined gun, but there's blood everywhere, and something's wrong. He falls backward into the water, but floats back up again, faceup, though that's missing: his jaw and cheeks are gone, his nose is a bloody hole, his eyes formless flesh and his forehead and scalp sheared away by coarse shreds of metal that burst from the gun. Blood wells everywhere, winking in every wound, a spreading slick of it.

Dee clings to the poles of the house above. His face is on fire, and there is blood all over him, his arms, his hands, everywhere. The man spins slowly in the current, and after a while, Dee pushes him out into the river proper. He feels his strength sap. Darkness clouds his vision. His head spins. He clings to a post, the shaft slick with weed and God knows what else. He presses his cheek to it, feels it slide, cold, up as he goes down. The water rises to meet him.

"Dee! Dee!"

It is Walsingham, his face pressed through the privy hole above.

"Stay awake! Stay awake, Dee!"

But he is falling, and fading fast.

CHAPTER SEVENTEEN

The White Tower, London, October 17, 1572

Any number of ailments might afflict a man after his flesh is shredded by pieces of steel that have first passed through the body of another man, and then he is dunked unconscious in the river Thames. But after he is bled a pint or two and plied with various purgatives and emetics that leave him racked with pain and weak as a kitten, Dr. John Dee is left to lie in bed for a few days, heaped with blankets so that he sweats out any further corruptives and pollutants, and so balance his humors.

He dreams, constantly, the same dream, of the girl whom one part of his mind believes to be Rose Cochet, but whom the other part—the rational part—cannot believe is so. His dreams show her playing again, this time with a battered straw doll, much loved, on a broad swath of grass below a painted dovecote. Once again she is prettily dressed and her cheeks are rosy with good health and there are other children gathered about. He can hear singing and the playing of a reed flute, and the scene is warmed by the golden light of a low sun. Isobel Cochet emerges and calls for her daughter.

When he wakes to proper consciousness, Dee finds himself unable to move.

"Don't move," the Queen tells him.

"I can't," he tells her.

He is weighed down by his covers, and bandages over his face, his hands, and his arms.

"My physician says you are very lucky."

Lucky?

He has a partial view of the room. A physician is holding up to the light of the window a jar of what must be Dee's urine. The Queen sits in an upright chair at the side of his bed. She is in pearlescent material, with a collar that frames her slender neck, her pretty ears.

Dust motes in the window light.

"How long have you been sitting here?" he asks.

She smiles.

"A week, no more."

He laughs, though it draws up phlegm. She has tears in her eyes. He finds she is holding his hand, and he hers. They clench them together, the gesture of two who have loved and lost and learned to love again.

After a silence he speaks. "Rose Cochet," he says.

The Queen looks away. But she does not seek to break their handhold. She clutches all the harder, her guilt all too clear.

"I am sorry," she whispers. "I did not know. I did not know. But I must take responsibility for her mother's death. I *do* take responsibility for her mother's death. Isobel Cochet died for me. I see that. She died for me. And for her daughter. And I will . . . I will do all I am able, to put that right. Please believe me."

He does.

⌖

Later Walsingham comes with the man Dee recognizes as Master Beale. There is no sign of the Queen.

Walsingham asks a few questions, the answers to which he already knows, or could deduce from observation, and which he doesn't care about anyway. *He looks tired*, Dee thinks.

"The Queen has examined the letters," Walsingham tells him.

He remembers. The two letters he stole from Van Treslong. He gave them to her the moment before the mirror was shot.

"And?"

"Well, we were right about both letters being in the same hand."

Dee closes his eyes in resignation, until a strong memory of her, on the ship, clutching these very letters, comes roaring back in protest.

"But . . . wait. She said . . . didn't she? That she had never written— She didn't write either of them?"

Walsingham shakes his head.

"Who then?" Dee asks.

CHAPTER EIGHTEEN

Hill Hall, Essex, October 25, 1572

They have all been to Epping Forest before: Dee in search of sites that might yield information on Druidical rituals; Walsingham to see the Queen in her father's ugly hunting lodge; and Beale with a woman who was married to the master of the Painter-Stainers' Guild.

"The hunting is supposed to be very good," Beale tells them.

Dee says nothing. He doesn't care about hunting, good or bad, nor does Walsingham, sitting beside him in the caroche, have an opinion to offer. Dee is well wrapped in heavy worsted, with marten at the collars and cuffs, and soft leather boots, all paid for by the Queen on behalf of a grateful nation. He feels delicate, and though his wounds have healed well, his cheek is flecked with a smooth pink scar that runs counter to the grain of his skin, and from which no beard will ever grow.

He keeps his gaze directed out of the window, where a faint mist softens the oak and beech trees, leaves already on the turn, and there is a faintly fungal smell in the air. By the wayside, russet pigs rootle in the mast.

It will soon be Martinmas, and they are traveling with a company of the Queen's guard to arrest Sir Thomas Smith at Hill Hall.

It was Margaret Formby's evidence that has him charged with conspiring to have Dee killed. Walsingham said that if it had been any other man Smith sought to have killed, then perhaps the Queen would have been more anxious to have him charged with the forgery of her signature, and the misuse of her seal, but there is, as Walsingham had admitted, something special between Dee and the Queen. Some bond that he cannot quite fathom. It made Dee very happy to hear that.

"Does he know we are coming?" he asks.

Walsingham shakes his head.

"He might not even be there," Walsingham supposes, and it turns out he is right. When they reach Hill Hall—late midmorning—they do not stop at the lodge on the track but carry on up to the house. It is built in the new style, and, like Smith's colony in Ireland, it sits unwelcome and awkward on the land.

A panicked groom greets them on the steps. He eyes the troop of soldiers, but mostly Walsingham, with something like terror.

"No, Master Walsingham, sir," he says. "Sir Thomas is gone north to see to his— He is stocking the estate. Only Master Gethyn is here."

Dee wonders what that means: stocking his estate?

Walsingham curses.

"Take us to his office," he tells the groom. There will be papers and so on, Dee supposes. "And have Master Gethyn come to us."

Gethyn is already there, standing at the lectern in Sir Thomas's study, a handsome room, with many windows affording much light, open now to afford a view over a sloping garden wherein the focal point is a very fine stone-built dovecote. The room has painted walls, rather than the usual hanging arras, showing what might be scenes from the life of Nebuchadnezzar, and there is a Turkey carpet underfoot that might in another house be pride of place above the fire.

He does not seem a bit surprised to see them.

"God bless you this day, Master Gethyn," Walsingham starts. "When is Sir Thomas expected back, do you know?"

"Not now until next week," Gethyn tells him. "He is away up north again."

"Seeing a man about a dog?" Beale asks.

"Ha." Gethyn laughs. "Something like that."

Only Gethyn knows why this is funny. There is something sad and sardonic about him, Dee thinks. He likes him.

"But if I am right as to your purpose today," Gethyn goes on, "then it is not Sir Thomas you seek, Master Walsingham."

"Oh?"

Gethyn is darkly dressed, in the old-fashioned manner, and holds three or four papers in his hands. They tremble slightly. Walsingham slows down now, tilts his head, narrows his eyes, and becomes less brusque. It is as if Gethyn is no longer an obstacle on the road, or a postway, but a destination in his own right. A thing of interest.

"There is something you wish to tell us, Master Gethyn?"

Gethyn says nothing but he holds up one of the pieces of paper. It is irregular, as if someone has cut—

Walsingham strides across to take it from him. He scans what is written. It is a grant of land from the Queen to Sir Thomas Smith, three hundred and sixty acres in Ulster, sent a few months earlier. It is missing the seal, and its bottom right-hand corner. Walsingham looks up at Gethyn very keenly.

"Smith?"

Gethyn shakes his head.

"*You?*" Walsingham asks.

Gethyn nods. He is pale, but also flushed, with glassy eyes. He is suddenly terrified.

"Why?" Walsingham asks. He is incredulous.

Gethyn shrugs minutely.

"I am of the true faith," he says, as if this explains everything. But Walsingham shakes his head.

"But—no. Gethyn. Not you. You are—"

Gethyn's smile becomes glassier yet. "Reasonable?"

"Yes."

Walsingham turns to Dee.

Dee feels blank. He is looking at a man confessing to having tried to have him killed, yet he cannot feel any rancor for him. It is not only because he looks like no homicidal firebrand Dee has ever seen, but because . . . what? Dee cannot say. Only that he is certain there is something odd here. Walsingham feels it too.

"So," he stalks, "when the Queen came here on the third to last day of August this year, she asked you to write, in her name, to Master Raleigh, of the *Pelican*, to instruct him to have this man, Dr. John Dee, collected from the coast of Normandy?"

Gethyn looks over at Dee with interest. In another time, would they have passed the time in quiet discussion of the ways of the world? Perhaps. Why not?

"I am sorry," he says.

"Nothing to be sorry about," Dee tells him. "It is the next letter that I found"—he searches for the right word, but can't—"upsetting."

Gethyn acknowledges his point. *We are not enemies*, Dee thinks.

"So you wrote the letter?" Walsingham continues with his question.

"I did. She wanted to write it herself, but she had been traveling two days, and on horseback from the Tower, and so I wrote it out for her, in as close to her hand as I could."

"Why? Why imitate her hand?"

Gethyn shrugs again.

"I wanted to please her," he says. "And to show her I could. And I had a template."

He indicates the grant with the section cut from its bottom corner.

"So you showed it to her, and she signed it? Is it her signature on the first letter?"

"Yes. And her seal. She impressed that sitting there."

He points at a bench.

"Smith watched?"

"Oh yes," Gethyn agrees.

"And then what?"

"Master Walsingham," Gethyn starts, "before I go on, I want you to know everything that happened, everything I did, and everything I did not do. Because I am not a brave man. You might put me in a room with the rack or the brake, and I would tell you everything you need to know, but I also want you to know that I will say nothing of this at any trial."

"Trial? *Trial?* What makes you think there will be a *trial*?"

Only now does Gethyn begin to look terrified.

"Please, Master Gethyn," Dee interrupts. "Go on. About the second letter."

There is a moment while Gethyn gathers himself.

"The second letter," he says. "The second letter. Yes. I did not understand everything that was afoot, of course, but I knew that the Queen had just come from seeing you, Doctor, in the Tower. She told Sir Thomas, while she was impressing her seal, that the fate of the nation now depended on you. Sir Thomas disagreed. He is not of first-rate intelligence, Sir Thomas, I hope you will forgive me for saying so?"

Walsingham agrees, as does Dee. Beale, too, murmurs that he has always thought it so.

"So that made you write the second letter? Just to get rid of Dee as an agent of Her Majesty?"

For the first time Gethyn looks uncertain. Beale takes out some paper and has an ingenious inkpot. He will take notes.

"I knew that the doctor was sent to retrieve some documents that had fallen into the hands of the Cardinal of Lorraine."

This is not an answer, really, Dee thinks, *but a lure*. And Walsingham seizes upon it like a hawk.

"Was it Smith who told you that?" Walsingham asks.

Gethyn shakes his head slowly.

"Then—?" Walsingham presses.

"A man in Rheims," Gethyn says. "One in the cardinal's pay."

There is a thick silence.

"So you are in contact with the Cardinal of Lorraine?"

There is a pause before Gethyn nods very slowly.

That is all they need, Dee thinks. He dreads to think what will now happen to Gethyn.

"Go on," Walsingham instructs.

"An Englishman," Gethyn says.

"Named?"

"Edmund Campion."

Beale shrugs slightly, scrubs over his previous note, and writes the name down. None of them have ever heard the name before.

"But still why?" Dee asks. "Why did you want me killed?"

This is the real question.

Gethyn opens and closes his mouth. Then he starts coughing again, long and hard, into his kerchief. It racks his body. His face reddens, veins spring up, and his eyes stream. It is like watching someone tear their own self apart. When it is over, he hides the kerchief.

Dee looks at him very closely. Gethyn's eyes are fugitives now and will not be caught. There is something amiss here. As if Gethyn did not know why he wanted Dee killed. *Did* he want Dee killed? The longer Dee looks at him, the more certain he is that Gethyn didn't want him killed, and so then, why?

He thinks back to those days after Van Treslong's men had shot the cardinal's man on Nez Bayard: how he had struggled through Normandy and Picardy, sleeping in hedgerows, living off sweet cider and green apples; how he had found first Boulogne then Calais being watched, so too Dunkirk, and he had to make his way through countryside to the north that was crawling with Spanish and French troops, until he finally found passage in that cog from Damme. Every moment of every day had been given over to rage and confusion, and guilt, too, which threatened to prostrate him, for leading Isobel Cochet to her death. He can still taste the bitter rancor that had seeped through him, staining him from within.

That it turns out to be the fault of this man is—impossible to believe.

After a moment, Gethyn recovers enough to speak.

"When I heard what you had found, the location of the mouth of the Straits of Anian, I thought, I believed, that it would be a sin against God were a Protestant nation to gain access to the riches of Cathay."

He speaks as if he has rehearsed this line. *He is changing the subject*, Dee thinks. *He does not wish to talk about why he wanted me killed, because he has no very good reason, because he did not do it!* Dee is certain, but Walsingham has caught hold of the lure. He has swallowed it whole.

"So you did what?" Walsingham asks.

"I devised the way to get Isobel Cochet to retrieve the documents that you had stolen from Admiral DaSilva."

That is a nice way of putting it, Dee thinks, and he is about to intervene with a question of his own, when he hears, distantly, a woman's voice summoning someone whose name Dee does not catch. But the sound takes Dee elsewhere, to his dream, and he walks across the Turkey carpet to where the window lets in a long stripe of light. Outside on the grass, in a garden not unlike Her Majesty's in Greenwich—save this one has a rather fine dovecote, newfangled, on a wooden post—under the watchful eye of two nurses and a man leaning on a nocked longbow, is gathered a number of children. They are having what looks to be a party. A game is in progress. Blind man's buff? Is that its name? One child in a blindfold, the rest racing around.

Gethyn joins him, and they stand shoulder to shoulder, their backs to Walsingham and Beale. It is a very pleasant scene.

"Are they all Smith's?" Dee asks.

"None of them," Gethyn says. "Smith had a boy, George. Killed in Ulster this last year."

"Yours?"

"Mostly," Gethyn says with a smile. He turns to Dee, waiting. Dee looks back at the children. His eye settles on one of the girls. She is dimpled, in a pretty dress, and one of the older girls is tying a length of linen around her eyes.

"You see, Dr. Dee?" Gethyn says. "No harm came to her."

The Queen's guard take Gethyn to the Tower, while Dee and Walsingham and Beale wonder what to do with Rose Cochet.

"Leave her with Gethyn's family," Dee suggests. "She is happy here, for the while. I will go to her grandfather. Swap his misery for his granddaughter's death with that of his daughter's."

Walsingham has the decency to look sick with guilt.

They ride back through the forest, having given up the caroche for Gethyn and two guardsmen. Dee is so weary he might fall from his saddle and they stop fairly often. Walsingham and Beale are deflated that it is not Smith on his way to the Tower.

"Gethyn seemed like a good man," Beale says.

He places him in the past tense.

"Perhaps he is?" Dee supposes. "Perhaps he is doing what he believes to be good?"

"He tried to have you killed," Beale says.

"Yes," Dee agrees. "That was bad, but he did it for reasons he thought were good. You two: you are the same as him. You risked Isobel Cochet's life for reasons you thought good. But what if they are bad?"

As he says this, Dee wonders if he is right: Does Gethyn really think what he is doing is right? He does not seem zealous in any way. And why did he stand and admit his guilt? He could have run? Taken a horse and ridden to the docks at Tilbury. A ship to Spain. France even. Easy. Why did he stay and take the blame?

He thinks of the blood in the man's cough.

Of course.

He is going to die anyway.

CHAPTER NINETEEN

Westminster Hall, Westminster, October 30, 1572

Dee attends the trial. He still feels weak, but a chair is brought for him and he is pointed out with some respect by those who know. He hopes for answers to his questions, and he gets them, but they come—or *it* comes, for there is only one big answer to the plethora of questions—not in the way he expects, in words, but in silence.

Gethyn refuses to speak. He keeps dabbing his mouth with a kerchief. *That's it,* Dee thinks. *He is going to die anyway.*

"Do you know what it is you are bringing upon yourself?" Leicester asks.

Gethyn still says nothing.

"It is contempt," Leicester says.

Gethyn just looks at Smith. Smith cannot hold his gaze but looks away and fiddles with something on his lap.

Walsingham arrives late, and somewhat flustered. He sits alongside Dee.

"What's he said?"

"Nothing."

"I knew it," Walsingham mutters. "This is a nonsense."

"Meaning?"

"It means he will die in *peine forte et dure* but he implicates no one, you see? And it means the Crown will not confiscate his estate: his children will inherit. They will be left provided for."

Dee looks once more at Gethyn, poor dying Gethyn. He is doing this for love. For love of his God, and for love of his wife and children, of Romilly, the faded beauty. But also: Smith? It is him they must look at now.

"Why have you not put him to the rack, Walsingham?" Dee asks. "Why not get him to confess he is doing this to cover Smith?"

Walsingham looks at Dee beadily.

"You think I did not want to?"

"I'm surprised you did not want to."

Walsingham nods. "The Queen will not grant a license to do it," he admits. "Smith has . . ."

He gestures to show that Smith has gotten into the Queen's ear.

"I am glad," Dee says, "that Gethyn will be saved somewhat."

Walsingham nods.

"Me, too, in a way."

The thought of putting Gethyn to the rack is horrible. The popping of his cartilage, ligaments, and bones. All because he is a loving father.

"But Smith?"

Walsingham says nothing. Dee understands though; there is nothing anyone may do about Smith, for the moment at least.

Burghley has no choice, and anyway even takes some pleasure

in announcing the death sentence. Hearing it, Gethyn clenches his eyes and then opens them and nods once, because what did he expect? The guards are gentle with him, and as he turns, he nods to Dee and even Walsingham.

Smith sits glaring at the floor.

He dies two days later, on the last good day that year, at Smithfield. There's a lively crowd, for this kind of thing doesn't happen too often, and the day's atmosphere reminds Francis Walsingham of that day in Paris, all those weeks ago, when the celebrants danced through blood-red streets.

Dee refuses to come.

"No," he had said. "I've had enough of this stinking business, Walsingham, and I've had enough of you."

Walsingham had managed a laugh.

"So your recovery is now complete, eh, Dee? Back to your old self?"

"Fuck off, Walsingham."

So it is just Walsingham and Beale who come to see Gethyn die. They stand alone, in a roped-off area reserved for dignitaries from court, and together they watch Gethyn brought up Giltspur Street from Newgate tied to a hurdle dragged by an ox. When he is untied he is helped to his feet and he rubs his wrists, but he seems unharmed by the ordeal even though someone has flung every sort of excrement at him.

He climbs up the steps to the scaffold and the executioner shakes him by his hand, and Gethyn looks about him for a priest of his own religion, but he finds only the grim-faced visage of a priest of the new faith, who is quoting a verse from the Bible, shouting above the crowd and still unable to make himself heard.

Walsingham watches Gethyn's gaze slide past the priest, to the rocks that lie piled like ship's ballast at the back of the scaffold. The executioner has two men to help him this day, and a lad, too, to carry the plank. Gethyn gives the executioner his doublet and then is persuaded to hand over his shirt to the boy, from whom it will hang like a nightdress.

Then he kneels and says his prayers and now the crowd would ordinarily bellow and throw offal and whatever was to hand, but there is something about Gethyn that stills their malice, and they calm into a placid sea of coinlike faces, and only the priest's voice can be heard.

". . . Princes in her midst are like wolves tearing the prey, shedding blood, and destroying lives to get dishonest gain. . . ."

When Gethyn has crossed himself, he stands and puts himself into the hands of the executioner, who leads him to the front of the scaffold where he lies him down on his back. It is strange to think he will never get up again. It is also strange to see how the executioner is solicitous of Gethyn's comfort.

"Get him a fucking bolster why don't you!" a wit shouts.

The executioner summons his boy, who passes him the plank. It is as tall as the executioner, not as tall as Gethyn, and he lies it on him so that his head and feet are clear. Again he checks his comfort, and the people in the crowd laugh. But his concern does not prevent him placing a first layer of rocks on the plank, two hundredweight, Walsingham supposes: the weight of two heavy men. Under them Gethyn is flushed and puffing. A second layer of rocks is piled upon the first, and Gethyn's face turns purple. He sucks and blows like a horse at a trough.

"What actually kills them?" Beale asks.

"I think breathing," Walsingham says. "Or perhaps the heart? It cannot beat when it is so . . ."

He mimes compression.

It is difficult not to talk nonsense in a moment like this.

The third layer of stones.

Gethyn sweats blood. His eyes boil red, too, and then something gives. His rib cage, maybe, and that's that. The plank jolts. Blood froths from every orifice. The people cheer. The executioner's men scramble to keep the rocks from sliding from their perch.

"Fuckin' rubbish!" is one opinion.

Walsingham agrees. Hang a man, burn bits of him, and then chop him up. Let them bathe in his blood. That is what you really want.

"Well," Beale says. "A martyr's death. I suppose that is what he wanted."

Walsingham agrees.

"A martyr, yes," he says, "but a martyr for whom?"

Walsingham dines alone with his wife that evening and listens when she tells him of Frances, his eldest daughter, who is as clever as any boy, and of Mary, his youngest, who sleeps well, which is a gift to all concerned.

But what is it that bothers him about Gethyn?

That he was innocent, he thinks, that was it.

He stood in another man's place and took the punishment for the future of his family.

Bloody Smith. Bloody Smith and his bloody Irish project.

But how to get him? How to expose him now that Gethyn is dead and his secrets are taken to the grave?

In Sheffield, Queen Mary watches the sun blink out over the hills beyond the western range of the castle, and she thinks of the wide open spaces, and of the endless black sea across which she now understands that Admiral Quesada's fleet tacks.

It grows quite dark before she hears Mary Seton come up the steps with a candle, and she turns to watch her bob her sleek little head. She feels a sort of weary fondness for the woman.

"How long have I known you, Mary?"

"Twenty-five years, Your Grace."

"We are old friends."

"I hope so.

"I am melancholic tonight," she admits.

"You are tired, after today's hunting."

"Perhaps." She sighs. There is an ugly pause. Queen Mary knows that Mary Seton expected her to rage and rant, having heard the news of Gethyn's arrest and death through the usual route from Sir Thomas. But she is not angry. She is sad. She knows nothing of this Nicholas Gethyn, but she supposes him to be just another beautiful young man who would willingly go out of this world for the love of her.

She may have failed this time, she thinks, and Master Walsingham has succeeded perhaps, but she can fail as many times as necessary, whereas Master Walsingham need only fail once.

And then she shall be queen.

"And there is a new girl come?" she asks.

"Yes, Your Grace, from Paris."

"Not one of Walsingham's stooping whores then? I am glad."

"She is as demure as a dove." Mary Seton laughs. It is a silvery tinkle, nervous.

A thought crosses Queen Mary's mind.

"A virgin?"

There is a tiny intake of breath.

"Of course, Your Grace."

Queen Mary's blood, thick and cold, stirs.

John Dee and Thomas Digges are back in Dee's orchard, measuring the movement of that star again, this time with Digges's perspective glass.

"None," Dee says.

"It is definitely fading, Doctor," Digges says.

"I believe you are right, Thomas. But what does it mean?"

Digges is silent for a long moment. Then he says: "I wonder if the stars we see at night are just a fraction of those that exist? Perhaps there are many millions more of them, running off from our sight in numbers we cannot imagine, into eternity?"

That night Dee dreams of doves in a dovecote, and of Gethyn laughing when Beale joked that Smith was up north to see a man about a dog, and of Sir Thomas Smith himself, but at dawn, before he's able to make much sense of his dream, he is woken by thunderous knocking at his door.

"John Dee! Open up! We know you are in there! You are under arrest for debts owed to His Grace the Bishop of Bath and Wells amounting to the sum of five marks, eight shillings, and sixpence. Plus interest."

Later, the Queen summons Master Francis Walsingham to Hampton Court. She is wearing silk the color of alabaster, and a very fine eau-de-Nil collar. Her hair is up, kept in place with jeweled pins that look like the nails you'd find in a sacristy door.

"I thought you'd be more cheerful, Master Walsingham," she tells him. "After all, your scheme worked out in almost its entirety?"

Almost, he thinks. He did succeed in diverting Quesada's fleet, and he foiled James Hamilton's attempt on the Queen's life, and he discovered—albeit too late to stop her—how Queen Mary sent word to the outside world, but he did not get so much as a glimpse of her cipher, nor did he discover how she herself received word. He asks himself why not? Why did he not put Nicholas Gethyn to the rack? He cannot say. Or he can, really. It was because of what Dee had said, when they stopped in Epping. That he thought what he was doing was good.

Had Gethyn harmed Rose Cochet, then Walsingham would have stretched the man himself, but the girl was happy, beloved, well cared for in the center of Gethyn's sprawling family, and Romilly Gethyn seemed to care for her likewise. It will be a shame to send her back to her grandfather, he thinks, but he supposes grief will have already intruded in that particular paradise.

And the Queen is waiting for his answer.

"Yes, Your Majesty. It worked out almost in its entirety."

She waits.

"This time," he finishes.

She nods.

"Thanks be to God," she says. "And to John Dee."

Walsingham laughs.

"And to John Dee," he echoes.

By God, he has almost become fond of the rascal.

"But what of next time?" he wonders aloud. "We cannot pretend our enemies have gone away."

"Admiral Quesada has." She laughs.

"Yes," he agrees, "but you know how many more like him there are in France and in Spain, and when they come—we have no men to defeat them on the battlefield, nor yet ships at sea."

"I cannot raise taxes further, Master Walsingham. Already my barons are squealing like squeezed pigs, and the wool trade is ground to nothing by the Dutch wars."

Walsingham nods. This is old territory.

"We need a new kind of weapon."

"Such as—what?"

"We need a company, or a guild, of men—and women—to collect intelligence and implement procedures that are paid for and directed outside the prescribed structure of oversight."

The Queen is puzzled. "Go on," she says.

"These men and women, they'd be obligated in certain instances to effect action central to the completion of a specific and critical task without regard for ancillary repercussions."

"I see."

"I mean, men loyal to Your Majesty, but whose actions cannot be connected to you. Men who work in the shadows. In the underworld. Who can pass unnoticed, unheralded, to take our fight to the enemy, to their very heart."

The Queen thinks for a long moment before nodding her approval.

"A secret service," she says.

"Yes," Walsingham agrees. "Your Majesty's Secret Service."

"That has a ring to it."

"I have taken the liberty," he says, "of compiling a list of those I think might contribute their skills."

He has with him the book he has brought from his room in Seething Lane, the simple clothbound book, the sort in which any wool merchant might keep his figures of profit and loss. He opens it and turns the pages until he comes to a back page on which is written a short list of names and numbers.

"Who is he?" the Queen asks, pointing at the name Christopher Marlowe.

"He is a bit young," Walsingham tells her, "but shows great promise. A playwright."

The Queen sniffs. "Master Raleigh, lately of the *Pelican*—him, I know. He should be back to Cambridge this term. And '006 – Francis Drake.' He was with Hawkins, wasn't he? In New Spain?"

Walsingham agrees he was. "I suggest that to preserve their identities, they be known only by the numbers as they appear here in my manifest."

"Double oh one. Double oh two," the Queen says, running her finger down the names. "Yes. I like it. But there are only six names here. Tell me. Where is John? John Dee. Why is he not numbered here?"

Walsingham sighs.

"He . . . he has certain scruples," he tells her. "This business with Isobel Cochet, and Willem van Treslong, and with Hamilton, too, of course: they have left him somewhat—ginger."

"I am not surprised," the Queen says.

She looks at Walsingham's manifest.

"Nevertheless," she says, "enter him in your book. He is a man of singular talents without whom I dread to think where we would be."

When Walsingham pauses, the Queen sighs and snaps for the feather in Walsingham's hand. She dips it into the inkpot and with a flourish writes: "007 – Dr. John Dee."

"There," she says.

The End

ACKNOWLEDGMENTS

Many thanks to Jake Mitchie, a pirate of the most excellent class, and to Toby Clements, a glorious magical wordsmith: my creative partners in bringing John Dee's story to life.

To my terrific editorial team, Rakesh Satyal and Loan Le, and to everyone at Atria for their support, especially Libby McGuire, Lindsay Sagnette, Jason Chappell, Kyoko Watanabe, James Iacobelli—what an incredible jacket—Nicole Bond, Gena Lanzi, and Isabel DaSilva.

To my consigliere, Lisa Gallagher. You are not only the greatest agent but I'm deeply grateful to you and to the stars that aligned us. Our partnership is a thing of beauty, legend, and madness. Thank you.

To Judith Curr, for believing in Leopoldo & Co. from the beginning.

To Gigi Pritzker and Rachel Shane, for unleashing a Mexican.

To my family and friends . . . I love you.

ABOUT THE AUTHOR

Oliver Clements is a writer and philosopher based in Mortlake, London.